D0977601

RUSH

A Novel

Inspired by a True Story

By Jayme H. Mansfield

HERITAGE BEACON

FICTION

RUSH BY JAYME H. MANSFIELD
Published by Heritage Beacon Fiction
an imprint of Lighthouse Publishing of the Carolinas
2333 Barton Oaks Dr., Raleigh, NC 27614

ISBN: 978-1-946016-29-4
Copyright © 2017 by Jayme H. Mansfield
Cover design by Elaina Lee
Cover illustration by Kelly Berger (www.kellybergerart.com)
Interior design by AtriTex Technologies P Ltd

Available in print from your local bookstore, online, or from the publisher at:
lpcbooks.com.

For more information on this book and the author visit: JaymeHMansfield.com.

Brought to you by the creative team at Lighthouse Publishing of the Carolinas:
Eddie Jones, Shonda Savage, Ann Tatlock, Andrea Merrell, Elaina Lee, Brian Cross.

Library of Congress Cataloging-in-Publication Data
Mansfield, Jayme H.
RUSH/ Jayme H. Mansfield 1st ed.

Printed in the United States of America.

Praise for RUSH

In *RUSH,* Jayme Mansfield weaves a story of Mary Louisa Roberts' determination to fulfill a dream, to overcome insurmountable circumstances, to stand and fight for her beliefs and her son, and to find unexpected love. Jayme sets the story in the colorful world of the Oklahoma Land Rush and pulls no punches on the dangers and threats Mary must face to achieve her dreams. An exciting read that will stay with you long after the final chapter.

~ **Henry McLaughlin**
Award-winning author of the *Journey to Riverbend* series

RUSH captures from the first page and doesn't let go. With breathtaking descriptions of the Oklahoma Land Rush and characters who are stunning in their depth, Jayme Mansfield leads readers on their own quest with this remarkable work of fiction.

~ **Cara Luecht**
Award-winning author of *Devil in the Dust*

Another intriguing must-read by Jayme Mansfield. *RUSH,* her second novel, invites you to experience the riveting adventures of Mary Louisa Roberts, a spunky pioneer woman who rides in the Oklahoma Land Rush and wins a 160-acre claim. When Mary faces both prejudice and evil that threaten her life and success, this determined woman overcomes, lets go of her past, trusts God with her future, and wins the love of a Boston artist. Mansfield paints a vivid picture of the 1893 land rush with incredible imagery, exciting adventure, and historical accuracy. Best of all, it's her family story.

~ **Susan G. Mathis**
Author of *The Fabric of Hope: An Irish Family Legacy*

RUSH is a lush, sweeping historical novel about a widowed woman who joins the Oklahoma Land Rush. The story has it all—lovers, heroes, villains, and fools. But with the added twist of Jayme Mansfield's own family history interwoven, you'll find yourself caught up in your own rush across the prairielands of this frontier tale.

~ **David Rupert**
Writer. Editor. Encourager.
Patheos Blogger. Founder of Writers on the Rock.

With the eye of an artist and the heart of a writer, Jayme Mansfield brings another amazing story to life. By weaving historical fact, high-impact fiction, and vivid imagery, she brings readers a memorable tale—inspired by true family events—that pays tribute to those whose pioneer spirit helped shape America.

~ **Andrea Merrell**
Author of *Murder of a Manuscript*, *Praying for the Prodigal*,
and *Marriage: Make It or Break It*

The best stories are the ones you've been hearing all your life. Jayme has taken a remarkable family story and transformed it into a tale of courage, independence, and redemption. Mary Louisa Roberts believes riding in the Oklahoma Land Rush will be her greatest challenge, but finding her way through a tangle of relationships and love proves harder still. This story will pull you in and take you on an amazing ride. And best of all—it's (mostly) true!

~ **Sarah Loudin Thomas**
Author of *Miracle in a Dry Season*
Winner of the 2015 INSPY and Selah Awards for Debut Fiction

Dedication

For my grandmother, Mildred Roberts Owens
1919 - 2007

Granddaughter of Mary Louisa Johnston Roberts
Daughter of Charles Wesley Roberts

Because of you, "Oklahoma Grandma" lives on.
Grandma Millie, you are loved
forever and a day.

Acknowledgments

There's truth to the saying, "It runs in the blood." As a child and well into adulthood, I heard the tales of my Oklahoma Grandma. Even though I was born nearly one hundred years after my great-great grandmother—a bit late to share in the 1893 race across the open plains of what would become the 46th state—her fierce determination and adventurous spirit trickled through the family tree and filled me to the brim. To her, I say thank you for following your heart and being part of what made America the Land of Opportunity.

My heartfelt thanks also go to the following:

- To Lighthouse Publishing of the Carolinas for continuing to believe in my ability to bring stories to life. Eddie Jones and Cindy Sproles, a special thank you for providing the Badge of Honor Contest—the book's first thumbs up. Ann Tatlock, your rock-solid knowledge and guidance are very much appreciated. And, Andrea Merrell, you continue to elevate my writing with your expertise, dedication, and friendship. You are all editors extraordinaire.

- To Henry McLaughlin for your guidance and initial editing process that helped me reach the end of the story amidst juggling many elements of life.

- To Kelly Berger, dear friend and wildly talented artist, your artwork has graced the cover of my first two books and for that, I am indebted.

- To Heidi Hamamoto, Berni Reynolds, and Denille Obermeyer for keeping the marketing afloat and all that goes with giving a book good legs to run.

- To Elizabeth Brunsdon, for sharing your roots and buddying with me on our modern day Oklahoma adventure to dig up solid research and laugh until our bellies hurt.

- To my cousin, Sally Wright, we're fortunate gals to come from such a heritage. Thanks for compiling and gathering the old photos, letters, documents, and precious jar of Oklahoma dirt. Trisha Head Cobb, we are indebted to you for being the "keeper" of the story and sharing it with all of us.

- To my mom, Janet Hanna, great-granddaughter of Oklahoma Grandma, your wisdom that the past holds treasures and has tales to be told is the reason the story was born. Grandma Millie would be proud!

- To my husband James and my family, for putting up with me riding off on wild imagination adventures and hanging out for ridiculous amounts of time with my characters … I love you (and they do too).

CHAPTER 1

Mary ~ Alone, Missouri, July 14, 1893

I can't stop shivering when I sleep alone.
As I pulled the threadbare quilt higher, daybreak peeked in the window. Morning already, and he didn't come home again last night. Disappointment and relief played tug-of-war in my mind. But what kind of wife did that make me, relieved my husband didn't come home?

My eyes followed a crack in the ceiling that ran like a river going nowhere. My hands rested on my flat belly, wishing for it to swell again with a baby. But that was nonsense. There was no new life in me. How could there be when I felt as though I were dying inside? Besides, having another child wouldn't make things better.

Tossing the quilt aside, I slid out of bed. The floorboards creaked beneath my feet. Despite the heat, I still wore Tuck's grayed wool socks, slipped on last night before crawling into bed. When darkness fell on Adair County, Missouri, my hope was that my husband would come home—at least for our son's sake. But it was to be another lonely night.

I pulled my shawl from the iron hook and wrapped it tightly around my bare shoulders and thin, cotton nightdress. The logs from last night's cooking had burned down hours ago. Only a faint glimmer of red pulsed from the ashes, determined to gain a last breath. I used the poker to rustle the fragile remains, urging them to life once again. A small flame darted, then receded as quickly as it had lashed out, reminding me of my own hurt and anger that was squelching the love I once had for my husband. But love was a requirement, wasn't it? Especially for our son, six-year-old Wesley, who lay sleeping in the other room.

I, Aaron "Tuck" Roberts, take you, Mary Louisa Johnston, to be my wife, to have and to hold from this day forward, for better or for worse, for richer, for poorer, in sickness and in health, to love and to cherish; until death do us part.

The promises were made nearly ten years earlier when the leaves were brilliant, and I was twenty-two. Like so many others, my husband's sights—as well as my own—were focused on eventually heading west for a chance at a better life. Now, the words he promised played over and over in my mind, slowly losing momentum like the record on the phonograph, winding down, then silent.

The window felt cool as my head rested against the glass. "He'll be home soon," I whispered, wiping away tears that lately came too easily. Outside, the dirt road took on an auburn haze—the mid-July sun promising a new day.

* * * * *

I must have dozed from the combination of reading William Blake's poetry and the incessant ticking of the clock that perched on the ledge near the kitchen table. The book, a gift from my mother, lay open across my lap. Most evenings, after tucking Wesley in bed, I enjoyed the company of my books, especially *Pride and Prejudice*. Elizabeth Bennet's quick wit and intelligence made me smile and realize, deep down, she and I were much alike. But it was Alice who gathered me into her wonderland, allowing me to momentarily escape the solitude of Adair.

Occasionally, Tuck would ask me to read aloud. We would journey together to some faraway land. And—if only in my mind—those were the sweet moments with my husband that made me hope he would open the front door at any moment.

"Mrs. Roberts?" A deep voice bellowed behind the door, followed by a loud pounding. "You in there? It's Sheriff Murphy."

The chair toppled as I jumped up. "Yes." The timidity of my reply made me clench my fists.

"Need to talk with you right away." The voice was one I had heard too many times and not one for a good conversation. The fist pounding repeated, shaking the door.

Tuck must have gotten in trouble again. *Maybe he's hurt ... or worse.* Unlatching the lock, I opened the door.

Sheriff Murphy peered from under the wide brim of his hat, his eyes moving from my face down the length of my body, pausing too long in obvious places. "Ma'am, it looks as though I've intruded." His bushy mustache couldn't hide the smirk.

I gathered my shawl around my body, disgusted with myself for being caught off guard and indecent.

"Excuse me." Tangled hair fell across my face. "Must have fallen back asleep. Hard to sleep last night." I averted my eyes, feeling foolish for being barely dressed in front of the man who claimed to uphold the law in our small town but had gained a reputation for desiring nothing more than to break it for his own benefit.

"Must be hard to get a good night's sleep when you're here all alone, taking care of that boy by yourself. Downright lonely, to be sure." His left cheek twitched.

"Where's my husband?" I straightened my back and forced myself to hold the door open instead of slamming it in his face. "Is he all right?"

"That's why I'm here." He stepped back and paced the warped, wooden planks of the porch. With each moan of the boards, he paused, clearly enjoying a game of cat and mouse.

"Sheriff ..." The words caught in my throat like a fish in a net. "What have you come to tell me? What's your business here?"

He stopped mid-pace, then walked toward me. His broad shoulders and muscular frame blocked the morning sun, but I forced myself to meet him eye to eye.

"Tell me where my husband is."

His ice-blue eyes, alluring to some, sent a chill down my spine. "He's in the jail."

Relief washed over me that it wasn't what I often feared when Tuck went missing for a few days. "Whatever he did, it was surely a misunderstanding."

"No such luck for that man. Got caught stealing one of Sam Taylor's finest horses." He chuckled. "Didn't work out too well for him though." His fingers caressed the Colt poised on his hip. "Nope, got beat up pretty bad by Taylor's men."

"What'd they do to him?"

"Nothing he won't get over. But he'll be sure to feel it when the booze wears off." He glanced at the sun. "Which ought to be about now."

My stomach twisted at the thought of Tuck drinking again. He had promised. But he had made a lot of promises. "Tuck wouldn't steal anything, especially a horse."

"That's not what folks are saying. And quite frankly, your husband doesn't have the best reputation around here."

And neither do you. "That's not proof he did anything wrong. You should know the law."

"I know the law, all right. And a horse thief too." The sheriff adjusted his hat and walked toward his gelding, its reins lopped over the rickety fence. "A pretty woman like you deserves something better. It's a shame your husband's chance at claiming some land in the Rush is over. Hard to participate if he's locked up in jail."

"Tuck will be out in time, especially since he's innocent." I set my jaw and swallowed hard. Surely he wouldn't have tried to steal a horse to make the race for the new territory. Or would he?

Sheriff Murphy hoisted himself onto the saddle. "You better get inside. Put some proper clothes on." He stared me down again, and this time my bareness felt complete. "You're too vulnerable, being such a pretty little thing."

CHAPTER 2

"**M**ama, why did Daddy steal a horse?"

Wesley's sleepy voice brought me back from my thoughts as I stared at the closed door, causing me to spin around. "Your father did no such thing." The widening of my son's eyes made me wince and soften my voice. "The sheriff doesn't know the real story. It was all a big mistake."

"But he put Daddy in jail. That means he did something real bad." Wesley's lips quivered. Standing there with tousled dark hair and a wrinkled nightshirt, he seemed so small under the doorframe that led to the back room where all three of our boys once slept.

All three of our boys ...

Unbidden, those painful thoughts came rushing in—how the twins, James and William, had arrived a year after my marriage to Tuck. How a couple of years after that came Charles, who soon came to be called by his middle name, Wesley, or "from the west meadow." Such a fitting name for this sweet child. But then the unthinkable. A lump formed in my throat when my thoughts replayed how the influenza took our two oldest sons. Something in me died that day as well. And in Tuck. Our attempts to hang on to each other in the raging storm of emotions failed. We were out of one another's reach, drifting apart and drowning in separate waters. And now? I feared he was already gone—to an even darker place where drink and sadness would be his only companions.

A tug on my shawl brought me out of my painful memories. "Mama?"

Placing my hands gently on his face, I looked down into his trusting brown eyes and swallowed the words that would only crush his young heart. "Your father's a good man. We'll go to the jail and get this cleared up. He'll be home before lunchtime. Just wait and see." I wrapped my arms around Wesley and pulled him in close, hoping he couldn't feel my heart pounding with the lies. But maybe this time my husband would prove me wrong.

Wesley squirmed out of my arms and eyed me, his head cocked to one side in his typical questioning pose. "Is Daddy gonna be in the land race? The other kids have been talkin' 'bout it. Billy Crofton's family is leavin' to get a new place to live. Ruth Ann said her dad is goin' with her uncle out west to get some land of their own. Lots of it."

"Not much gets past a smart boy like you." My smile was tight and forced. "Let's get you something to eat. Both of us need to get dressed." I walked to the shelf and pulled down the canister of grits.

"Ruth Ann said her father's gettin' a hundred and sixty acres for free." Wesley's voice perked up. "Is that what Daddy's gonna do?"

I scooped a cupful of grits from the tin. "Your father and I have thought about the race. Plenty of people have been talking about it. It's in the New Territory that the government's opening up. Used to be Indian land."

"Indian land? Can we get some? Sure would like to live with the Indians." Wesley climbed on the chair at the end of the table and propped his chin on his folded hands. "It wouldn't cost us nothin'."

"Anything," I corrected. "First of all, the Indians have been moved off the land to other areas." My son's serious expression made me smile as he tried to understand that his idea of living with Indians and chasing buffalo on horseback was no longer a reality. "Besides, everything costs something. Even if it's free."

The water in the cooking pot bubbled, inviting me to add the grits. "We have our home here." *Even if it doesn't feel like it any longer.*

*****

The walk to the jail felt longer than the few streets we actually passed. Maybe it was because Wesley was preoccupied with kicking a stone that bounced and rolled haphazardly on the rutted ground. While he was intent on keeping the whereabouts of his rock, my thoughts focused on what my reaction and words might be at seeing Tuck behind bars. I dreaded the thought of how he might look after a night of hard drinking and from the roughing up by Taylor's men.

Was it wrong to bring our son along? Maybe he should have gone to Mother's. But then she would ask what happened. And it's impossible to lie or keep a secret from her.

My sweet mother wasn't fond of Tuck's behavior either, but she was forever encouraging me to forgive. *Forgive. Forgive. Forgive.* Just like the Lord has forgiven us.

We passed the last street and made our way to the front of the sheriff's office. Our town didn't need much of a jail since little happened around here. Unfortunately, Tuck had been a visitor quite a few times since the twins died, to sleep off a night of drinking—and causing problems in the saloon. The last time it happened, Sheriff Murphy said Tuck needed to have time to think on a hard cot and an empty stomach. But that wasn't all he had to say. "He needs to know what it feels like not to be snuggled up next to you for a night. A respectable man wouldn't take for granted sharing a bed with a woman like you."

Replaying the lawman's words caused me to stumble on the steps leading to the door. I gathered my courage and blew out a sharp breath before stepping up to the entryway.

"Didn't think I'd see you so soon." Sheriff Murphy reclined behind an oak desk, hands folded behind his head, feet propped on the desk. His leather boots were shined to perfection. "Even brought the boy along." He winked at Wesley.

"He's come along to escort his father home." I pulled my son closer to my side.

The sheriff slid his feet off the desk and stood, towering over me. "Now, I wouldn't be in such a hurry, Mrs. Roberts. There's a few people I need to speak with to determine exactly what happened."

"And who would those folks be?" I tried my best to keep my voice from quivering, but the combination of the sheriff's ominous stature and smug stare unnerved me.

"The Taylor men ought to be showing up any time now to give their account. They have better things to do than come up with false stories, so I reckon' they'll have plenty to say."

"Let me talk with my husband." I stepped forward, feigning more courage than I possessed. "Privately."

"Suit yourself, but he ain't a pretty sight." He nodded towards Wesley. "He can wait here with me."

The thought of leaving my son with this man did not sit well, but seeing his father beat up and half-drunk behind bars was not good either. "Wesley, mind your manners and stay put. I'll only be a few minutes. We'll be heading home with your father shortly."

"Take your time. Me and the boy'll be within earshot if you need us. Right, Son?"

"Yes, sir."

Wesley's eyes were firmly fixed on the shiny badge proudly displayed on the lawman's pressed shirt.

* * * * *

Tuck was unrecognizable except for his dark hair, which was matted against his cheek and caked with dried blood. One eye was swollen shut, ringed with purple, and his lips were distorted. Like an animal, he huddled in the corner of the cell, knees drawn to his chest and head leaning back against the brick wall.

"Tuck." His name sounded foreign since the man on the floor appeared a stranger.

"Mary?" His good eye opened.

"Yes. You all right?" My question was ridiculous, but I found myself at a loss for words that usually came easily. "It's time to take you home."

"That's the best news I've heard in a long time." He almost produced a smile, then grimaced at the apparent pain in his split lip. "I didn't do nothin' wrong, promise."

"They're saying you tried to steal a horse. You wouldn't do that, would you?" My voice cracked. "Taylor's men are coming here to give their account."

My husband edged onto his side and pushed himself up on hands and knees. I had never seen him in such pain. Watching him wince with each motion caused anger to swell in my gut.

"What did they do to you?"

"Must have busted my ribs 'cause I can barely breathe." Grasping the bars, he pulled himself to a half stand. "Like I said, I didn't do nothin' wrong."

Not anything like taking a horse to ride in the land race? "Nothing you can remember," I said coldly. "You promised you wouldn't drink like that anymore."

He reached through the bars to take my hand. Instinctively, I stepped back. My husband had betrayed me before, and the pain still lingered.

"Mary, I'm sorry."

His breath reeked of bad whiskey, causing my hand to cover my nose.

"I love you." The usual pleading brown eyes weren't as convincing this time, especially with his left eye shut. "I'll make it right with you. You have to believe me." Again, he reached through the bars and held a fold in my skirt. "Will you forgive me?"

I want to believe you and forgive you. You've been given that gift time after time. I don't know if I have it in me any longer. "I forgive you." I touched his bloodstained hand and then pulled away. "But this time it's for Wesley's sake, not yours or mine."

"Mary—"

"Let me see about getting you out of here." I spun on my heels and walked toward the office, willing myself not to look back.

"I'll be escorting my husband and son home now," I said to the sheriff's back.

Wesley and the sheriff were in deep discussion over the rifle collection standing at attention in the gun case. "This one's a beaut, ain't she?" The sheriff handed a rifle to him.

"She sure is." My son rubbed his small hand over the smooth wood. "I'd like to learn to shoot one like this someday."

"Hasn't your father taught you to shoot a rifle? A big boy like you?"

"No, sir. He—"

"That's enough talk now, Son." I stepped forward, lifted the rifle from his hands, and handed it to the sheriff. "Here. It's time for our family to head home. *All* of us."

"That's a pure shame. Young Wesley and I have been having a good man-to-man talk." He patted the top of Wesley's head. "Right, Son?"

Wesley nodded with wide-open eyes, as though this lawman were larger than life.

"There's some good news for you and your husband. The Taylors think there may have been a mistake. They sent one of their men a few minutes ago. Seems your husband was cavorting with a rough group of drunkards last night. The Taylor boys ain't sure which one of the carousers unhitched and tried to take a mare belonging to their father, Sam. Fact is, it may or may not have been your husband. Anyway, he's off the hook … for now." The sheriff returned to his desk and plopped into the chair.

"You mean this is what happened to my husband over a *mistake*?" I waved my hand toward the back of the jail. "Or for that matter, any man who simply unhitched the wrong horse?" My face burned, and I was sure redness swept across my cheeks.

"A man knows his own horse," he said, crossing his arms across his chest, "whether he's stone drunk or not. And to my recollection, your husband doesn't even own a horse." He chortled. "Not that he could afford one."

I averted my eyes and tried to calm my swelling anger that would only fuel his ego. "Would you please release my husband and let us get on our way?"

"Not quite yet. He should be home before dark. Some tables were busted up at the saloon. The owner may have something to say about restitution before I let Tuck go."

Pleading with this man would only produce a trite refusal. It would be easier to deal with my husband when he was completely sober. Besides, time was needed to prepare my son for his father's appearance. "Very well. We'll have supper waiting for him." With Wesley's hand in mine, we headed for the door.

"Thank you for showing me the guns, Sheriff," Wesley called out as I pulled him down the steps.

"You're welcome, Son. Anytime."

Whether it was my imagination or his voice carried on the breeze, I could hear the pompous lawman chuckle at my folly.

CHAPTER 3

Mary ~ Shattered Innocence, July 14, 1893

By eight o'clock, the remaining stew was cold. Reluctantly, Wesley crawled into bed, but not before asking if his father would check on him once he arrived home. I avoided answering, but my son was insistent. A false promise was made. His father would kiss him goodnight. I hated myself for lying, but something in my gut warned we would not see Tuck tonight.

Once Wesley was asleep, I gathered my shawl and quietly slipped out the door. A few lights from neighboring homes cast enough glow for me to navigate my way toward the jail to see why Tuck had not returned home.

Others were outside, enjoying an evening stroll or sitting on porches to escape the heat that still lingered on late summer nights. The O'Reillys called a greeting, but I merely waved, not in the mood for small talk about the weather. My pace quickened until I rounded the corner and stood in front of the brick building. On the rise above the steps, Sheriff Murphy leaned against the wall. The butt of his cigarette glowed as he raised his hand and tipped his hat.

"Good evening, dear lady. What brings you back here, especially in the dark?"

"You know exactly why." My hands fisted as anger grew. "You said Tuck would be home by supper. Obviously, that time has passed."

The sheriff took a long drag and then released a plume of smoke that swirled around his head. "That's interesting."

"What does that mean?"

"Your husband was released well before suppertime. Can't imagine he got lost trying to get home, can you?" The cigarette dangled from his mouth. "Told him to get on home and count himself a lucky man that the Taylors and the saloon owner felt sorry for him and let him go."

I crossed my arms tightly, trying to steady myself. "Was he too injured to make it home on his own? He must have stopped somewhere along the way." My excuses were weak, but they were all I had.

"Come on now, you don't live far. Even a man weak in the knees would make it home to a woman like you." He dropped the cigarette and smashed it under his boot. "Maybe he headed to the saloon, but he'd be a fool to think Amos would open his doors to him, especially after just letting him off the hook for damaging things last night."

"He wouldn't—"

"But then again, that man of yours is a fool." He stepped to the edge of the porch and bent over, leveling his eyes with mine. "Mary, you deserve much better than a husband like him."

My mouth opened, but words refused to form. Lately, my mind was caught between reality and dreams of what my life should be. Could the sheriff's hurtful words be sprinkled with truth? Our eyes locked, but I backed away with measured steps as though cornered by a wild animal.

"You let me know if you need help finding him." He resumed his stance by the wall. "If I can help with anything. Anything at all." He tipped his hat and pulled another cigarette from his shirt pocket.

My feet hurried down the street toward the saloon. I needed to pull myself together. Be strong. Surely, Tuck was at home by now. Probably went another direction, and we missed each other. I would peek inside to make sure he didn't stop to make things right with the owner or clear up another friend's name with this misunderstanding.

At the saloon, I paused to gather myself. This was not an establishment most women would enter. Inside was dingy, and a cloud of smoke hovered over the heads of a small group of men at the bar. Others sat among scattered tables, lifting glasses and playing cards. A survey of the room confirmed the absence of my husband.

A man behind the bar, presumably Amos, called out to me. "Can I help you, ma'am? You seem lost."

"No, sir. Just looking for my husband." Several chuckles rose from the cluster of men. "Aaron Tuck Roberts."

The group turned as one and looked directly at me. A few laughed again, and a fat one snorted and banged on the table.

"Tuck Roberts, you say?" The bartender tossed a towel over his shoulder. "First of all, he ain't welcome here ever again. Busted up the place last night."

"So I heard. You haven't seen him at all today?"

"Yeah. Had the nerve to come in and say his good-byes to the few he would dare to call friends."

Again, chuckles erupted. A gravelly voice added, "and to bum whiskey and a cigarette from Ruthie."

"Ma'am, with all due respect, your husband was lucky to get out of town with his hide." Amos poured whiskey into a shot glass and placed it on the counter. "Here, it's on me. You look like you might be needing this."

Blood rushed to my face, and I grasped the back of a chair to steady myself. "I don't drink."

"You may want to start," the gravelly voice chimed in.

"Enough, Ebner." Amos tossed the wadded-up towel at the bald-headed man. Then he leaned over the counter and motioned me closer.

I approached the bar, careful to turn my back to the group of men. "Good-byes? What do you mean he came by here to say his good-byes?"

"Don't you know? I mean, being his wife and all." Amos wiped a large hand across a crooked nose. "He was heading to Colorado. Cripple Creek, he said."

"Colorado?" Without looking, I knew all eyes in the saloon were on me.

"That's right. Said he was off to make his fortune at a gold strike in the Rocky Mountains. Some say there's more gold to be found in those parts." This time, he lifted the glass and offered it to me again.

"I wish I did drink." My spirit sagged under the reality that was punching me in the stomach.

"Sorry to be the bearer of bad news. Thought you knew your husband's plans."

"I thought so too." As I turned away from Amos, all the men now stared openly at me. It was hard to read their faces, but I imagined that some of them had an ounce of compassion for a wife abandoned by her husband.

CHAPTER 4

Daniel ~ Boston, July 30, 1893

"Daniel, you look pathetic. Worse than a stray dog with no hope for a home." Finn shook his head in disgust as I frowned back at him.

For the third night in a row, sleep had evaded me. Without invitation, the nightmare had returned to remind me of my cowardice. "That bad?" I tried to force a smile, but my best friend and sidekick photographer for the newspaper knew me too well. Even though I was ten years plus his twenty-five, we had developed a strong working relationship when Finn arrived four years ago from Scotland—hungry for food and work.

"'Tis the dream, it 'tis." His left eye squinted even though my small studio room was depressingly dark. Finn spent a good part of his life with his left eye closed—peering through the lens of his camera with his right eye wide open, or when summing up the quality of a person. Finn knew me better than anyone, particularly when I slipped toward the guilt that regularly tried to consume me.

I stood and stretched my arms above my head. "A walk is what is needed." The draperies hung helpless in front of the window, pooled on the floor in dark green puddles. Pulling them apart allowed entrance for the little sunshine available on a dreary East Coast morning.

"Friend, allow me to correct you. A woman is what you need." Finn snickered.

"Hardly. I don't get enough sleep as it is."

The red-brick facade of a six-story building stood directly across Washington Street. THE GLOBE, emblazoned in stately lettering, crowned the entrance to my daily existence. For the past eight years, I had diligently worked as the illustrator of "urgent news and future historical importance" as Chief Editor McKelvey reminded me each shift—every day except four years ago, January 5, 1889. That was the day after the famous Burning of the Boston City Stables.

"How about we go to Melville's for a bite of breakfast?" Finn patted his stomach, and it rumbled in response. "I'm starving, and you look like you could use some fattening up."

"Too much work to do." I pointed across the street. "The deadlines keep piling up. This city isn't about to go to sleep so I can get on top of all the happenings around here."

My permanently ink-stained fingers were a constant reminder of my long days hovering over my work table. Over the years, with pen and ink, I illustrated the news important enough to make the front section of the Globe, gathering every possible detail—texture, feature, color—before the moment slipped away. The work had branded me. Not merely my fingertips, but my view of the world.

Finn knew that ever since the fire, my disposition had changed. Observing life from a distance was now my permanent vantage point. Like a boat loosened from its moorings, I was slipping away into a fog that would eventually separate me from the past and the painful memories that haunted me.

"But it's Sunday." Finn crossed his arms and dared me with his eyes. "You can't be working today."

"Since when have you become concerned about what not to do on Sunday?" I crossed my arms as well. "You've never been one to care much about those things."

Finn ran long, slender fingers through his curly red hair—hair that enjoyed charting its own course most days. When he grinned, his cheeks took on a deeper hue. "Ever since Arthur Turney down in the printing department informed me the only way I can see his daughter is if I'm a church-going man."

"What did you tell him?"

"Told him I'm a regular attender. I figure the Lord understands those wee lies when it's in the interest of love." Finn winked and gave me a lopsided grin.

"Love?"

"Who knows? But she sure is bonnie. Never thought I'd see the day, but I might head over to Central Church this morning." He nodded as though approving his own idea. "If nothing else, it would have made me mum proud. Why don't you come along? Maybe we can learn a thing or two." He snapped his fingers. "Ay, Elizabeth might have a friend for you."

"No thanks." I rubbed my chin and contemplated the idea of love, doubting it was in the cards for me. "There's plenty to keep me busy without complicating my life with a woman."

"They say the church has an electric chandelier. Imagine that." Finn joined me by the window. "And those stained-glass windows you can see when you walk down Newbury Street. Bet they're even prettier from inside."

"You're quite a salesman, Finn Allaway," I said while mentally questioning his new fascination with church. "But save it for Miss Turney."

Finn turned serious. "You know, Daniel, God didn't intend for us to be alone."

I stepped back and surveyed my friend. He stood a head shorter than me with blue eyes the color of the ocean on a clear day. I hadn't noticed before, but suddenly it hit me that the boyish face Finn wore when he bounded into the newsroom of the Globe to ask for a job four years ago, had transformed. The once disheveled young man—who looked like he always used his fingers as a comb and wore clothes traveled in for weeks—had held fast to a black, leather box. It soon became apparent it was his only possession of any value—a Number 1 Kodak box camera.

"Not sure what to make of you this morning. You're acting like you've been hearing directly from God Almighty Himself."

"My dear friend." Finn shook his head slowly, the usual indication he was ready to impart his wisdom. "I don't need to hear from God to know that a laddie needs a lassie." He started for the door but stopped and looked back at me with a sly grin. "I just feel it in me bones." With that, he slipped out the door.

I smiled in spite of myself. Finn was a charmer for sure. Perhaps there was a thing or two to be learned from him.

CHAPTER 5

July was ready to slip away, taking its last breath on the hottest day of the year.

I blamed my lack of motivation on the heat. However, it was obvious I was stagnant, unsure what to do about the future of my depleted family, a thirty-two-year-old single mother with a six-year-old son. Beyond the two of us, my family extended only to my mother, Louisa—the one I was on my way to visit two streets to the west, as was my routine each Sunday afternoon.

"Any news?" A woman of select and often poignant words, my mother sat on the front porch, rocking methodically as the warped boards creaked beneath her prized chair.

"And hello to you as well." The three steps leading to the covered porch seemed nearly insurmountable in the heat. "Keeping cool?" I wiped my brow with the back of my hand and fixed my eyes on the pitcher of lemonade on the small table beside her.

"Any news?" Mother repeated with an added shake of her head. As always, her silver hair was pulled into a tight bun at the base of her neck. Her brown eyes loomed large in comparison to her petite nose. If she hadn't blinked, she would have been mistaken for a chickadee, delicately perched on a high branch, surveying the scene below.

"The lemonade looks delicious, especially on a warm day. And, no, I haven't heard from him." I picked up an aqua canning jar, one of an assortment that Mother always kept on the small table in the event a neighbor might want to join her for a refreshing drink on a sleepy afternoon. Mother swore the canning jars were the best invention ever—thick, sturdy, and tight-lidded for canning peaches, jams, and applesauce. And even better as a drinking glass. She bought a case of twenty-four "Ball blue" from a catalog and had them shipped from the Ball Brothers' Company in Muncie, Indiana.

Funny though, as little as she spoke—compared to other women who measured good conversation with the amount of talk and often gossip—friends found my mother's company a priority, even if it was just sitting and watching the sun slip behind the rolling hills in the distance. Mother was like a sweet-smelling lilac bush attracting the bees.

I settled into the other rocking chair. "How are you feeling? You didn't sing with as much enthusiasm this morning in church."

"Where's Wesley?" She rocked forward, planted her feet on the boards to cease the motion, and glanced up and down the street.

"He'll be along in a few minutes. He's throwing a ball with the Patterson boy. Maggie Ann's going to walk him over here in a bit." I leaned over and placed my hand on my mother's. "You didn't answer me. Are you feeling well?"

My eyes followed the blue veins that meandered along her wrinkled skin. Like uncharted rivers through rugged land, my mother's hands reflected her history, her determination to persevere through the adversity that chased her much of her life. In turn, my skin was deceivingly smooth and mostly unmarred. Until lately, the chasm between my mother's years and my years seemed to be widening as old age beckoned her to its doorstep. But now, admitting the possibility that my husband wasn't coming home, I had aged like sour wine.

"I'm fine, Mary." She turned her slight body and placed her other hand on top of mine. "It's you we should be worrying about."

My mouth opened to object, but how could I lie to my mother? Her wide-open eyes, though draped with sagging lids and defined creases at each side, were the same eyes that watched me take my first steps and sleep restlessly with the fever as a child. Those eyes smiled over my shoulder into the mirror as her nimble fingers braided my hair on my wedding day. My mother's eyes were the ones that wept along with mine on the two separate days we buried Thomas and Henry, my twins and her grandsons. Now, gazing into her eyes, I realized they had become reflecting pools, forcing me to look directly at my plight—an abandoned wife and mother alone in a man's world.

I cleared my throat and gripped the arms of the rocker. "Mother, I'm going to do the Run. Even if Tuck isn't back in time." There, it was said. I settled back in my chair, nodded to myself, and looked straight ahead, waiting for her response—and silently daring her to argue.

The silence unnerved me. When my head turned in her direction, she was staring straight ahead with the corners of her wrinkled lips turned up slightly.

"Mother, did you hear me?"

"Oh, I heard you, child." Her methodical rocking was like a ticking clock, moving forward yet going nowhere. "I'm not surprised a bit."

"Hmm?" I sat forward and searched her face. "How so?"

"Because you've been making your own way since the day you were born. Nothing is ever going to hold you back from your dreams." She gave me a knowing look. "I'm going to worry something fierce, and I'll miss seeing you on a whim, but you need to do this. Even if Tuck does show up in two weeks' time and you do the race together, it's your spirit that's pulling you that way."

"What a surprise. I thought you would protest for sure. Tell me I was crazy to think of trying to stake a claim by myself."

"I'm not saying it will be easy. I'm not even saying you'll be successful." Mother stopped rocking and sat forward on the edge of her chair. Her serious tone drew me into her next words. "Mary, a person has got to do what the Lord is calling her to do. If you really believe this is what God wants for your life, then you have to go." She lifted her forefinger and pointed it toward the sky. "Sometimes you don't know what He wants for you and from you until you stretch yourself further than you ever imagined you could fly."

My own words wouldn't come as my mind pondered the most words my mother had spoken in sequence in quite a long time. It had never crossed my mind that any of this idea to participate in the Cherokee Strip Land Run had anything to do with God. It was a discussion that had become more serious over the last few months between Tuck and me. The thought of staking claim to one of the thousands of plots was enticing, even though money was hard to come by. Up front was a fourteen-dollar filing fee. After five years of proving we were settled on the land, we'd have to pay two dollars and fifty cents an acre. One hundred and sixty acres of our own sounded like a dream. It had become a reality for others, most recently in the Run near Guthrie, Oklahoma, in the spring of 1889, in the unclaimed land the government had taken from the Indians.

Tuck and I spent many nights whispering to each other in bed, out of earshot of our son. We could build a home, plant crops, and start a new life with Wesley. We'd leave behind the unsteady jobs Tuck occasionally picked up and then lost days later. Most importantly—like protecting precious belongings in an heirloom cedar chest—perhaps a new home would help us store away the memories of a family of five that had tragically been reduced to three. But as I rocked faster, the realization surfaced like the bubbling hot springs to the north—my family was now two.

"You are most certainly aware," Mother added as she refilled my glass, "that husband of yours isn't making a living for you. If not for my Sunday meals, you'd be as skinny as a stick."

I grinned in response but knew there was truth to her statement. Tuck brought in very little money, and the house we rented from Mr. Hudson, the owner of the general store, was out of his generosity to provide a modest home for our family. His kindness had been accentuated with chocolates and caramels given to Wesley for sweeping the store a few times a week. For cleaning up spills and scrubbing the baseboards, he treated him to a handful of something none of us had seen the likes of before—pink-and-white candy with black licorice inside. *Good & Plenty*, special ordered from Pennsylvania.

Yes, it would be safer, more logical, for an abandoned mother and young son to remain where life was familiar and predictable—where there were good people and plenty of love and extra hands to raise a child. But even sweet-smelling apples, dangling from branches and dancing with bees, knew when change was coming. For me, like the unstoppable coming and going of the seasons, change was in the air.

CHAPTER 6

Daniel ~ Change, July 30, 1893

The long walk through elm and maple-lined pathways in the Common was refreshing as a gentle wind blew in from the ocean. In my mind, the morning's conversation with Finn replayed over and over. Why was I not the one giving him advice about life—especially women?

Eloise. She had not entered my thoughts in many years. Maybe when another attractive, dark-haired woman passed me on the street or sat in my vicinity at a restaurant, only then I'd think about what my life would have been like if she had said yes to my proposal. The pressure from her established Bostonian family to "marry well" had eventually trumped any true love she had for me.

For quite some time, she was infatuated with my artistic abilities to paint landscapes that made us dream of faraway places, or when I composed a still life that seemed as though we could reach out and pluck a ripened grape. But we were in our early twenties, and there was little money to show for my talent as an artist. My company had been a temporary diversion for her from the proper etiquette, rules, and expectations she was accustomed to. Eventually, she set her sights on familiar territory and sailed that direction with the wind at her back.

Soon after her rejection, my work at the Globe began. Ironically, my first assignment was to illustrate a nuptial banner to hover above a photograph of Eloise and her new husband in the local announcement section of the paper. Hoping to shake off humility's sting, my determination rose to establish a professional career and make a good living. Relinquishing precious time with my brushes and palette knives, I picked up pen and ink and attended to the business of others' lives. After that, I only met my easel and palette on an occasional Sunday afternoon or in the late and lonely hours when even sleep wasn't my companion.

If I wasn't painting, it was usually Finn who put me—and even the most tight-necked supervisors at the Globe—at ease with his keen sense of humor and infectious gut-laugh. But lately, neither Finn nor even the methodic stroking of the canvas to layer in a mesmerizing sunset could calm the restlessness in my soul. Like the old sea captains yelling orders in the harbor as the clouds rolled in, my senses told me a change was coming.

Though for me, it wasn't a change in the weather that made my bones ache like the leather-faced captains talked about as they downed another shot of whiskey or pint of beer in one of the taverns lining Marshall and Union streets. It was something far deeper. The change coming my way was surely intended to go directly toward my heart.

I stared up at the dense tree canopy and noted the menagerie of green-toned leaves. Though they would be brilliant shades of deep ochre, crimson, and orange in a few months' time, they would soon die and float listlessly onto the path. Even in the lingering warm weather of summer, I wrapped my coat closer, tucked my chin, and prayed that whatever change was coming, it would not be after my soul.

CHAPTER 7

Mary ~ News, September 3, 1893

Mother and I spent a good part of the afternoon in our porch chairs watching Wesley climb the crab apple tree in the neighbor's front yard. With great care, he plucked the fruits not yet snatched by the birds and aimed for jars and buckets he had placed in various positions in the grass. To his credit, his accuracy was quite good. A distant *plunk* rang out each time he hit his target.

According to the pastor—and my mother—Sundays were meant for relaxing and thanking God for all our blessings. So, while Mother rocked and most likely thought about those things, fear swelled in my chest. How could Tuck leave us? The question plagued me. I had been so forgiving with his drinking, and only God knows what else.

With the approach of Sheriff Murphy on his horse, anger joined my fear.

"He's a handsome man." Mother tossed out the comment as if she spoke of the weather. "Don't you think?"

"I don't trust him." My rocking continued as I looked straight ahead to maintain my composure. The sound of the horse's hooves slowed to a halt in front of the house, and it was impossible to ignore his arrival any longer.

"Good afternoon, ladies." The lawman tipped his hat.

"Likewise, Sheriff," Mother said. "Would you join us for the last of the lemonade?"

"That would be fine, Louisa. Much appreciated on a day like this." He slid from his horse and looped the reins over the fence. The horse nibbled on the crabgrass sprouting along the fence, its sorrel coloring shimmering with sweat along the saddle line and chest. Heavy boots sounded on the steps up to the porch. "Mary." He tipped his hat again and nodded in my direction.

"Sheriff." I nodded back, then did my best to avoid his piercing stare.

"Mary, would you get a fresh glass from the kitchen?" Mother's smile appeared forced, making it clear she wasn't asking a question. "Bring a plate of the muffins as well."

Rising from my chair and stepping around Sheriff Murphy took some effort. He was a tall man, and his presence filled the small porch. I opened the screen door and headed toward the kitchen, my eyes adjusting to the dark hallway after being outside most of the day. Rummaging in the cupboard for another mason jar, I took my time to fill a plate with the muffins Mother had made the night before—her weekly baking ritual to have something to bring along to church for the pastor in addition to her weekly offering.

"Why is he here?" I muttered. *Be polite. After all, it's the right thing to do.*

The spring moaned as I pushed the screen door open with my elbow. "The muffins smell wonderful, Mother." When our eyes met, hers were squinting, brows drawn together as if she were in pain.

"What's wrong? Are you ill?"

"Oh, Mary ..." She pushed herself from the rocker.

The sheriff rested his hat across his broad chest.

Mother stepped toward me, stopped, and pushed her hands deep into her apron pockets. "Honey, you should sit down."

"Would someone tell me what's going on?" My voice quivered, and my knees felt weak.

"Your mother's right. Best if you sit down. There's news about your husband."

I eyed him, not wanting to hear what he had to say. "I'd rather stand." My back straightened with my need for courage. "Go ahead."

"As you please. Mary, your husband is ... well, he's ... dead." He shifted his weight as though waiting for my response.

My heart pounded. My throat went dry. "That's not possible."

"I just rode in from Kirksville. One of the patrons from Amos' saloon said they'd heard of Tuck's whereabouts. Headed over there to find out what I could."

My teeth were grinding as he spoke. "Why are you so interested in—"

Mother reached her hand toward me. "Mary, the sheriff was only—"

"It's all right. This is hard news to hear." The lawman shook his head.

"What happened?" My voice was barely more than a whisper, and I still believed it was all a vicious lie.

"The man I spoke with went West with your husband—off to Cripple Creek to catch the tail end, or what they hoped would be another gold rush in the Colorado mountains."

"Yes, he spoke of the opportunity." I tried to reassert my words. "He was set to come home as soon as he earned some extra money."

"Perhaps." The sheriff pulled his kerchief from his rear pocket and wiped it across his forehead. "Word is, he got mixed up in a bar brawl after another night of drinking."

A clear memory pierced my mind of the last time I saw Tuck after a night of drinking and fighting.

"He made a poor choice and went at another drunk with a knife. Shot straight in the chest. Died on the spot." Sheriff Murphy twirled his hat in his hands. "Sorry to be delivering such awful news. Wish I could say something different. Don't even have his body to properly bury. Seems he was placed in the miners' communal grave, being he had no family there to speak of."

I tried to shout the words that spiraled in my head. *It isn't true! My husband isn't dead!* But all I could feel were my legs giving way, my head swirling, and the sound of shattering glass.

CHAPTER 8

Daniel ~ Assignment, September 3, 1893

"We're heading West, my friend." Finn removed his bowler, unleashing dark red curls. He slapped the hat on his leg, raised his arms above his head, and twirled in a circle across my wooden floor. I could only imagine it was a form of a Scottish dance, erupting from his boyhood days in the Lowlands.

"And don't you ever knock?" I turned, paintbrush in hand, and smiled at the young man who seemed to feel it his job to try to narrow the decade between us.

"McKelvey is sending us to the Oklahoma Territory." He spun again, this time adding a sidekick and nearly crashing into my easel and canvas.

"For heaven's sake, Finn. Would you settle down and let me get some work done?" I turned toward my painting and contemplated the next color.

"Don't you want to know why we're going?" He pulled up a stool and positioned himself adjacent to the large canvas.

"I already know." My eyes stayed focused on the penciled lines, sketched out late last night when sleep eluded me again. "Talked with McKelvey a few days back."

"Why didn't you say so?" Finn crossed his legs and rested an elbow on his knee. "You wanted me to keep dancing for you, eh?"

I cocked my head toward my young friend and studied him. "Hardly, and Mrs. Williamson on the level beneath us is certainly glad you stopped." I lifted my palette and swirled a mixture of dark umber and olive green. "Told him I'm not going."

"Of course you are. You can't expect me to go without you." Finn scooted the stool closer. "We'll be right there while history is being made. Can you imagine? They predict thousands of people will line up to race for plots of land on the wide-open plains. I'll take the photos, and you'll make your drawings. Folks back here have never seen such a thing." Finn was nearly bouncing on the stool as though racing along on an imaginary horse. "Documenting this event could make us famous, Daniel."

"You'll be fine without me." I wiped a corner of the canvas with my finger, leaving a black smudge. "Besides, there's plenty of news to cover right here."

"Why are you always using those dark paints? Why not add a bit of life?" Finn stood and eyed the painting closely. It wasn't completed, but the trees along the grayish-green river were bare. The bent and gnarled dark-brown branches had lost their leaves in anticipation of winter, and a dreary fog was settling over the landscape.

I stepped back a few paces to view my work. "Because ..." I hesitated, fumbling for words. "There's no ..." My head bowed in defeat.

"Life left in you?" Finn finished what I didn't want to admit.

"Is it that obvious?" Studying my palette, my eyes were met with the dark blends of browns, greens, and shades of gray mingled together—a muddy conglomeration. I eyed Finn. "Have I really become so lugubrious?"

Finn raised his eyebrows. "Not sure about that description since I've never heard the crazy word."

"Means sad, gloomy, dismal—"

"Okay, got it. He picked up a tube of cerulean blue. "How about this color? Folks say the sky out west is a blue like you've never seen." He tossed it aside and picked up alizarin crimson and cobalt violet. "And the sunsets and sunrises stretch for miles across the horizon."

My forehead pounded with another unwelcome headache. "As usual, you're only trying to help, but things can't change." I pulled a rag from my pocket and rubbed at my paint-stained hands. Darkened creases accentuated the lines on my palms and fingertips, and from somewhere back in my high school days, Lady MacBeth's words echoed in my mind, *Out damn'd spot! Out, I say!*

"Daniel." Finn's voice was abrupt, no longer having fun with the assortment of paint names. "Listen to me." He stepped toward me and snatched the rag from my hands.

I stared at him, not sure what to make of his sudden change in demeanor.

"You didn't kill that boy." He laid his hand on my chest and our eyes locked. "It was an accident."

Like a deluge of rain, the images raced back into my mind, vivid as the day it happened four and a half years ago. The Boston City Stables, a large brick building on Highland Street, filled with several tons of hay, hundreds of bushels of grain, and stalls filled with snorting and screeching horses, was ablaze in the middle of the day.

As if still standing on the grassy rise just to the west of the building with sketchbook and charcoal pencil in hand, my mind replayed what I had witnessed. The three-story building erupting with shattered glass falling from the windows, followed by belching, black smoke. The slate roof groaned under its own weight as the interior support beams gave way and sections of the roof crashed mercilessly to the floor below.

In the dim light of my apartment, I squinted into Finn's eyes, desperately hoping it had all been a nightmare—the horrific images, the stench of blackened smoke, the deafening sounds, and even the heat lashing out at my face from the inferno ... taunting me to keep enough distance to save myself from being consumed as well. One last time, I willed myself to believe there was a God who could take all of it—the images, the sounds, the smells, and the guilt—and bury them where they belonged. In the depths of hell.

"Daniel?"

It was as though my body had been temporarily knocked from the safe vantage point from which I witnessed the event. Now, my eyes watered as they did that day. But unlike the soot and heat that stung my eyes, my eyes were wet for another reason. Tears poured from somewhere deep in my soul, and, without invitation, they invaded my heart with ruthless intrusion.

"I saw him." My heart sank, and the tears came with a vengeance.

"Watched him go back in ..." I gasped for air as my chest heaved, "to get the last horses."

"Daniel, listen to me." Finn grasped my arm, giving me a quick shake.

"No! Don't you see?" My hand pushed at him, causing him to stumble. "I watched it happen from a safe place—taking it in, observing the entire scene—just as a journalist is trained to do." My face contorted at the reality of my cowardice. "I could have thrown my paper and pencil to the ground and ran in after the boy, helped him get the horses, helped him—"

"But the firemen were there. They—"

I shook my head at Finn, though actually ashamed of myself. "I'll never forgive myself for letting that boy die. All the horses got out alive because of him and some other brave men." Exhausted, I steadied myself against the wall and slid down to a crouch.

Finn approached and squatted next to me. The silence lasted several minutes. Then he barely whispered, "God knows I'm glad I wasn't there that day to see the same." He paused and drew in a deep breath. "But there has to be some forgiving of yourself or you might as well just lie down and die."

A guttural sound rose from my throat as though my subconscious agonized at my demise. "My friend, I believe I already have."

"Forgiven yourself?" He turned toward me.

"No, died."

✱ ✱ ✱ ✱ ✱

Neither of us had more to say. We sat on the hardwood floor, stretched our legs straight, and leaned our heads on the cool plaster wall. Moments later, like an antsy child, Finn began to whistle as he often did while he worked. Then he jumped to his feet, walked across the room with boots clomping, and rummaged through the paints on my supply table. This strange act continued until several tubes fell onto the floor.

"Hey, what do you think you're doing?" I pushed onto my knees and stood as a jar of brushes toppled over. "Knock it off. Don't touch anything." I stomped toward my easel.

"Catch."

Just in time, my hand reached into the air and caught a tube of paint.

"Nice catch. It could have clobbered you in the head." Finn laughed like he found my discomfort amusing. "But maybe that's what you need."

"You're acting like a fool." I rolled the tube over in my hand and read the label: Windsor Newton—Cadmium Yellow. "Throwing paint at me, are you?"

"No, just passing on the new color of the day, my friend." Finn snatched his hat from the chair. "You'd better stock up on that one. I hear there's plenty of sunshine where we're heading." He walked toward the door and turned the knob. "And get busy packing. McKelvey has us leaving on the train within the week." Finn opened the door and disappeared into the dark hallway.

Standing in my dimly lit apartment, Finn's off-key whistle diminished as he descended the stairs. Surprising myself, I smiled and went in search of a suitcase.

CHAPTER 9

The next morning, I awoke in my mother's bed. She was asleep in her floral reading chair—her slippered feet propped on the ottoman—snoring lightly like a purring cat.

Pushing myself upright caused a sharp pain to pulse in my shoulder. Ignoring the pain, I edged out of bed and landed softly on the floorboards so as not to wake Mother.

My clothes hung over the back of the chair in front of the vanity, and at the sight of my reflection in the mirror, I gasped. My hair was tangled and disheveled, and my left eye was slightly purple and swollen near the corner. *What in the world happened?*

Flashes of memory came racing back—of my legs giving way and the realization that I couldn't catch myself with both hands holding the plate of muffins and drinking glass. My left shoulder must have taken the brunt of the fall, followed by my face bumping against a chair, or perhaps the table. Strong arms—arms that must have belonged to Sheriff Murphy—carried me to Mother's bed. Then there was that voice that caused me to shudder.

"She'll be fine, Louisa. Put a cool cloth on her eye and let her rest." The voice and heavy breathing came from the edge of the bed. The scent of leather mixed with earth wafted from his body—the scent of a man who spent most of his days outside, and often upon a horse. "There's no need to call the doctor."

"All of this has been too much for her," Mother said. "She's always been a strong girl, but having him leave like that, and then hearing the news ..."

"Yes, ma'am. That's hard news to share with a woman left alone to raise a son by herself." The sheriff's voice was low, but I could still hear every piercing word. "If I may be so bold as to say that her fool of a husband made the worst decision of his life by leaving your amazing daughter. Bad enough it cost him his life." Heavy footsteps came closer to the bed. "I'll be by in the morning to check on the two of you. It may be high time Mary has some help once she realizes the state of her life."

His warm hand brushed across my forehead, but a chill raced through my pounding head.

I don't need anyone's help, especially from you, I wanted to shout, but the darkness of the night slipped into the house and blanketed me with only fitful dreams of Tuck grabbing his chest as I tried to scream his name.

* * * * *

As I stared into the mirror, my fingers tingled, and my legs shook. My entire body felt numb—all except my aching heart. Was Tuck really dead? Wasn't it all a horrible nightmare? As though confirming my greatest fear, tears of sadness and disbelief trickled down my cheeks.

With weak arms, I adjusted my dress over my undergarments and wondered how it had been removed last night. Mother was slight, and her sixty-plus years were beginning to show. She was still asleep in the worn and sunken chair, curled like an animal in a favorite resting spot. Had I been dealt the same uncertain and tragic plight as my mother?

No doubt, she was a strong woman—a survivor who had been abandoned by her hard-drinking and abusive husband. My father left when I was sixteen. Mother had done the unthinkable and divorced him after having eleven children, me being the sixth, to raise me and my five younger sisters and brothers back in Stockton, Ohio. My older siblings had found wives and husbands and moved on to new locations. John, my oldest brother, even went on to practice law back East while I helped Mother with the little ones and tended our small farm.

Looking back, my life had been held at bay for the sacrifice needed to help my mother. Suspended in the middle between the older siblings who were free to make their way, and the younger ones who needed both their mother and me, we became a team, strengthened by a love unique to a mother and daughter trying to navigate the difficulties of life.

Tragically, the youngest two, Albert and Anna, died of pneumonia in the winter of 1880. They were laid to rest in Stockton before Mother and I, and the remaining three children, moved to Adair. Two years later, a handsome young man from a neighboring farm caught my eye at the monthly social. On a crisp, autumn day, Tuck and I were married. After some time, my remaining younger siblings grew up, married, and moved to other Midwest towns. Mother managed well on her own, though I still offered help whenever needed. Even with a sore back and aching feet, her job at the general store, inventorying, selling, and taking care of the locals' needs kept her sharp and feeling appreciated.

"Oh, Mother." I placed a blanket over her arms. "You never wished for my life to be difficult like yours." My lips brushed her wrinkled forehead, and then I spun around in a panic. "Where is Wesley?" I started for the bedroom door.

"He's fine, dear." Mother waved a limp hand as though dismissing my fear. "He slept on the sofa last night. Wanted to be with you, but I told him you needed to rest well through the night, and his kicking and hogging the bed wouldn't make that possible."

"Does he know about his father?" My lips pursed in anticipation of her answer.

Mother shook her head. "It's best for you to tell him." She rubbed her hands together. "I told him you got overheated from the weather. Said we ladies get a little too hot sometimes. That's all."

"I'm going to go wake him and get us on home."

Mother slid her feet off the ottoman and pushed the blanket aside. "He got up early to go fishing. Sheriff Murphy came by before seven to check on you. Figured since you were still sleeping, he'd take the boy to the river to catch some trout."

My jaw dropped. When I found the words, it was better not to tell my mother what was on my mind. After grabbing my hat, I ran out the front door and jumped off the porch, not bothering with the three steps.

* * * * *

After a few minutes of running as fast as I could manage in a long skirt, I reached the river. A scan of the bank showed no sight of the sheriff or Wesley. Sweat stung the cut near my eye. My head pounded, and my shoulder throbbed. I cradled my arm next to my body to calm the pain.

The river meandered and gurgled now that summer had passed. It appeared only knee-deep in most places. The bushes and pines were thick along the bank, and it was impossible to see past the first bend. The best vantage point to look both east and west along the waterway would be to wade into the middle. Finding a grassy spot, my shoes were quickly unlaced and tugged off along with my stockings. The cool grass felt good on my bare feet, reminding me of earlier years when Tuck would take my hand, and we'd sneak away from town and swim in the deep waters where the river ran through the canyon walls.

Pushing the memory from my mind, I hiked my dress around my knees. The first step sent a shiver up my leg, and the sandy bottom squished between my toes. Another step welcomed the water gently swirling around my calves, inviting me to play in its presence. It was a strange sensation. Part of me was determined to find Wesley and put an end to his fishing interlude with the man who was clearly not his father as quickly as possible. Yet at the same time, the water was bathing me—cleansing me of my fear and worry. After wading three steps further and lifting my dress around my waist, the water splashed and hopped like a child released from school on the first day of summer.

Like a dry dishrag, the hem of my clothing dipped and absorbed the water, taking on an awkward weight. I tucked my right arm under its layers and lifted the pale blue fabric above the water, determined to free myself from the burden.

Nearly to the middle of the river, a sense of lightness washed over me—a release from the darkness that had invaded our home. With my eyes closed and my head tilted back, the sun warmed my face as the gurgling water whispered my name.

My foot stepped where the smooth rocks became dislodged and left a divot in the river bottom. Suddenly, the water pulsed against my waist. It encircled me and propelled my body forward as though ensnared in a crowd. Unable to hold my dress higher, the cloth drank the water—parched and greedy like the scorched dirt road running out of town. Losing my balance, I let go of the petticoat and extended my arms to steady myself. Like a rock, all the bulky material dropped into the water and encircled my legs, tripping and dragging me into the river. The sandy bottom, mixed with rocks and sticks, brushed against my hands, making it impossible to reorient myself.

The strong current pulled my feet out from under me. No longer able to stand, my head bobbed under the surface. My hair fell loose from its bun and tangled around my mouth and eyes. Up became down. Down became up. My instincts knew the river was fairly calm and should allow me to simply force my legs downward. Then my feet could plant themselves and stand, finding myself in only waist or chest-high water. But the tangle of my clothing, like an anchor securing a ship, defeated my attempts to be free. The chance of stopping myself from floating further downstream was only temporary.

Trapped.

The realization spun through my mind, and for one brief moment I was drowning. First a swirl of blue, green, and white—gasping for air—then everything went black.

* * * * *

As though being plucked from the river by the hand of God, someone grabbed me around the waist and lifted me above the water. Massive arms held me, and as they pressed harder, I coughed and gagged as a small river of its own sputtered from my mouth. Though the current still tugged at me, an arm scooped under my legs and nestled me.

Pushing the hair from my face with a limp hand, my eyes took in the face of Sheriff Murphy. His eyes were dark, his lips terse. It was difficult to be certain, but a look of fear—foreign for a man of his stature—swept across his face. He only stared at me, then waded toward the riverbank. Once at the edge and still cradling me against his chest, he climbed the embankment and laid me on dry ground.

"Mama!" Wesley sprang from the brush, panting hard, eyes as big as wagon wheels. "We saw you fall. I tried to swim upriver to catch you." He was shaking, and his shirt and pants clung to his tiny body.

"He's one tough little boy. Threw his rod into the water and started running upstream like a fish going to new spawning ground." The sheriff grinned at my son. "Problem is the water's too swift and the rocks too slippery for a boy his size."

"Oh, Wesley." My arms reached out and pulled him close. He rested his head on my chest and cried. "I am so sorry to frighten you." I hugged him tightly. "I wouldn't hurt you for the world."

The familiar saying echoed in my mind. My mother said it to me as a child, and Tuck and I coined it early on in our marriage and with our three sons. How drastically my life had changed. However, determined to keep that promise for Wesley, I repeated the phrase. "I wouldn't hurt you for the world." A coughing fit followed, and I rolled onto my side, spitting a rancid fluid into the dirt.

Spent, Wesley stepped aside and plopped onto the grass.

"Here, let me help you to your knees." Sheriff Murphy took my hand, helping me sit upright. "You have half the river in your gut."

Rocking forward, deep breaths slowly filled my lungs—air that had always been taken for granted. With bowed head and eyes closed, I silently prayed for the first time in weeks, perhaps even months. And even though death had just taken my husband, I thanked God for letting me live. Mostly, I thanked Him for Wesley.

"Mary." The sheriff's voice was urgent as he held my hair away from my face. "Are you all right?"

When my eyes opened, the man who had plucked me from the river was crouched in front of me. The fear on his face had waned, but squinted eyes revealed what seemed to be genuine concern.

"I'm all right." I nodded sheepishly, feeling ashamed of not only my foolishness, but also my appearance. My soaked clothing was in disarray around my body, and the bodice clung to my chest. My usually wavy golden hair with flecks of auburn hung limp and matted against the sides of my face.

Obviously exhausted, the sheriff sat on the grass and stretched out his legs. His pants were soaked, and his shirt equally wet from holding me against his chest. Slipping off his boots, he tipped them upside down and let the water dribble out. For the first time, we all laughed.

His squinting eyes locked with mine. "You really scared me, Mary." The man swallowed hard. "I mean, not much scares me, but I thought you ..." He grimaced. "I thought I had lost you."

Thought I had lost you. The words felt strange to my ears. Logically, I knew what he meant, but the way he looked at me made me uneasy. Why couldn't I be grateful for heaven's sake? The man just saved me from certain death.

The words were forced but had to be spoken. "Thank you for saving my life." I bowed my head to avoid those piercing eyes. "It was foolish to go into the water like that. It would have been easy to find you and Wesley by looking up and down the river. When Mother said you took my boy fishing, it was obvious you'd be somewhere near this area."

"Why did you come looking for him?" He cocked his head to the side and looked at me as if confused. "I'd have brought him home soon enough." He put his hat on and adjusted the brim. "I'd say after yesterday's tumble on the porch and now a near drowning, we've had enough excitement from you for a while."

Heat rushed to my face. For someone who prided herself on being capable with most things, in less than twenty-four hours, the same man who'd brought news of my husband's death carried me to safety.

Ignoring his latter comments, my words formed with as much composure as possible. "It was time to get along home. That's all."

Once on my feet, I felt light-headed, and my body swayed. The man offered his hand, but I pretended not to notice.

Wesley came to my side and slid his arm around my waist. "I'll help you home, Mama."

"Son, your mother may need a bit more help than you can offer." Sheriff Murphy stepped to my other side and took my elbow.

"We'll be fine." I followed with a forced smile. *After all, you did just save my life.* "You truly saved my life. How can I ever repay you?" The words were cliché and came too easily. But the moment they were spoken, I wished to take them back.

"You can start by calling me David. Sheriff Murphy is too formal for someone who has held you twice in his arms within the last twenty-four hours." He tipped his hat and walked away from the river. After a few steps, he stopped and looked back. "I believe someday you'll have the opportunity to repay me."

He snickered, and the sound caused a sensation to ripple through my body that was hard to describe—as if from some faraway and future place, a door-rattling, pounding on my soul.

"You could say I feel it in my bones," he added as he stepped into the thick brush bordering the river and disappeared from sight.

I looked down at my son and pulled him close. "Time for both of us to put on dry clothes."

"And time to eat." He smiled up at me with his missing-front-tooth grin. "I'm as starved as a coyote chasin' rabbits for days."

I chuckled in spite of my exhaustion. "Where did you hear that?"

"Daddy made it up." Wesley took my hand. Together, we made our way through the scrub brush and grasses toward the road.

Once we got home, he would need to know about Tuck—need to know his father would never be coming home. I squeezed his small hand. No child should ever have to hear those words. No child. Especially not mine.

* * * * *

Whether it was the moment in the river when death called my name or a mother's deepest instinct to protect her child at any cost, my decision was sealed. It was all too clear now. It was time to leave Adair to begin a new life. If not, all the heartache from the losses and betrayals would pull me under. I'd stop breathing … stop living. I couldn't do that to my son and wouldn't do that to myself. And in that precious, brief moment before the water pulled me under, the river cradled and refreshed me. In that moment, I believe God was reminding me that only He could calm the raging waters in my life.

CHAPTER 10

Daniel ~ Train from Boston, September 7, 1893

Finn dozed as the Atchison, Topeka, and Santa Fe Railway tracks led us across the border and into New York. Undoubtedly, he had stayed out late with his friends and—if he had his way—Elizabeth Turney as well. Suppressing a yawn, I pulled my bowler lower to shade my eyes from the sun's glare.

My fatigue was brought on by something else—painting well into the night, covering over the grays and muddy greens in the park scene I had begun weeks before. Now, the canvas was transformed with blue, crimson, ochre, and, admittedly, an abundance of bright cadmium yellow into a scene that forced me to smile. Surely, Finn would like to claim I finally came to my senses and took him up on his challenge to render my paintings—and my perspective on life—more optimistically. Maybe Finn's prompting did urge me to come up for air, fill my lungs, my mind, and possibly even my heart with life, at least one more time.

Logically, it made no sense to be so excited to temporarily leave the comforts of Boston, along with the modern conveniences and sophistication of the East Coast. Even in the plummeting national economy, the city offered many intriguing places. For me, it provided a job and a place to lay my head. Lucky, some would say. In my mind, I was blessed. The country's unemployment had risen to eighteen percent, and banks and businesses were closing their doors at an alarming rate.

Last February, days before Grover Cleveland was inaugurated, an unnerving panic rose over the rich and poor. Like a continual drizzle, the Globe and every other newspaper across the country recounted the dismal economic situation. Whether people read the paper to keep informed, to commiserate with others experiencing the same duress, or to simply watch for a glimmer of hope for their future, the stories, articles, reports, photographs, and illustrations captivated the populous and kept me working.

The Globe paid me a decent salary that allowed for a comfortable flat at ten dollars a month. A new coal-burning furnace in the basement of the building pushed heated water into the radiator throughout the cold winter months.

In the evenings, large windows welcomed the warm glow of the gas street lamps. For the little cooking I did, a small wood-burning stove was sufficient. After all, a market and several restaurants were a short stroll from my front door—a convenient excuse for my mostly bare pantry. Running water served my other needs and those of five neighbors down the hall.

With another quick glance at Finn, I folded my arms behind my head. Why would anyone leave all that to head to a desolate, rural, and—by all reports—wild and unruly landscape? *Maybe they have nothing left to leave.* My eyelids became as heavy as my thoughts. *Or perhaps they're running away, choosing to leave something, someone …* I swallowed hard … *or a haunting memory behind.*

I awoke much later to Finn rustling a newspaper in my face.

"Daniel, you've been sleeping for hours. Been missing all the excitement at the depot stops."

One eye opened enough to squint at the back of the *Wichita Daily Eagle, September 6, 1893.* "Either we've made it all the way to Kansas, and you're reading day-old news, or we've gone back in time." My thumb methodically rubbed the soreness from my neck.

"I believe we're somewhere in the heart of Indiana now." Finn creased the paper. "Someone left this in the dining car. Take a listen. 'Eight thousand people in line at Arkansas City, two thousand more arriving each day. The Santa Fe will run six trains for the boomers. The Rock Island will also run six boomer trains. These trains will be used mostly by those going to the town sites.'" Finn peered at me over the top of the paper.

"And?" My head automatically cocked in anticipation of his brilliant response.

"Just think, thousands of people swarming like flies on a horse's rear end coming on all those trains." He tapped on the glass. "And by what I'm seeing, the further west we travel, it's beginning to look like a horse's rear end."

"Not sure about that." I gazed out the window and took in the golden fields of prairie grass stretching endlessly to the south. The waving grasses, syncopating between a golden yellow and a deep, earthy rust, reminded me of the ocean waves I had lived near most of my life. "I find it to be … freeing."

"Poetic, my friend." Finn propped his feet on the seat opposite him. "Let's see if you find it as freeing when we depart the train into a sea of people who haven't bathed for weeks."

I nudged him with the toe of my boot. "Finn Allaway, you are becoming a snob."

"Alas, I'm afraid I've become a Bostonian."

"I don't think a Scotsman can officially do that. At least not one who hails from Galloway and Wigtown." My eyebrows drew together as I studied my friend. "Aren't you the one who maintained, once a Scot, always a Scot?"

Finn sighed and pushed my boot away from his leg. "Aye, I did at that. But that's all behind me. Now, I'd be classified an American." His boyish enthusiasm was infectious. "But with the wit and good looks of the Scottish."

* * * * *

The train slowed as we pulled into the next large town. Between the crowds on the platform, I pieced together the letters on the sign designating that we had arrived in Indianapolis.

More passengers climbed aboard, filling the cars to capacity. A miscellany of humanity, mostly men with a few women, filled the cars with various accents and languages. Like a patchwork of mismatched fabrics, Germans, Italians, Poles, Russians, French, Dutch, and many more, clambered to find seats as the train lunged forward toward what most were seeking—a better life and the opportunity to claim their own land in the West.

A burly man with a thick, black mustache wedged himself into the seat across the aisle. He positioned a brown leather case on his lap and began shuffling through papers.

Finn and I eyed one another. Whatever he was doing, it obviously had great urgency to be completed before he arrived at his destination. He cursed under his breath and then looked across the aisle at me.

"Would you happen to have a pen and ink?" In spite of his overgrown mustache, his clear green eyes and smooth, rosy cheeks revealed a much younger man than one might have guessed. "Must have left mine behind in my hurry to get packed and catch the ol' iron horse."

"I can oblige you." Fumbling in my bag secured in the rack above my seat, I found what the man needed. "It's not much of an eye-drop filler. Been having a horrible time with it leaking. Here's a pencil, if you prefer."

"Thank you, sir. I'll take my chances with the pen. Can't have anyone erasing the contents of these important documents." He reached for more papers and a handful slid onto the floor. More curt words followed as he bent at his rotund waist.

"Let me help." Finn gathered the papers, handed them to the man, and extended his free right hand. "Finn Allaway at your service."

"Bartholomew Reid." The man held the papers against his chest and extended his right hand. "Attorney at Law."

"Pleasure to meet you, Mr. Reid." Finn nodded toward me. "This is my friend, Daniel McKenzie."

I reached across the aisle and shook the attorney's hand. "Welcome aboard."

"Lucky to get a ticket. Had to pay extra and take a first-class seat. Second class is sold out to the Boomers. They're even letting folks huddle in the freight cars." He took a handkerchief from his front pocket and wiped the sweat forming on his temple. "Feel awful for those people back there. The heat is merciless, and there's no letting up in the direction we're heading." He shook his head and wiped it again. "No, I've never experienced temperatures and dust like those in Guthrie. Can't believe I'm going back."

"To the Oklahoma Territory?" My eyebrows shot up. "Amazing what happened. They say a town grew up overnight. We hear Oklahoma City is going to give Guthrie some fierce competition as the state capitol if things go that way."

"My bets are on Perry to be the next metropolis." Mr. Reid pulled a paper from the stack. "See this map? Some forty-two-thousand claims to be made. Most of them are one-hundred-sixty acres each, just waiting to be snatched up."

The map was neatly divided into a perfect grid, each square labeled with a number. He pointed to a section in the bottom left, also equally segmented into smaller rectangles set apart by longer, narrow strips running north and south, and east and west. "But it's not a big homestead I'm after. No, sirs." He tapped a pudgy forefinger on town lot number twenty-three. The attorney lowered his voice, "That prime piece of land is the future site of the law offices of Simon, Levy, and Reid."

"But you don't have it yet." Finn strained his neck to survey the map.

Mr. Reid glanced around and then leaned in closer. "That's true. But I will." He ran his finger along a thin line bordering the grid. "See, the train will run all the way to this point. Just about here it should slow down to a crawl. That's when I'll jump off and run like a bat out of hades for my lot, pound the flag in the dirt, and stand my ground until a registrar documents my claim." He wiped the sweat from his brow once again, obviously excited at his plan.

I think my eyes had opened as wide as Finn's. "You mean you're going to jump off a train, run through the sagebrush for who knows how far, and beat the others who are racing on horses and in buggies?"

The lawyer frowned. "Sir, I may not look like one who can run at lightning speed, but I assure you, I have the brains and determination to beat any other man when my future is at stake." He lowered his voice even more. "Not to mention, Mr. Simon and Mr. Levy will not be pleased if I don't secure our parcel."

Finn chuckled. "And where are Mr. Simon and Mr. Levy?"

Mr. Reid frowned and looked rather annoyed. "Most likely napping after indulging in an ample and expensive meal."

"Why aren't they making the Run with you?" I asked. "Seems if the three of you were going for the same lot, you'd stand a better chance if at least one of you made it there before the others." I looked at Finn. "Don't you agree, partner?"

Finn nodded and grinned. "Sounds right to me."

"That might work for you, gentlemen, but Mr. Harold Simon and Mr. Rubin Levy, Esquires, they are not the sort of men to be getting themselves involved in situations like this, at least not directly. They've made me the offer that if I secure lot number twenty-three, they'll make me partner—the youngest in the firm's history. Simon, Levy … and Reid."

"So, these wise businessmen see a future in the new territory?" I asked. "And they see you as the right man to set up shop?"

"That's exactly right. They know I'm not only smart but brave enough to expand the firm into an area that will need my expertise with law." He leaned back and gave us a contented smile. "That's what all these papers are for. There are hundreds of cattlemen begging for help to keep the land they've been leasing from the Cherokee for years, not to mention all the homesteads that will be changing hands once the Rush is over. There will be businesses setting up left and right." He lifted my pen, and a thin trickle of black ink dribbled onto his thumb. "Yes, Bartholomew Reid will become a household name in the Oklahoma Territory."

"Well now, that might make jumping off a moving train worth it." Finn gave the man a mock salute. "If you don't die trying, that is."

As our conversation stalled, I turned to the window to keep myself from laughing. Only the sound of rustling papers came from across the aisle. A few minutes later, the sound of screeching metal was followed by passengers being lunged forward as the train came to an abrupt halt.

Mr. Reid scrambled from his seat to retrieve his open case that had slid from his lap. I joined him on my hands and knees to retrieve the papers scattered haphazardly under the seats ahead and a few feet down the aisle.

"Where is it?" he muttered to himself, grabbing more papers and clutching them to his chest. When he lifted his head, the color had drained from his face. "They'll kill me."

"Who?" I handed him crumpled papers.

He ignored my question, ruffled through the sheets, and then tossed them onto his cushion. "You have it, don't you?"

My baffled expression must have answered his question as he returned to poking his head under other seats. He searched as though his life depended on finding whatever had been kept in his leather case.

What did he have in there besides all those contracts?

In the commotion of passengers gathering items that had fallen from the racks and a few young children being calmed by their mothers, my gaze settled on a gentleman two rows ahead of Mr. Reid. Unlike the other passengers who were trying to settle back into their seats, he clutched his belongings and hastily made his way toward the vestibule leading to the next car. Finding it odd that this passenger was moving at such a hurried pace, the journalist in me decided to follow him.

"Where are you going?" Finn put down the newspaper he had been reading as if nothing had occurred.

"Acting on a hunch." I stepped over Mr. Reid, who was still crawling in the aisle, swiping his hands from side to side near the passengers' shoes.

"Then I'm coming with you," Finn called after me.

Instead of passing into the adjoining car, the man I was following took a sharp left and bounded down the steps leading to the outside of the train. He was lanky and his stride long as I scrambled in the loose gravel to catch up to him alongside the passenger cars. Though too hot for the weather, he wore a long, leather coat, its tails flapping like a bird caught in a windstorm.

I ducked my head and ran faster.

"What in the …" Finn shouted.

"Gut says that fellow took something of Mr. Reid's." I panted as Finn came alongside me.

He nodded and took off at a youth's pace.

When I caught up, Finn had the tall man pinned against the railing on the first passenger car. A good head shorter than the man, Finn held him by the shirt collar. The gray-bearded man struggled to free himself, but the wrinkles on his forehead and around his glassy eyes betrayed his age. He gagged as Finn tightened his hold.

"You got something that isn't yours?" Finn sneered.

This was a new side of my friend—at least one I had never experienced. "Take it easy, Finn."

He released his grip. The man straightened his collar and glared.

"We don't want any trouble. Just what you have in your pocket." I stepped forward and thumped the man on his chest. "Or we can call those conductors over here, and they can get the proper authorities."

Standing next to the coal car, two men in dark suits and short-brimmed caps were exchanging heated words, presumably about who was to blame for a train still sitting at the depot when another was approaching. Both conductors shook their fists in the air and yelled over one another until the engineer called from the window that the train was ready to resume its course.

"I got nothing of yours." The man darted his eyes toward the crowd milling around the platform. "Leave me be unless you want real trouble." He began to slip his hand inside his coat but stopped.

"Like this kind of trouble?" Finn growled as he poked a Colt revolver into the man's gut.

My eyes widened, but for that moment, it was necessary to act as though this event was a common occurrence for my friend and me.

I opened the man's coat enough to pull a crumpled envelope from his pocket. It was bulging and partially torn open, exposing money. Assuredly, a great deal of it.

"Looks like we've caught us a train robber." Finn pushed in closer, causing the man to groan. "I'm sure the sheriff of this town would like to meet you since you stole money belonging to Mr. Bartholomew Reid."

Without warning, the train's whistle screeched. Like startled possums, the three of us stared at one another. Smoke billowed from the train's chimney as it inched forward. Grabbing the man's arm, I pulled him away from the tracks where he then stumbled and fell.

He pushed himself to his knees and cursed, eyes wild like a rabid dog. "Better catch the train, gentlemen." He gave us a look that said he would not forget us. "And I know just where yer headin'." He coughed as if years of dirt had settled in his throat. "I'll be sure to see you and yer friend again. Mr. Bartholomew Reid—a memorable name." He stood and hobbled toward the congestion of travelers on the platform.

With another blast from the whistle, I nodded at Finn to put the gun away, slipped the envelope into my pocket, and we raced back to our car, barely in time to leap onto the steps as the train moved down the tracks.

CHAPTER 11

Mary ~ Mother Talk, September 7, 1893

Leaving a life behind is much easier when you have little to leave. Except for Wesley and my small rented house, the rest of my belongings were sparse that needed to fit into the cramped space allotted to me on Lizzie and Joseph Contolini's buckboard wagon. The older couple had graciously offered to let me join them and their horse, Sadie, on the four-hundred-mile, nearly week-long journey to Arkansas City. Short of walking, there were no other means of travel to one of the designated jumping-off towns to register for the Run. From there, I would make my way to the starting line on the sixteenth of September and wait for the noontime gunshot that would launch me and thousands of others on a mad dash into the future.

* * * * *

"Not much room except for a change of clothes and a few books." I pressed down on the top of the small case mother had retrieved from her attic. She had set it on the extra bed that Wesley and I had been sharing since we vacated our house in August. "Lizzie said she'll help me sneak a few extra items into the back of the wagon when Joseph isn't looking."

"That man never smiles. He's either had a hard life from the start or regrets he ever left Italy." Mother lifted the hem of her skirt. "But he knows how to mend a boot. Put a new heel on for me when mine caught in a rut on the street."

"It's hard not to be concerned about them making the trip, let alone being in the race. It's a long way in this heat, and Lizzie said she hasn't been feeling well lately. I worry about her." I ran my fingers gently across my mother's cheek. "I worry about you too."

"Why?"

"For one, you'll be here alone. And you're—"

"Old?"

Sitting next to my mother on the edge of the bed, we both looked at our reflections in the vanity mirror. Her once dark hair had turned the silver of the full moon on a cold winter's night. Mine was golden, like the harvest moon, mixed with the added warmth of auburn—the same moon, made by one Creator, yet revealed so differently in the phases of our lives.

Her hair, smooth along a delicate hairline and pulled back in her usual bun until bedtime, revealed a thin neck and slight frame. Wrinkles coursed their way across her forehead like the lines on a map, reflecting the detours and journeys her life had followed. I studied her cheekbones, and then her soft lips—the gateway to wise and discerning words shared with those she loved over so many years.

In comparison, my hair curved around my face and cascaded onto strong shoulders—its thickness and waves determining its own course. And even though the proper style was to keep it brushed and pulled tightly in a bun and clips, it gave me pleasure to release it at the end of a long day and set it free—allow it to be untamed like the desires and dreams of my heart. My cheekbones shared a similar high position to Mother's, but my lips were different than hers. Mine wore the fullness of more years to come—more years to learn to speak kindly and wisely, to smile, to laugh, and … possibly to touch another's.

How could I think such a thing? I'm never going to rely on love again.

Mother giggled like a schoolgirl.

"Why are you laughing?"

"In so many ways you are still the little girl who climbed high into the trees and crawled to the ends of limbs, bouncing in the breeze. You are the girl your schoolteacher described as very intelligent, but even more obstinate. And most definitely, you are the same girl who challenged the boys to races in the field and beat them every time." Mother clapped her hands together. "I'm glad you did."

"Even though the neighbors told you I should—"

"Act more like a lady?"

She smiled at our reflections in the mirror. "Yes. I'm glad the Lord served you a healthy portion of courage and determination." She turned toward me, leaving the two people in the mirror to eavesdrop. "Because you're going to need that and so much more to succeed at what you're taking on." Her smile faded, and her eyes locked with mine. "I'm older for sure ... slowing down in many ways."

"But, Mother, you're doing well. Every day you—"

"It's hard to accept. But you see it. My steps are slower, each one contemplated. Opening a canning jar used to be easy. The names of folks I once knew dangle on the tip of my tongue and then slip away as if swallowed—still inside me but unreachable." She gave me a sad smile. "Surely, I couldn't ride a horse like before."

"But you're feeling healthy, right?" A knot settled in my throat. "Nothing's wrong?"

"No, I'm fine. The good Lord knows to keep me around to take care of Wesley until you get settled and come back to fetch him." She tilted her head as if looking straight through the ceiling toward heaven. "Lord, am I right with thinking you need me here more than there for quite some time?" She hesitated as if waiting for a response, then looked at me again. "Now, I want *you* to think about something."

"I know what you're about to say. We can have a good life here, and I should drop this wild idea of going into an unknown and dangerous situation, especially for a widowed woman. It would be better to stay and be a good mother to Wesley and find a responsible man to marry. Even Sheriff Murphy. But I'll tell you—"

"Stop, child." She cupped my face between her soft palms and gently placed her forefinger across my lips. "Listen. That's all I'm asking."

My lips automatically pursed, and my eyes closed. So many times, I'd had to calm the defiance that raged in me—the instinct to justify my position and maintain my independence. *Pride.* The misguided badge of honor I'd worn for much of my life.

"I'm not asking you to give up a dream or be someone you were never meant to be. I'm not even asking you to reconsider staying here, even though it scares me to death at the thought that something or someone might ..." Her voice wavered.

When my eyes opened, hers were moist. My heart ached, but I continued to listen for the words she would be sure to choose carefully.

"You're right. This body is getting older, and if I had my way, I would want you to be part of as many of those days as possible. But my hopes, and perhaps yours, are not necessarily the plan God has for you. That's what really matters. It's the only thing, really." She took my hands in hers and gently ran her thumb over my skin, just as she had done hundreds of times when I was a child, sad or hurt. "Go to Him and ask if this is His plan for you."

Tears blurred my vision, further clouding the confusion playing havoc in my mind since Tuck left. "I have prayed. At least I've tried. Maybe He doesn't want to hear from me." An unexpected sob released a torrent of tears held back for over a month.

Mother pulled me into her arms and kissed the top of my head. "Oh, my sweet Mary. He's not only listening to you, He's working in you. You just have to make room for Him."

My arms wrapped around her, and we clung to each other as the setting sun dimmed the room. Resting my head against her chest, I memorized the sound of her beating heart—tucking away a part of her that I could carry with me forever.

* * * * *

Later that evening, Wesley and I snuggled in bed to read more of *Treasure Island*. I read longer than usual, wanting to savor each minute with my son before leaving the next day with the Contolinis.

Joseph's plan was to spend the first night in one of the small towns on the way to Kansas City. Eventually, we would head directly south toward the Territory, hoping to reach our destination in about a week if all went well with the wagon, the horse, the weather, and whatever other obstacles we could stumble upon.

"Who's gonna read the rest of the story to me?" Wesley yawned as he rubbed his eyes.

"Your grandmother is *going* to finish the story with you. But you have to promise me that you won't tell me what happens to Jim Hawkins. I want to find out when we read it again in our new home."

"Where's that *going* to be?" He rolled onto his side, propped his head in his hand, and stared at me with brown eyes the size of the moon. "Will it be a big house like Teddy Reynolds'?"

"No, not nearly that big. That's quite a house."

"Can we have cows and horses? And a dog too?"

"Maybe someday." I forced my smile to remain as reality flashed across my mind. *Sod house. Struggling garden. Windswept fields of prairie grass. Freezing winters and blazing hot summers.*

Tuck and I had talked with others who knew folks who made the 1889 Rush near Oklahoma City and Guthrie, towns of ten-thousand-plus people that literally sprang up in half a day on the twenty-second of August. The people we talked with and the newspaper stories we read shared many success stories but also acknowledged thousands of failures and lost dreams. Maybe that's partly why my husband left, hoping the gold in the mountains of Colorado would be a better way to go—an easier way to happiness. Too bad he never made it.

"Are you sure there aren't any Indians?" Wesley's eyes grew wide.

"Some have stayed on the land where they've been allowed."

"Hmmm." He squinted as he did when in deep thought. "That doesn't seem fair."

I leaned back on the pillow and let out a sigh. "You're right. Not everything in life makes sense."

It was silent except for the lingering chirps of the crickets outside the open window. Then, an almost inaudible whisper broke the quiet. "I miss Daddy. I wish he was still here."

For a moment, I couldn't respond. I missed the old Tuck— the man with whom I first fell in love, married, and shared in the creation of three wonderful children. But he had ceased to exist. Even before "death do us part," the Tuck I knew and loved had died at the expense of drink and the desire for those other than me. But what does a mother say to a six-year-old boy missing his father?

I pulled Wesley close, holding him as only a mother can—unconditionally and completely. "I miss him too. If only he could be here with us." Kissing his hair, ears, and cheeks, I tried to stamp the essence of his scent into my memory for the long journey ahead.

"How long will you be gone?" He wiggled out of my grasp and eyed me with one eye squinted again, revealing the seriousness of his question.

"Only a month. I plan to be back by the middle of October." I fastened the top button of his nightshirt. "Besides, you'll be busy with school. You'll hardly notice I'm gone when you're with all your friends. You may not even want to leave school."

"Yeah, I'll do good in school, especially 'cuz I'm smarter than most of the other kids."

"You'll do *well* in school *because* you like to learn." I tapped the end of his nose. "Now, time for sleep. Morning isn't going to wait for us."

"You always say that."

"That's because your mother is smart too." I kissed his forehead and pulled up the sheet and blanket even though the late summer heat lingered longer than usual. "I love you more than the drops of water in the sea."

"I love you more than the all the apples on Grandmother's tree." Wesley giggled. "Even though I picked most of them."

"Goodnight, honey."

"I like it when we play that game."

"Me too." It was a game learned in my childhood. My mother had played it with all of her children, and I couldn't help but wonder how long it took her to get us all to sleep.

Nearing the bedroom door, a piece of paper caught my eye tucked in the wooden frame of the mirror above the dresser. My mother's slanted and precise handwriting was easily recognizable, always presented as carefully as her spoken words.

Dear Mary,

The Lord wanted me to share this with you. He wants you to know there is a divine plan especially for you if you will seek Him. He loves you even more than I do. That's hard for me to comprehend, yet I deeply believe it is true.

Loving you more than all the leaves in the trees,
Mother

For brethren, I count not myself to have apprehended: but this one thing I do, forgetting those things which are behind, and reaching forth unto those things which are before, I press toward the mark for the prize of the high calling of God in Christ Jesus. Philippians 3:13-14

I met my reflection in the mirror. A sliver of moonlight danced on my face as the curtains swayed with the gentle night breeze. Like a game of hide-and-seek, the light shifted, illuminating parts of me, hiding others in the darkness. I stood there for several minutes until Wesley's breathing changed to a slight snore. I was alone with God.

God, I know You're real, and I want to believe You love me. It may be true that You have a calling for me, some plan that's hard to understand. But I need to do some things on my own for now. Prove to myself that I'm capable to make my own way. I don't want to depend on anyone else to be happy or content. Even You.

Carefully, I folded the paper and set it on the dresser, took a slight step backward into the darkness, and then slipped out of the room.

CHAPTER 12

Mary ~ Lizzie Talk, September 10, 1893

A few days into our journey to Arkansas City, it was easy to understand why Joseph was a man of few words. Lizzie did all the talking. Not that I minded. She had a thought about nearly every farmhouse, town, and traveler we encountered. Even though I hardly got in a word, her way of recalling details from the past and vivid descriptions made her stories come alive like an illustrated book. Best of all was her ability to see the beauty in endless fields of yellow, brown, and occasionally green-feathered grasses. The talking went on and on for hours, but it helped pass the days of traveling on the rutted and dusty roads.

Her sixty years of living included a childhood spent in upper state New York before being sent to Chicago by her parents to attend art school. Her adeptness with a brush and palette had been noticed when she was coming of age, and a plan by her parents to send her away was soon realized.

"But the real reason was that Thomas Horner had fallen in love with me." Lizzie leaned in closer to me as we bumped along in the back of the wagon. "And," she whispered, "I had feelings for him as well."

Joseph glanced back at the two of us. "I heard that, Lizzie."

We were wedged between a large wooden chest, a barrel of water, bags of flour, slats of wood, and a roll of canvas for our makeshift tent that would serve as our home until the start of the race.

"Oh, Joseph. You know that was only infatuation. Nothing like my love for you and our forty years of marital bliss." Lizzie pinched my arm, and I had to suppress a giggle.

"That's the truth, *amore mio*." He turned his attention back to the road. "And may God give us many more years together."

"How did you meet?" I shifted my position to relieve the numbness in my backside. Surprisingly, neither of them spoke as if they hadn't heard my question. "In Chicago?"

More silence followed, and then Joseph spoke. "At the art school."

"I didn't know you studied art as well."

Lizzie's face reddened, and she looked away.

I reached for her. "Are you all right, Lizzie? Your face is all flushed."

"Whoa!" Joseph called out to Sadie. The wagon came to an abrupt halt.

Wondering why we had stopped so quickly, I propped myself onto my knees to see if something had blocked our way. Nothing ahead appeared out of the ordinary, so I figured Joseph had to relieve himself behind a cluster of trees, especially when he hopped off the front board onto the ground. He walked toward the back of the wagon, folded his arms over the sideboard, and stared, first at Lizzie and then at me. That's when he started to laugh. It began as a low rumble, but then his laughter turned into a full belly laugh as his eyes watered and snorts erupted.

"Here we go." Lizzie sighed, though she couldn't help but disclose a smile. "This is what happens when he's kept his emotions in check for too long." She shook her head. "Comes out like a prisoner set free."

I'm sure my eyes were wide, but I never expected to witness the stoic and serious Mr. Joseph Contolini nearly doubled over from a fit of laughter. This was as good a chance as any to stretch, so I stood and arched my back. "Are either of you going to tell me what is so funny?"

Joseph cocked his head at Lizzie. "Should we tell her?"

"I don't know, honey." Lizzie pushed herself to a stand as well. "It's hard to explain."

"Explain what?" I asked, continuing to stretch. "Come on, Lizzie. You've talked for days, so you can't hold back on me now."

"True enough, and you've provided me a good audience. Joseph gets tired of being the only set of ears."

Another snort followed. "Don't let her fool you. I've learned to pretend I'm listening."

Lizzie waved off his comment. "Go ahead, Joseph. Tell her what's got you in such a fit."

As though contemplating the decision to share, Joseph proceeded to pace alongside the wagon. When he stopped, he looked me straight in the eyes. "I wasn't a student of art. I was an object of art."

My eyes traveled from Lizzie and then back to Joseph, whose mouth widened into a broad smile.

"I don't understand." Now heat was rising to my own face for not being privy to their inside story. "What do you mean you were an object of art?"

"He was a model," Lizzie stated as though sharing the day's weather.

"A model?"

She tugged on my sleeve. "You know … the person who poses in the middle of the room, and the students sketch the human form."

Joseph had struck an absurd pose on the side of the road—one hand on his hip, the other under his chin with head tipped back, staring at the sky.

"He was a divine subject. Full of muscle and form." Lizzie giggled like a schoolgirl.

A flashback to the pictures of Michelangelo's paintings and sculptures in an art history book tucked on Mother's bookshelf brought a startling realization. I placed my hand over my mouth and blinked my eyes a few times to try and shut out the images.

"No, ma'am. It's not what you're thinking." Joseph waved his forefinger in the air. "I was clothed, to be sure." He spread his arms as if to take a bow. "The young ladies were so smitten, all they could do was sit and stare. Hardly any painting happened in that studio."

"And Monsieur Patelle, our French-born instructor, would turn purple in the face and tell us we were doomed to become nothing. Or at least he said something like that." Lizzie rolled her eyes. "I never did very well in French class."

"Regardless, that's when Lizzie fell in love with me." Joseph reached toward his petite wife and lifted her from the wagon.

She wrapped her arms around his neck and kissed his cheek. "That's partly true, my dear. There I was, trying to concentrate on sketching the human figure. Then it occurs to me, *that man is staring at me*." As if pulled back by time, she surveyed her husband.

"It was my wink." Joseph ceremoniously closed his left eye. "That's what made her swoon."

Lizzie nodded in agreement. "I believe *that* is true, Mr. Contolini. And from head to toe, you were quite a sight—even fully clothed."

"Lizzie!" Now my face was surely the color of a ripe apple. "There's more to you than I ever knew." I shook my head at Joseph. "And much more to you than anyone could have ever imagined."

"Freely admitting my guilt, ma'am." He pushed his hat back, revealing tousled gray hair. "The moment my eyes beheld that blonde-haired beauty with the emerald-green eyes. I was in love, and there was no turning back."

"But your parents. Whatever did they think? You going off with—"

"An artist's model?" Lizzie's laugh was as delicate as her small frame. "They never knew. I couldn't tell them the truth. Not only did I meet Joseph under the most unusual and improper way for a high-society girl, he was a poor Italian boy. He barely spoke English. Besides, he hardly had more than a penny to his name."

"No disrespect to your fine husband, but what did you do?"

"Wrote them a letter telling them I had fallen in love with one of the instructors. You know, a professor of the arts who had a high position at the school. I knew they wouldn't be too happy about that either since they planned on me marrying a son of one of their New York friends upon graduation." Her smile faded. "I'm still not proud about lying to my mother and father. But even though they loved me, they would never have understood."

"I wanted to face her parents, ask for Lizzie's hand in marriage. You know, do the respectable thing." Joseph grimaced. "But we both knew her father's answer. We couldn't take a chance on losing each other."

"And there was the matter of his temper." Lizzie spoke quietly and glanced around as if assuring herself we were alone. "Even out here, far away from another soul, I can still hear his yelling and feel the sting of his hand."

Joseph slipped his arm around his wife's waist. "We headed out and never turned back."

In front of me stood a leather-faced, slightly hunched-over man like a tree that had been blown by the wind for ages. Next to him was a silver-haired, frail woman, reminding me of the last leaf, holding on until the snow would release it from its branch. Together, aged versions of what I imagined were once a dark, handsome young man and a lovely, fair-skinned young woman. Now, they held on to one another on a barren and unpredictable path to the next, and most likely, final season of their lives.

Joseph pulled his wife closer. "Mary, true love has a way of triumphing, even when it doesn't seem to stand a chance."

"Don't think poorly of us, child," Lizzie said.

"Not on your life, my friend. It's a delightful love story." A sadness long kept at arm's length crept into my heart, and I wondered if I had ever really experienced true love.

"You will." Lizzie patted my cheek.

"Excuse me?" *Did I say that out loud?*

"But stay away from that sheriff." Joseph gave Lizzie a quick kiss and then hoisted himself onto his seat.

I frowned at Lizzie. "What does he mean by that? I have no feelings for that man."

Lizzie took me by the arm, and none too gently. "That doesn't matter 'cause he has some for you." She wrinkled her nose, reminding me of my mother. "You be careful, child." She stepped toward the sideboard and pulled herself up to where Joseph had gathered the reins and was talking with Sadie. The chestnut mare bobbed her head when he spoke, and I could only imagine she was thanking her owner for the brief rest from the arduous journey.

I climbed into the back of the wagon and settled as best I could, wedged between the supplies we would need when we camped in Arkansas City before the race and in the open prairie when we staked our claims.

Like so many times before, Joseph clicked his tongue and Sadie quickened her pace to a slow trot. For several hours, the road behind me faded into the distance, and I wondered if my life as I knew it would soon do the same.

* * * * *

That evening, we camped along a small creek somewhere fifty miles or so north of Arkansas City. If we got a start at daybreak and held a steady pace, Joseph said we would reach our destination at sunset. If not, we'd settle for one more night and pull into Arkansas City in two days. Either way, we'd have a handful of days to stand in the necessary lines to register and each pay fourteen dollars to participate in the race.

I must have been in a deep sleep when Joseph's voice awakened me.

"Mary, get up. I need help." His voice was strained.

I pushed back the blanket and rolled onto my hands and knees in the rough grass. We had laid our bedrolls under a large cottonwood to be protected from any rain that may have fallen in the night. Since it hadn't rained for weeks, even a drizzle was unlikely but would have been a welcome visitor.

"What's wrong? Is there trouble?"

We had been fortunate. So far, there had been no substantial problems other than a bear wandering near our campfire one evening and an angry swarm of bees that had nearly set Sadie off running as she grazed near a rotted tree stump.

"It's Lizzie." Even in the dark, the whites of Joseph's eyes were visible in the moonlight. "Been turning and tossing all night, and she's hot as a baked potato."

I jumped up and ignored my tangled hair that had come loose from its bun. "Where is she?" I looked around, trying to adjust my eyes.

"In the back of the wagon. Didn't think it best to have her on the ground." He jogged toward the wagon, and I hurried after him.

We climbed into the back, careful not to jostle the rickety boards or wake her if she was able to sleep again. Lizzie moaned and called out for Joseph in slurred words. Immediately, he was at her side, whispering something in Italian.

Kneeling on the other side of her, an odd sensation of fear sweep across me, and I realized how quickly anything in life can change. I pushed the thought from my mind and spoke to her. "Lizzie. It's all right, honey. Seems you took on a slight fever. Maybe the sun or too many mosquito and horsefly bites got to you today."

Joseph glanced at me and nodded, looking hopeful.

I hope that's all it is. I nodded back at him, wanting to believe my quick diagnosis.

The moonlight cast a pale glow on her moistened face. Her forehead and cheeks were covered with tiny droplets as if the late autumn dew had visited in the night. Her eyes opened slightly, and even in the dim light, they appeared blurred—as though a fog had rolled in from the creek bed, unwilling to lift.

"I'm going to the river to soak my shirt again. The cold water seemed to settle her down." Joseph leapt over the sideboard and disappeared towards the gurgling creek that, before this dry season, probably swelled four-fold. Until that moment, I hadn't realized he was bare-chested, using whatever he could to bring comfort to his wife. Instinctively, I knew he would sacrifice anything, even himself, to keep her from harm.

Her small frame shivered, and she let out another moan.

"You're going to be all right, my friend. When the sun rises, you'll be brand new." *Lord, don't let anything happen to her.*

With my face toward heaven, I gazed at the pinpricked sky dotted with millions of stars.

Unworthy. That's me. I can take care of myself without You. That's what I said, didn't I? Not so sure if that's true any longer. But this is the truth, Lord. Lizzie is a much better person than me, and she doesn't deserve to travel all this way for something to happen to her now.

CHAPTER 13

Daniel ~ Arrival, September 10, 1893

It took some convincing for Mr. Reid to believe our story. He admitted that when he surfaced from crawling under the seats only to find us missing, he was sure we had taken the money and were long gone. He vowed he would find us if it meant looking for the rest of his life—which he figured would be shortened by Mr. Simon and Mr. Levy. Not until the envelope was securely in his own coat pocket did he reach across the aisle to shake our hands.

"Sirs, you are honorable and brave. Perhaps dense as well." He whispered the last part. "The two of you could be lying dead on the side of the tracks, and I would be soon to follow if my bosses found out the money was gone." He leaned in closer, mouthing the words. "Security money."

"If you aren't as quick as the others to make your claim?" Finn raised one eyebrow.

"A possibility, but rest assured, gentlemen, there are other ways to get what I came all this way to secure." He slipped his hand under his lapel.

"Hopefully, your plan doesn't involve getting us killed," I said.

"Let's hope not." He leaned his head back and closed his eyes, with his hand still in his pocket.

After my heart resumed a normal beat, I knew he was right. Maybe it was gut intuition after years of observing my surroundings on the job that made me go after the stranger. It was ingrained in me to notice the details of people and places, sometimes obvious, but often subtle or unnoticeable.

Or could it have been that still, small voice I had ignored for so many years, ever since Eloise chose another man ... and the stables burned? I closed my eyes, hoping to push the memories away that lingered like smoldering embers until words I hadn't heard since childhood, echoed in my mind. *Call unto me, and I will answer thee, and shew thee great and mighty things, which thou knowest not.*

After my mother died when I was fourteen, my father continued the tradition of gathering my older brother, Joel, and me around the wobbly table in front of the fire before supper. What I remember most was my growling stomach—hungry from a day of working in the fields on our small farm outside Boston—not the verses he read over and over. But suddenly, I missed those days, huddled together with only the light of the fire and a single candle on the table.

Without Mother, the three of us held to one another like moorings in the sea. But after Father passed a year later, my brother and I were cut loose from the safety of the harbor, only to float away—me to the neighbors to the north and my brother to New York City, hoping to make a life for himself.

I was fortunate. The McPhersons were a kind, young couple—Kate a seamstress and Robert a tailor. With no children, they took me in as their own. And although I could never call them Mother and Father, they didn't expect it. Rather than working the farm as I had with my father, my time after school was spent helping them maneuver heavy bolts of fabric onto a cutting table and delivering completed dresses and suits to the wealthy in the city and the clothing shops in town.

Best of all, I learned to paint. Robert McPherson's real love was art, and when the jobs were few or the day's work complete, we sat near the fire as he drew the skeleton of a scene with a bit of charcoal or the stub of a pencil. He taught me how to make the paints, combining just the right amount of pigment, linseed, and turpentine.

Over the course of days, weeks, and even months, the canvases—derived from spare scraps of linen or cotton fabric and coated with rabbit glue—were stretched and tacked onto discarded boards, slowly transformed. By his hand, pictures were born. There were flowers cascading from vases, horses immersed in fields of green, and landscapes of places I dreamed of and hoped to visit someday. A favorite painting depicted a house that would be perfect in which to raise my own family.

For several months, I tried to sketch pictures from my mind—images of my first dog curled up on the front porch, my family's weathered farmhouse, and the apple tree with sagging branches. But when trying to draw the likenesses of my real family members, their features continued to fade as if a fog had crept in and their faces were no longer clear, especially my mother's. *What was the color of her eyes?*

Maybe the McPhersons sensed my growing sadness, or perhaps Mr. McPherson really did see some promise in my sketches. Because one day, when my chores and schoolwork were finished, he handed me a rolled-up piece of flour sack. It was tied with a strip of burlap.

Go on, open it. I remembered Kate's words as she patted my arm, and Robert's broad smile as I pulled the tie loose and unrolled the fabric. My own brushes—one round, the other flat—made from hog bristle. The neighbor's pig was surely short a few patches.

* * * * *

The train slowed as it pulled into our destination, and I stood to retrieve my case from the luggage rack. In it were the few clothes needed until my return to Boston after Finn and I had enough photos and initial paintings to document the race. A wooden box contained tubes of paints, bottles of linseed oil and mineral spirits, a roll of canvas, and my brushes, including the ones with the hair from a hog that had died so many years before.

Beneath those items was my pistol—just in case.

* * * * *

Stepping from the train was like being caught in a raging river. Hordes of people pushed and argued as they waited to get their possessions from the baggage cars. Covered wagons jostled on the dirt road that ran alongside the tracks. Sweaty horses and mules snorted and brayed as they pulled overflowing buckboards. Men on horseback weaved between the wagons, people on foot, and even an unfortunate soul attempting to ride a bicycle on the rutted road.

"This is where we must say our good-byes. I'll be making my way to the registration booth." Mr. Reid extended his hand. "I owe you a favor if our paths ever cross again."

Finn shook his hand. "Perhaps they will. God Almighty has a funny way of making that happen."

I eyed my friend, surprised that he may have actually listened to some of the pastor's sermons while sitting in church with Elizabeth Turney.

"Mr. Reid." I reached out my own hand. "It's been a pleasure. We wish you every success. If you get your claim, we'll try to include your story for the Globe."

"Boston Globe reporters?" He shook his head. "Thought you must have been outlaws. Yes, I'll have a story to tell. Front page news, gentlemen." He stepped into the crowd, calling out, "Front page to be sure."

With parched mouths, Finn and I worked our way through the crowd toward a makeshift building topped with what appeared to be the remnants of a circus tent and painted lettering. A crowd of gritty men and a few women, equally thirsty and desperate for a whiskey or beer, were gathered inside what was aptly lettered, the Elephant. As we wove our way to the bar, it was obvious we were no longer in Boston.

CHAPTER 14

Mary ~ Arrival, September 13, 1893

Despite Joseph's best efforts to keep Sadie at a quickened pace, Lizzie's condition forced us to make more stops than planned. Though her fever had subsided, her stomach was cramped, and the bumpy ride didn't help matters. I held her in the back of the wagon, but now it was me doing the talking. I told her how much she and Joseph would enjoy their new home that would be above their cobbler store, and how she could help me start a vegetable garden and make curtains for my future house.

"Imagine. With your talent, you can paint scenes of Italy on the walls in the shop. Joseph says the countryside outside Florence is incredible—olive groves, poppies, and tall cypress trees all over the hills. And the sunsets ..."

She moaned, and my grip tightened. Joseph snapped the reins, and Sadie trotted toward the buildings we were beginning to make out in the distance—jagged silhouettes cast from the low-lying sun.

After passing the flour mill, we entered the edge of town where the Arkansas and Walnut rivers met. The smell of campfires filled the air, and a smoky haze hovered above the water. People milled around tents that dotted the open fields like winter's first snowflakes, though the end of the day's heat was still unbearable. The scent of cooking meat made me realize we hadn't eaten much the last few days, being more worried about Lizzie's stomach than our own.

"I'm heading to the buildings. One of those must be a doctor's office." Joseph clicked his tongue, and Sadie dutifully continued her pace.

We turned onto what must have been the main street. A general store, saloon, and a hardware store were first in the row of establishments.

"Is there a doctor in town?" I called to a woman who held tightly to her child's hand on the bustling street corner.

"On the left, past the justice's office." She pointed in the direction and said something else that was lost in the commotion of the wagons, horses, and crowds of people. We continued on, making our way into the heart of town.

*****

When the doctor stepped from behind the curtain after examining Lizzie, his face told me he had bad news. Dark circles under his eyes provided a perfect match to his frown.

"Seems like your wife may have a tumor of some sort in her stomach. I was hoping it was bad water she drank on your travels, like so many of the others, but she said she hasn't been feeling well for a couple of months." He paused and rubbed the gray stubble on his chin. "And there's a noticeable mass on her right side that's giving her a fit. I can give her some medicine to help with the pain for now."

"You mean she will get better?" Joseph nodded as if to answer for him.

"Hopefully, she'll have some good days, but more discomfort is sure to come if what I'm feeling gets larger. The medicine will allow her to travel to one of the larger towns where you can get her to a physician who can tell you if surgery is possible." He rolled down his shirt sleeves. "Sorry you're so far away from home."

"This will be our home." Joseph blurted the words. "My wife and I have plans for our new home and business."

I had remained in my chair to give Joseph privacy with the doctor. This type of conversation was reserved for a husband concerned about his wife. Now, I stood next to him hoping to provide support but knowing I was unable to help either of my dear friends. A single tear trickled over Joseph's wrinkled cheek. It was sure to be the first of many.

Doctor Bennett offered to let Lizzie rest for the night in the back room since the boarding houses and the Gladstone Hotel were overflowing like buckets of water with all the people streaming into the town. Besides, it wouldn't suit her to be sleeping on the ground under a makeshift tent.

After a bit of talking, Joseph convinced the doctor it was imperative that he be with his wife, even if it meant sleeping on the hard floor. He started for the back room but then turned and looked at me.

"Mary, you understand, don't you? I don't want to leave you, but—"

"I'll be fine." With a quick kiss on the cheek, I urged him toward the doorway. "Your wife needs you. And you need her. Besides, Sadie and the wagon need to be taken care of. The kind doctor told me to drive her around to the back of the building for the night. He'll have one of his sons bring by a bale of grass for the ol' girl and help keep an eye on things until morning."

"That boy better keep an eye on you as well." Joseph's voice became even more intense. "Get the rifle from the chest and keep it near. You know how to use it, right?"

This would be my first night alone in the wagon since we left Adair. Might as well get used to sleeping with one eye open. That's the way it would be once I had my own land. And when Wesley came, he would have to be kept safe.

"First thing in the morning, we'll go to the registration booth and get the paperwork." Joseph produced a weary smile and went into the dimly lit room.

He still believes we can do this. I stepped into the evening air alone and took a deep breath. "Can *you* do this?" I asked myself out loud.

Standing in this foreign land with an unknown outcome, my own voice seemed that of a stranger's. Perhaps tomorrow's sunlight would bring new hope for all of us.

* * * * *

The medicine allowed Lizzie to sleep most of the night, but Joseph looked as if he could have used a good night's rest as well. Unfortunately, the opium was costly, and Joseph would only be able to provide her its relief in the worst moments.

As other patients filed into Doctor Bennett's office, we thanked him for his hospitality and helped Lizzie onto the front bench of the buckboard. Heading down Summit Street, we made our way toward the outlying fields to erect our tent for a couple of evenings. After that, if all went as planned, my friends would have their tent pitched on a town lot—the future site of Contolini's Cobbler Shop. And I would have mine propped on a claim of one-hundred-sixty acres to call my very own.

* * * * *

Lizzie insisted she would be fine if she rested while we waited in line to register for the race. Joseph and I both needed the papers to prove we were legitimate land seekers once we staked our claims—not one of the Sooners who were known to sneak into the territory well ahead of the race, even at the risk of being arrested … or worse.

Word among the people clustered around the tents was that the crowds lined up to register had grown well beyond the number expected.

"We've been sleeping in shifts," a man camped only yards away said to Joseph and me. "Yep, my son dozed on the ground while I kept our place. If we both would have been sleeping, those possums would have sneaked right past. Not thinking for a minute to wake us to move along in line."

The boy, nearly matching his father's height, still wore the wiry build of youth. "Yep, Ma brung us biscuits and coffee. If it weren't for that, I think I may have laid down and died."

As the boy scratched his red-tinged hair, my mind conjured up pictures of the father and son pair, rusting away like abandoned farming equipment in fields.

"We appreciate the advice. We'll have my wife bring us some food and water if the wait is too long." Joseph glanced at the opening to his and Lizzie's tent. "Sir, I don't even know you, but will you keep an eye on her for me?"

"In a place like this, good people have a way of finding one another. The Lord is making sure of that." He extended his hand. "Pastor Allen. Walter's the first name. St. Louis is, or I should say *was*, our home."

"Good to meet you, Pastor." Joseph shook his hand. "This is Mary Roberts, a close friend from back home. She traveled from Missouri with my wife, Lizzie, and me."

The pastor tipped his hat. "A pleasure, ma'am. This is my son, Gabriel. My wife is at the general store getting a few last items—if there's anything left, that is. With the Run only a couple days away, Arkansas City has never seen the likes of this many people. It's like bees swarming a hive with all the activity."

Joseph and I looked at each other. It was time to get on our way.

But first, Joseph stepped closer to the pastor. "Sir, I'm not very good at praying, but you must have a way to talk with God." He gripped the pastor's hand. "Will you ask Him to heal my wife?"

Pastor Allen was silent for a moment. "I'll pray for your wife." He squinted at Joseph as he gathered his thoughts. "But when you return from getting signed in properly, we'll pray together for her." The pastor smiled. "The Lord knows you just as well as He knows me. I'm sure He'd love to hear from you."

$$* * * * *$$

Like a meandering crack in dry earth, thousands of people moved in slow motion through the parched fields towards the mill, the makeshift location for registration. Its eastern side doorway was tiny in comparison to the hordes that would need to pass through it to pay the race fee.

"Threading a needle, I'd say." Joseph frowned at me as he surveyed the area. "Looks like the officials weren't ready for all this."

"We'd best get in line and hold our ground." I stepped behind a gentleman—so covered in layers of dust and grime he looked like an aged bronze statue—and had to suppress a smile when he spoke.

"No need to hold on to your hat, ma'am. Line hasn't moved more than an inch the last hour." He pointed to a small piece of paper displayed on the brim of his hat. "See this number? Eventually, they'll be coming by to give you one. Don't want to lose it since it's your way of proving your place." He pushed the paper deeper behind a frayed leather strap. "Yep, keeps folk from breakin' in line."

After only a few minutes, the line had lengthened behind us by at least several dozen more souls. I pulled my hat lower to shade my eyes from the intensifying sun—shining too brightly for not yet being at its peak.

✶✶✶✶✶

When the sun was well on its descent, a newfound energy bubbled throughout the line. People chattered and stretched to peer around those ahead. I pushed up to my tiptoes to see what was causing the excitement and tapped the bronze man's back. "What's going on?"

He only shrugged, but then leaned into the conversation in front of him. "It's about time," he shouted, then spun around towards me. "Word is the marshals are opening a second booth." He grinned, making the dirt-stained lines in his face even more pronounced.

"I could have suggested that a long time ago." Joseph smirked. "But I'll take it. Best news we've heard today."

Just as he spoke, a gangly boy raced towards us. When he stopped, he was panting. "I've been running up and down the line trying to find you."

"Gabriel?" I grasped the boy's arm.

"Ma'am." He gave me a quick nod but turned to Joseph. "It's your wife, sir. She's in plenty of pain and calling out for you. My ma and pa are with her, but they think you need to come right away."

Joseph's hands began to shake. "Mary, you stay right here."

"No. I'm coming with you, Joseph."

"This is no time to argue." He pointed at the ground. "You hold our spot, and if this line splits in two, make your way to the shortest one."

"But …"

The distorted look on Joseph's face caused my heart to twist. It was a mixture of frustration and confusion. But mostly what I saw was fear. I gave him a hug. "Tell her I love her and …" A lump grew in my throat. "And to be strong."

But he had already run off alongside Gabriel, both of them disappearing into the crowd.

CHAPTER 15

Daniel ~ Observing, September 14, 1893

McKelvey had made arrangements for us to stay at the Gladstone Hotel. A relief, in spite of the fact the desk clerk was busy turning away a constant stream of weary travelers, even those willing to pay extra for a place to sleep. The conditions in the growing city of tents along the outskirts of the town caused a sick feeling of guilt, reminding me of my many comforts.

"Hardy folk, to be sure." Finn shook his headful of curls. "Like back home. Mum and Da took on anything to make a better life for themselves."

"There's a good smattering of Scottish brogue here, especially in the Elephant."

"Aye, like the Scots say, never drink whisky with water and never drink water without whisky."

We'd spent a good part of the time since we arrived in Arkansas City talking with rushers from all parts of the country. For most, the chance to own a sizeable piece of land for farming or raising livestock was the draw. For others, the town sites and the opportunity to set up whatever kind of shop—in what they hoped would be a growing metropolis—was the dangling carrot. A good many laughs were had with several who came merely for the excitement—the thrill to see whether their horse, buggy, wagon, or even feet, could carry them faster than the others.

Most in the crowd were men, but women dotted the landscape. Some busily cooked over fires while others washed pots and utensils or mended holes in tents and clothing. Small children hung to their mothers' aprons while the older ones entertained themselves playing leap frog, hide-and-seek, and challenging each other to running races and wrestling matches.

"Ever consider signing up to run?" Finn shot me a sideways glance. "I see a bit of wanderlust in you since we've been here."

"That's ridiculous." I shoved my hands deep into my pockets. "Everything I need is in Boston. A job. Decent apartment—"

"No prospects."

"Of what?"

"You know. A woman. Maybe even one to marry."

"Finn, we've had this conversation—more than once—so I'm leaving the lady love to you." A wagon pulled by two mangy mules rattled by, causing me to step aside.

"Just may do that. Thinking about asking Elizabeth to marry me when we get back."

"Really?"

"Aye. She's smitten with me, and I'm not wanting her to get away with someone else."

"And you believe she'll say yes?"

"First, I plan on asking her father. He likes me. Knows I'm a hard worker at the paper." Finn leaned closer and whispered, "Do you think she'd want to marry me?"

"She'd be loony if she didn't. And you don't have to whisper. Nobody knows you here."

Finn visibly stiffened. "Except him." He looked past me. "The bum from the train. I think he spotted me, and he's not looking like he got any friendlier."

"Do you have your barker?" My own gun was packed in my bag. I kept my back turned and quickly played possible scenarios in my mind.

"Sure do." Finn glanced down at his vest pocket. "Might be illegal to carry it within the city limits, but anything could go on in this town right now."

I slowly turned around, and, sure enough, the lanky stranger was staring directly at us. His cheek twitched above his matted gray beard. He whispered something to a stocky man next to him, who then displayed crooked, tobacco-stained teeth. The thief tipped his hat at us, then the pair walked across the street toward the entrance of the saloon.

"That's a sure cure for me wanting an afternoon whiskey." Finn released a deep breath.

"Next time we run into them, it might not be so easy." I started the opposite direction, with Finn catching up to my side.

"Where're we headed?"

"The registration booth. Need an idea how many people are going to be fighting for those forty-two thousand claims."

"Doing your homework?"

"As always." I secured the strap on my leather bag holding my art supplies—and my revolver. "Then we'll head to the starting line and see what kind of rise we can find for the best vantage point. I'm counting on you to get photographs that will make the readers' jaws drop." My pace quickened. "We have work to do. No time for getting beat up, or worse."

"Not to worry, ol' man. Got you covered."

"That's my concern." I rolled my eyes at my friend, and he grinned. "Why do you think that crook's here?"

Finn shifted the strap of the camera. "Same as everyone else. Or he's up to no good. Plenty of people to rob that have little money to lose."

"May have come to find us," I said.

"Thugs like that can find trouble with anyone. We're nothing special."

"Except you pinned him up against a train with a pistol in his belly."

"And took back plenty of money that wasn't his." Finn whistled. "More than I'd ever seen in one bundle."

My eyes widened as I looked at Finn and thought about the trouble that could come our way. "I wonder where Mr. Reid has been these last few days?"

* * * * *

With the Rush less than forty-eight hours away, the rumored second registration booth opened to accommodate the overflow of registrants.

The single line that stretched for well over a mile, now split into two like a long piece of twine that had been snipped in half. The new line shuffled toward the booth as the officials tried to keep some semblance of control and order.

When we neared the jury-rigged booth, clearly hammered together with ill-fitting pieces of wood, it was easy to spot the rotund Mr. Reid. Most of those around him were coatless, wearing only a shirt and suspenders, or some with a vest. In contrast, he appeared quite businesslike in his suit and tie, covered with dust that turned the dark wool to an ashen gray.

"Gentlemen." Mr. Reid extended both arms as if greeting old friends. "I wondered if I'd see you two again."

"In this horde of humanity, it is a wonder." Finn shook his head. "Figured you'd be signed up by now."

"Should have been. He knuckled his bloodshot eyes. "After we said farewell, I went straight to get in line. Never imagined it would be such a wait. I've been out here day and night since … well, two nights sleeping on the ground. The first day's mistake was stepping out of line to get some water and food. Gave a husband and wife behind me a few bucks to hold my spot. When I came back, the line had moved on a bit." He shifted his weight from leg to leg, teetering like a massive bear. "Do you know what happened?"

I shook my head. "Can't imagine."

"That couple told me to head to the back of the line. Said they had never seen me before—unless I was willing to give them more money. When I argued, others around them got riled up and said anyone trying to jump in line would regret it."

"Rough crowd," Finn added.

"Speaking of that, our friend from the train is in town." I surveyed the crowd. "Probably a good idea if you keep your wits about you. He certainly hasn't forgotten what he had of yours."

Mr. Reid looked around. "Good to know. At least good fortune has been with me." He leaned in closer. "See that woman about a dozen or so in front of us?"

Finn and I bent to the side and glanced. Finn blew out a puff of air. "Sure do. You'd have to be blind not to notice her."

"For hours, talk had been hanging over us like a swarm of gnats that there was going to be a second booth added. When the officials did it, they split the line right in front of her. These government folks don't know how to organize thousands of people, but they can spot a good-looking woman." He cinched his tie that had sagged around his neck. "Lady luck for me."

"Needle in a haystack," Finn agreed. "Daniel, what were the chances of that happening for our friend, Mr. Reid?"

Even though Finn's question reached my ears, my eyes were set on the woman. And though I wanted to blame it on the heat, I felt a bit light-headed.

CHAPTER 16

Mary ~ Official, September 14, 1893

It was a welcoming sound when my boots thumped on the flimsy piece of plywood inside the shed marked booth number nine.

"Ma'am, step right up." A burly man sat behind a table much too small for his mass. "Full name, birth location, and date."

"Mary Louisa Johnston Roberts. Ohio, January 24, 1860."

"And your husband? Need both of your signatures on these documents."

I leaned forward, resting my hands on the edge of the table. "Sir, my husband is deceased. I'm a widow."

The clerk scrutinized me over the wire-rimmed glasses perched precariously on the tip of his nose. "My apologies. A pretty woman like you wouldn't typically be alone in a place like this."

"Actually, I'm not." Straightening to my full five-foot-four height, I looked down at the seated man. "My dear friend is with his ill wife at the moment. I'll be registering for both of us."

"Sorry. He'll need to be present. Can't register anyone who isn't here in person."

"But his wife is extremely ill." The chattering and shuffling behind me magnified the growing impatience of the crowd. "He can't leave her to stand in this line."

"Not my rules, ma'am." He flipped through an enormous ledger. "K, N, P, here we go, R." He turned a few more pages and ran his finger down the length of the yellowed page. "Did you or your husband participate in any other land race?"

"No, and why would it matter if my husband had?" My frustration was rising.

"You still share his name," he said, "and if he had rushed before, I couldn't grant you permission."

I swallowed hard to push down my anxiety and tapped the page with my finger. "Regardless, you won't find either of our names in that book. You won't find Joseph Contolini either."

He narrowed his brow into a question mark.

"The dear man who is taking care of his wife. They were kind enough to help me travel all this way." I forced a smile and folded my hands in front of me. "Please …" I softened my voice. "He's a cobbler, looking for a chance to start a new business on a town lot."

"Just like everyone else." He crossed his beefy forearms on the table.

I set my small bag on the table and bent close enough to smell stale tobacco on the official's breath. "I'll sign and pay for both of us. Please."

The man's gruff appearance softened as he took a deep breath and relaxed his features. "I shouldn't do—"

"Mr. Nelson." A slight man with a high-pitched voice appeared next to me. "What's the hold-up? We have an angry group out there that says this line still isn't moving." He slammed his fist on the table.

"No issue, Mr. Hoyt. Finishing up with this lady."

"Ma'am." The man gave me a quick nod and then pulled a handkerchief from his front pocket and dabbed the sweat on his brow. "No offense, but we need to speed it up." He circled around to the back of the table and spoke to the clerk. "You help the next person, and I'll complete her papers. We've got less than twenty hours until we shut down registration, and more people keep coming. It's like flies on manure."

The clerk rolled his eyes as he shuffled through other papers. My heart sank. The chance of a new start for Joseph was slipping away as quickly as Lizzie's life.

* * * * *

Even tightly holding a certificate stamped Number 5370, my hand felt empty. Pushing aside the canvas flap revealed Joseph sitting cross-legged next to his sleeping wife. He raised his finger to his lips, and I took a step backward into the night air.

Settling onto a log next to the campfire, my legs welcomed the chance to rest as I leaned back and gazed at the darkening sky. Stars were beginning to appear, and as more came into view, I felt insignificant—one out of so many who had come, all desiring a piece of this unclaimed land.

Lord, why am I allowed to race and the Contolinis aren't? You know there isn't time for Joseph to make it through the lines. Foolishly looking around to see if anyone heard my thoughts, I spoke aloud to the sky. "It isn't fair. I'm the one who shouldn't be doing this." Suddenly, the urge to run away washed over me. An anger swelled inside that hadn't been present since seeing Tuck bruised and bloodied in the jail cell.

When I began to push myself up from the log, a gentle hand rested on my shoulder. *"La vita non è giusto."*

I took Joseph's hand and held it against my cheek. When he gently cupped my face, he seemed to hold my heart as well. Tears rolled down my face at his tenderness.

"Life isn't fair," he whispered. "It's not supposed to be." He settled next to me, and we stared at the sky, now powdered with glistening stars.

"I tried," I said between sobs.

"I know you did."

"How do you know?"

"Lizzie and I talked. It was obvious you would try to take care of us."

Neither of us said anything for a while. The only conversation was the hissing logs speaking to the crackling twigs.

"What will you do?" I asked.

He turned toward me, and the creases around his eyes deepened when he grinned. "We have a plan. Lizzie says it's the Lord's plan, and we're His helpers." Joseph's face was like an ancient map, the deep-set wrinkles traveling among his features.

"What is that supposed to mean?"

"Lizzie does a lot more talking with God than I do, but she says, and I think she's right, that He wants you to have a new life—you and your son." He lifted his face to the night sky. "Do you see all those stars?"

My gaze tilted upward. "Sure do."

"If we got a star for each year of our lives, all our blessings, and all the love God has for us, we'd have been given more than we could ever count." He reached his hands toward the sky and cupped them together as if filling his hands with fresh water from a stream. Then he carefully lowered his hands and turned to me with his offering. "Look." He nodded at his hands. "I do understand one thing ..."

I gazed into his cradled palms.

"God has plans to fill the sky with stars for you." His eyes widened as a child's would at the sight of a present. "And the largest bucket in the world would never be able to hold them all."

He wrapped his arms around me, and my head rested on his chest. A long-forgotten memory of my father holding me when I was young tiptoed into my mind and knocked on my heart. It made me feel safe.

"You'll ride out on Sadie," he spoke into my hair. "She's still quick and sure-footed."

I sat upright. "But what about you? She's your horse."

"She's my ol' girl, faithful animal. But she'll run as fast for you as for me." He stood and walked to the other side of the fire. "Lizzie and I will wait until you run the race and stake your claim, then we'll head to St. Louis. Pastor Allen said there are good doctors there who might be able to help."

"But that's a long way to travel again. Is she up for it?"

"We don't have a choice, Mary." Joseph rubbed his forehead. "He's sending word to his congregation to help us out—perhaps a place to live until we get Lizzie back on her feet."

"You and I can make the run together in the buckboard, just like we planned. You get your town lot first, and I'll continue on."

"It will be much faster on horseback." He looked at me through the rising smoke. For a moment, it felt like a dream. "From the start, our plan had some faults. Even if luck went our way, most likely only Lizzie and I would have gotten a claim. Now, seeing how many people are rushing, it would be mighty difficult for you to get back in the race at that point."

I stood, my arms crossed in defiance, hoping to muster a solid argument, even though my legs were shaking. "But your shop. You and—"

"We can do that in St. Louis. People wear shoes there as well. "Besides, we believe this is God's plan. I'll admit I don't like all of it, but it's not mine for choosing."

I paced back and forth, trying to steady my legs as my thoughts jumbled around. It would definitely be faster on horseback. There would be a much greater chance of driving in a marker stake before others beat me to the spot. *And what about Wesley? I've traveled all this way to make a new life for my son and myself. No, it's ridiculous. Who do I think I am that I could do this race by myself, let alone successfully get land? Maybe it's time to go back to Adair and live with Mother until I find work.*

I stopped pacing and stared into the fire. The embers glowed beneath the dancing orange and blue-tinged flames. A few flames lashed out, and with them, an unsettling vision of Sheriff Murphy's smug face. But as the flames retreated, the image was smothered—replaced by a sense of peace.

The note from my mother had been read several times over the course of the journey, and now the carefully written verse from Philippians played across my mind. *For Brethren, I count not myself to have apprehended: but this one thing I do, forgetting those things which are behind, and reaching forth unto those things which are before, I press toward the mark for the prize of the high calling of God in Christ Jesus.*

As I took a deep breath and lifted my face once more to the sky, the fire crackled and let out a loud pop—the sound I would soon hear at the starting line for the Rush.

CHAPTER 17

Daniel ~ Starting Line, September 16, 1893

As though an electric wire hovered along the border, each person, horse, mule, and even barking hound skittered with excitement. Finn and I wove our way through the array of spoked wheels—prairie schooners, open-top wagons, buggies, spring wagons, two-wheeled carts, and buckboards—as they rolled into position, their wooden slats groaning under the weight of supplies and family members.

"Not sure how that bicycle will fare, but I'll give that gentleman his due for courage." Finn held up his camera toward a man in a straw hat. "Taking photographs for the Boston Globe. Mind if I capture the moment?"

"Not at all." The young man smiled widely and adjusted his bowtie. "Be sure to include the name, Douglas Stone. Proprietor of the future Stone and Sons Bicycles."

"And your sons?" I asked.

"None to speak of yet. I'm counting on this new adventure to provide me a wife as well."

Finn shot me a grin. "My friend here may need your help."

"For a bicycle?" He swung his leg over the bar and settled onto the seat.

"No, a wife." Finn laughed and then steadied the camera.

"I'd rather risk my life on one of those two-wheeled machines." I pulled a notepad from my bag and jotted down the entrepreneur's information—a journalistic habit as natural as breathing. "Best of luck to you, Mr. Stone."

Other spectators dotted the hill from which we would view the race—townsfolk, fellow reporters, and others simply wanting to witness what was being called the last Rush of the final frontier. About two hundred yards into the Strip, a team of deputy marshals readied a cannon to sound off in tandem with the official gunshot.

A gruff voice rang out in front of us. "It's high noon!" Suddenly, a surge of horses and wagons lunged forward, nearly running us down. I yanked Finn by the back of his shirt and pulled him to the side.

"It's got to be a false start." I pulled the chain on my pocket watch and glanced at the time. "Twenty minutes to go."

Shouts and stomping hooves added to the confusion as horses were drawn back. A few wagons tried to circle back into position, only to become log-jammed with other teams of horses and mules.

"We'd better get to the rise. The officials won't be able to hold this throng much longer." I tucked my watch back in my vest pocket and headed toward the mound.

* * * * *

Sure enough, from the rise, we witnessed fifty to one hundred horsemen draw out of the line at least a half dozen times more, only to be driven back by cavalry patrolling the Strip. In the dust-filled air, tension hovered like a swarm of wasps between the soldiers and the mob—determined forces in opposing directions.

Finn was on his knees, digging small divots with his fingers to steady his tripod on the bumpy ground. "Matters aren't helped with word spreading about the Sooner being killed yesterday. A soldier shot him from his horse as he rode across the border."

"Can't say I feel too bad for the man."

Finn grunted. "Daniel, you've become a hardened bloke."

"I've heard the stories. People disappearing from the camps, supposedly hiding out in the timber within a reasonable distance of a town site or choice claim. Once the race is underway, they'll run their horse enough to show a good sweat. That's cheating."

"True enough." Finn stood and secured his camera to the mounting plate. "Some will even come out of their hiding place once the others have run from the line. With their fresh horse, they can catch up and beat the others."

"And those they beat out become the unknowing witnesses to prove they passed each other in the race if anyone is ever questioned."

"Risky to be sure." Finn looked through his camera lens. "But smart."

"Risking your life for a plot of dirt is foolish, especially if you're willing to cheat out the others who play by the rules." I pointed to the crowd below that had become surprisingly quiet—the calm before a storm.

"Take a look." Finn gestured to the Kodak and stepped aside. "Hurry up."

I lined up my right eye. "What am I looking ..." My heart jumped.

"You see her, don't you?" Finn whispered.

CHAPTER 18

Mary ~ Rush, September 16, 1893

Even though sleep should have come easily after little to no rest since arriving in town, I couldn't stop the thoughts running through my mind. Sadness about the Contolinis warred with my excitement at the impending challenge to ride out on Sadie. It was a childhood thrill that remained in my blood.

Although I rode frequently as a child, a few years had passed since I had last ridden a horse—and in a race, at that. Tuck had worked as a ranch hand on the outskirts of Kirksville. The owner's young wife, Bess, and I had struck a friendship. On warm afternoons, we raced each other across the open fields, laughing when our hair loosened from the constraints and fell around our faces. We rode along the river, stopping to cool the horses and our feet in the rippling waters and rest under the draping canopy of the biggest willows.

Like a long shadow in the afternoon, the part I tried to escape but couldn't evade was fear. The likelihood of being injured alongside aggressive and more skilled riders—those equally determined to get land—was real. But that wasn't my only concern. I was afraid of failing, then dragging myself back to Adair to admit my failure to the naysayers, especially Sheriff Murphy and his accusations of me being selfish and foolish to leave my mother and son behind.

My fear became real when, in the middle of the night before the race, a rustling and stomping of hooves came from behind the tent. Without a proper corral or stall, Joseph had tethered Sadie to a fence post. I slid Joseph's pistol away from his bedroll and crawled out of the tent. Under the glow of a half moon, the silhouette of a man stood next to the horse. He ran his hand along her neck and then fidgeted with the knot in the rope. In no time and without thought, I was behind him with the gun shoved in his back.

"What are you doing here?" I said in a low, threatening voice.

"Looking for my horse." He grunted as the gun pressed harder into his ribs. "Thought this might be her in the dark."

The smell of whiskey brought back a putrid memory of Tuck's drinking. "You're looking to steal a horse." I stepped backward, still pointing the pistol at his back. "You'd better be going while you can."

As he turned, his eyes widened—the white circles on his filthy face making him look like a raccoon. "I ain't havin' no little bitty woman like you tell me what to do." He teetered to the left and then straightened himself. "Especially when this here is my horse." He slapped Sadie on the rump.

"I said, you better be going … now!" I cocked the gun and held my finger securely on the trigger. "You wouldn't want a gunshot in your belly waking the rest of the camp, would you?"

He sneered, then stumbled off in the direction of the river.

I put the gun down, realizing my arm was shaking. *I'm going to need to be awfully tough for this. Guess that was a good start.*

"Well done, *tesoro mio.*"

I spun around and found myself face-to-face with Joseph. "You scared me to death."

"You are *coraggiosa.* Now I feel better about sending you, my treasure, to race by yourself." He slipped the gun from my hand. "Let's put this away for tonight. Tomorrow you will keep the gun."

"But it's—"

"You'll need it more than me." He lifted it toward the night sky, the silver barrel and cylinder catching the moonlight. "Besides, you probably didn't know about Lizzie's pearl-handled pistol. She keeps it … let's just say, in a private place. She has quite an aim too." He tucked his gun into his pant waist.

"Let's get some rest. Big day tomorrow."

* * * * *

Sleep must have found me because I awoke to Joseph clanging pots and supplies outside the tent. Lizzie was up too, her sweet, though weak, voice peppering her husband with questions.

"What else can we leave for her? She'll need every bit of wood, food, and water."

"She's fixed to ride out today with enough oats and grub to last about two days. She's got a canteen of tea and another with water."

"What about cover? She can't ride out with the tent. What will she do?"

"She'll be okay. Once she's established her lot, she can ride back in and get us so we can drop off more supplies."

"This doesn't feel right, Joseph. I'll never forgive myself if something happens to her."

A long silence followed.

"Me either, *cara mia*. She's become the daughter we never had. But this is right. Something in my gut tells me she can do this."

Please be right. I pushed aside the thin blanket. *I'm doing this not only for Wesley but for them as well.*

*****

It was a sight never to be forgotten. Every inch of ground near the starting line was occupied by animal or person. People dashed to and fro, securing supplies with ropes and leather straps and holding the bits of eager horses. Even the mules tried to lunge forward in anticipation of the start. Whether a Kentucky thoroughbred, farm horse, or cowpony, horses whinnied, and some reared, nearly throwing the riders. Whoops and hollers rang out as rushers vied for a prime starting position.

Lizzie's walk was labored, but she was determined to watch the race and wish me well. With Joseph leading Sadie, the three of us made our way through the masses, looking for a thin place to join the line. Sadie whinnied and bobbed her head, no doubt letting the other horses know she was ready to run.

Next to us, a woman standing in the rear of an uncovered prairie schooner held her hand above her eyes and called to her husband behind the reins, "They're cutting sections of the fence, Floyd. Letting people through already."

With that, her husband slapped the reins, and his team of four horses surged forward, nearly tossing his wife from the back.

"Should we go too?" I asked.

"No, hold your ground." Joseph raised the brim of his hat. "Let them get all snarled up like tar in a sieve."

"You'd better mount up." Lizzie patted the saddle. "Joseph, get her stirrups adjusted."

Joseph leaned over and interlaced his fingers, making a foothold. "Step on up, your majesty."

I slapped him on the back and lifted the hem of my dress. "I'm not much of a princess showing my legs."

"It's a shame we don't have a sidesaddle, but you'd have a hard time staying put with a leg wrapped around only the horn."

Joseph hoisted me onto the worn leather—an awkward seat as I maneuvered the fabric beneath me and gathered the layers towards my knees. "I prefer it this way. This is how I rode as a child."

"Hold in your belly, Sadie." Joseph tugged upward on the cinch as Sadie grunted.

From atop the horse, the view changed. Smoke billowed from the first Santa Fe that was edging toward the starting line. Many more were scheduled to carry rushers across the available heartland. This one had at least ten or more cars attached—a slithering, black snake, oozing with people on the inside as well as those clinging to the roof. The train's whistle sounded, and my heart leapt.

"Lizzie, we'd better clear out of here before we get trampled. Can't be fifteen minutes more now." Joseph rubbed Sadie's muzzle and spoke to her softly. *"Prenditi cura di lei. Buona fortuna."*

It was difficult to hear his voice over the pandemonium, let alone understand Italian.

Lizzie reached for my hand. "He told her to take care of you." Her small hand shared a strong and assured grip. "And Godspeed."

I squeezed her hand. "Thank you for everything." Tears blurred my vision. "I'll be back soon with my claim. Maybe we can still find a way to get yours."

"If the Lord is willing. This is in His hands now." As if to confirm her thoughts, she patted my leg with surprising firmness. "Mary, you have to believe that truth."

"But ..." I squinted against the sun, searching for words to respond.

"Pray, my dear." She took Joseph's hand and, together, they scurried into the crowd, disappearing into the plume of dust rising as the line tightened.

I edged in as close as possible to the front with the other horse riders. Behind us, the wagons lined up, drivers holding the reins and whips ready.

A woman's voice called out from the buckboard behind me. "She's a disgrace. Imagine riding with your skirts pulled up like that."

Even though thousands of eyes could have been staring at me, I turned in my saddle and shouted, "You ought to try it sometime. Stop by my land, and I'll show you how it's done."

A cowboy next to me tipped his hat. "After you, ma'am." He waved his hand, ushering me in front of his black gelding.

I smiled a thank-you and moved one position closer to the start.

An odd silence blanketed the rushers. Everyone, even the animals, seemed to stop breathing as they leaned forward, waiting for the signal that would send us into a wild chase.

CHAPTER 19

Daniel ~ Rush, September 16, 1893

My heart leapt again, but this time it surged all the way through my core as the single gunshot fired in tandem with the roar of the cannon.

"Ah, darn … let me behind the camera." Finn pushed me aside and started snapping photos as quickly as he could replace the plates.

In all the confusion, my eyes tried to remain focused on the woman with the ivory-colored hat and pale-blue dress. She was near the front of the solid moving mass, but as the thickening dust cloud engulfed the riders, a terrifying image of the smoke rising from the Boston City Stables replayed in my mind.

"I've lost her!" I shouted at Finn.

"Who?" He continued to peer through the lens, rotating the camera to follow the direction of the race.

"The woman." I stepped forward and scanned what was visible of the riders.

"You're in the way!" Finn shouted behind me.

The line continued to surge forward, stretching like a piece of black licorice taffy.

Those on horseback took the lead with smaller carts close behind. Buckboards, buggies, and spring wagons followed at top speed, bumping over the relentless prairie. Once they caught their stride, the larger teams of horses were powerful and fast, their thundering hooves vibrating the ground even where we stood.

A short distance away, two wagons collided, sending one into a ditch and the other toppling. An injured horse let loose a great screech. A man, holding his forearm, tried to calm the animal. Men on foot, most likely hoping to get the close-in claims, ran in haphazard directions as though they had all gone mad.

"Take a look at that." Finn pushed his hat back. "Mr. Stone on his bicycle. Poor fellow."

The man was pumping his bicycle for dear life but was sandwiched among a cluster of wagons. Every time a horse's foot struck the ground, a mouthful of dust and dirt was thrown in his face.

"He'll be beaten to a pulp before this race is over." Finn clicked a photograph.

Soon, the riders pulled far enough ahead of the others, leaving the first signs of earth and the bulk of the dust behind them. In a remarkably short time, the line—now more than two hundred yards wide—disappeared in the distance.

* * * * *

Most of the spectators descended the small hill and headed back to town. Some good Samaritans attended to the injured man and his horse. Finn and I remained on the hill watching another man take a switch to his mules, who refused to move. The more he hit them, the more stubborn they became. Now that the roar of hooves and wagons had disappeared, his swearing shattered the calm. A woman, most likely his disgusted wife, snatched the long, blacksnake whip from him. We couldn't make out what she said, but she pointed to the south, and within seconds, the man ran toward a cluster of marker rocks adjacent to the border.

Finn whistled, and the sound cut through the air. "Unbelievable. That claim could have been ours." He walked back and forth. "In all the excitement, the sites right under their noses got passed by. We should have strolled over there and claimed that lot, don't you think?"

But I didn't answer. My eyes were focused on a speck of ivory that lay in the open field.

CHAPTER 20

Mary ~ Claim, September 16, 1893

The noise was as though hell itself had let loose. Yells and hollers raged with snorts and screeching as the reverberating boom launched the line forward—an uncontrollable, unstoppable wave of humanity.

My legs hugged the saddle tightly, giving Sadie full rein. She needed no direction as our course was narrow between the other horses. For now, our only destination was straight ahead.

A cloud of dust lifted like an angry beast behind the front-runners, pouring itself into my eyes and nose. I tried to cover my mouth, refusing to drink its poison. At one point, the veil was so thick, I shut my eyes and simply trusted Sadie's instinct to follow the others.

She must have despised being caught behind the other horses as much as me. Without my prodding, she surged forward and broke into stride with the foremost riders. To my left was a dapple-grey thoroughbred, its rider crouched over its neck and straddling an English saddle—not a common sight on the plains of the frontier. The horseman's mouth and nose were covered with what once must have been a white handkerchief. When he looked in my direction, his eyebrows lifted atop his dirt-splattered spectacles. I had to grin in spite of myself. Apparently, I was not the only one surprised at my position in the race. Or perhaps the sophisticated rider was awed at my ability to ride astride and quite unladylike.

As if the wind intended to humble me, a gust caught the brim of my hat and pulled it from atop my head. I tried to right it and secure the loose ribbon under my chin with one hand, but the satin slipped through my fingers. My hat whirled in the air before landing on the ground for a brief moment before pursuing hooves beat it into the ground. My hair that had been bundled and held prisoner beneath the straw hat now tumbled and waved around my face in fiery streams.

Maybe it was the repetitive stride of Sadie's gallop or the droning of the hooves and wheels cutting down the once virgin prairie grasses. For a moment, it was as though I were dreaming—set free from the memories of the past and the confusion of the present. Running away from or running toward something. Neither seemed to matter.

The English rider veered, pushing his stirrup into Sadie's rump and jolting me from my solitude. The horse stumbled, and my hand found the saddle horn in time to save me from tumbling to the ground— surely to be trampled by the oncoming crowd. Like a peal of thunder, a wagon pulled by a team of six black horses and moving like a steam engine veered ahead of us. Like an ax laid to wood, I split to the right and the rider to the left.

Sadie was breathing hard, and her withers damp with sweat. "Come on, girl, it can't be much farther. If I remember right from the map, the spot we want is over that bluff." We took a sharp right and headed into a tall, grassy section speckled with goldenrod and wax goldenweed. There was so much yellow it looked like the bounty of a king. And as much as my body wanted to rest, there would be no treasure of my own until the two-foot wooden stake, carved with my initials and tied to my saddle, was driven into my claim.

Other riders and wagons zigzagged across the plain now, heading for a specific claim site or wherever they stumbled and could grab a plot. The rock markers placed by the surveying teams in the northeast corner of each site would be almost impossible to find in the mayhem.

It would be easy for several rushers to stake the same piece of land and then have to decide—or fight—to determine who would be the owner. Horrible stories had surfaced from earlier land rushers—especially from the Guthrie and Oklahoma City area—of cheaters, bullies, and even murderers who stole claims from honest people. Tuck and I had read articles, some truthful and others most likely stretched like a rubber band. We also listened to defeated rushers who had returned empty-handed, forlorn that they didn't get land but happy they were breathing.

Once we were on the rise and the other side was visible, I pulled on the reins, stood in the stirrups, and surveyed the area. The remnants of a trickling creek tiptoed its way through a steep, sandy bank directly below me. On its other side was a pebbled bank dotted with a few sparse trees and bushes. Beyond it was an open area, parched and brown.

At least it has water close by. That's surely worth it.

Carefully, I navigated Sadie down the hillside, the sand and dirt giving way beneath her weight. I was leaning back in the saddle, trying to keep my balance, when a rumbling of wood and the clanging of metal came from above.

"Can't take her down this hill, Pa," a raspy woman's voice called out. "Too steep and soft. I'll tumble for sure."

"Where's your courage, woman?" a gruff voice answered. "This is the spot."

I was nearly to the bottom when a wrinkled face, framed in a bonnet, stared down at me.

"A claim jumper!" She pointed at me and cursed. "Get on it, Pa!"

Just as Sadie reached the flattened ground, a horse and rider jumped over the edge of the bluff, swooping from the sky like a hawk.

Instinctively, I gave Sadie a kick, and she leapt across the creek bed. I headed toward the open field, intent on being the first to drive in my stake. But the other horse was swift and gained on me within seconds.

Soon, the rider was alongside me. The man raised his wooden stake and swiped it at my head. Throwing myself to the side to avoid being struck, my footing came loose in the stirrups. In an instant, I slid off the saddle and fell to the ground with a thud. Like a fly caught in a spider's web, the bottom of my petticoat tangled around my legs and held me to the ground. Rolling onto my knees and pushing myself to a stand, my eyes were met with a terrifying sight—the man spun his horse around and charged straight at me.

Lord, he wants to kill me. The thought jolted through my mind as he galloped toward me, the stake raised in his right hand.

"Don't kill 'er, you fool!" the raspy voice yelled.

The man pulled his horse to a stop, still holding the stake in the air. He scowled down at me with cloudy eyes, and then let out a laugh that quickly turned into a hacking cough. "No one ..." he wiped a brown tobacco dribble from the corner of his mouth with his shirtsleeve, "is gonna jump my claim." He squinted at me, peering through a matted mass of gray hair. "Especially a woman ... if you call yourself one."

I pushed my hair to the side and brushed the dirt from my blouse.

The bonneted woman shuffled towards me. Her face reminded me of a walnut—dark brown with deep creases running its length. "That's right. This is our land, and you'd better get on your way before I take that stick to you myself."

"Who says this is yours?" The man had momentarily dangled the stake at his side. "I got down here before you." With Sadie's reins gathered in my hand, I started limping into the open field.

"You'll get hanged for sure, Pa," the woman hissed.

A shiver ran down my back to match the pain reverberating in my hip. I stopped and turned around to see the end of a rifle pointed at me.

"Git on your horse, little lady, before my wife changes her mind." He made a sideways nod. "She don't stay kind for long."

I walked around Sadie and ran my hand along her neck and side. Dark sweat stains darkened her chest and along the girth under her belly.

Not sure of what possessed me to be so bold—maybe the wretched couple's injustice and dishonesty—but the moment my words were spoken, I knew they could be my last. "Your horses look awfully refreshed for running such a grueling race." I pointed to the workhorse laden with bags and supplies. "For carrying all that and not even having a lather."

The couple sent sideways glances at each other.

"It would be a shame if you were found out to be Sooners. The government isn't too fond of folks who've been dishonest."

"We'd better git rid of 'er." The man's upper lip twitched as he glanced at his wife.

"Then you'd be in even deeper." Keeping my eye on him, I lifted my foot into the stirrup.

A loud whoop sounded from the rise. The three of us looked up to see two dark-coated riders ascend over the top.

"That's a prime piece of land we got," the first one to reach the bottom called out to the other who was close behind.

"Dang it, Pa." The wife swatted at her husband. "Now we've lost it for sure." The woman, like a stiffened broom, swept across the dusty ground toward the men who didn't appear the type to be intimidated by an old man and woman.

Quickly pulling myself onto the saddle, I headed Sadie in the direction of the drizzle of water. I would follow the creek and hope it would lead to a more welcoming piece of land.

* * * * *

The wasted time forced me to dig my heels into Sadie. Once more, the faithful mare broke into a gallop. After several minutes of hard running, we rounded a cluster of cottonwoods and followed to the left of a ravine that cut into the hardened earth.

Surprisingly, the creek widened enough that a few stagnant pools formed on either side. Had they been clear, it would have been tempting to stop and cool both Sadie and myself. But even at that thought, other riders and bouncing wagons stirred up dust in the distance.

"Come on, girl. You can do this." I stroked her neck, realizing my words were more for myself than the horse. She whinnied and jumped forward.

Side to side and straight ahead, the landscape became the same— one giant swath of brown, dotted with traces of faded green and tarnished gold. Even with the surveyors' attempts to mark the land, it was now impossible to distinguish specific sites from the claim maps. Any distinguishing landforms had lost their identity.

My heart pounded with the truth that I didn't know where to stop. I could drive my stake into the earth, only to find that several others were on the same claim less than half a mile away.

Lord, I've been plucked from the sky and have fallen in the middle of nowhere. Please give me some direction.

Slowing Sadie, I trotted her in a tight circle, hoping to make sense of the landscape. The only form that stood out was a thicket of box elders in the forefront of a slight mound.

Sod house. Shade.

I gave Sadie a final kick as we headed to what would hopefully be the site of my makeshift house for the first winter on the piece of ground I would eventually call home.

*****

A tickly muzzle woke me, the sun still high but drifting toward the west. "Sadie, you were amazing." I patted her nose as she nibbled on the few stubbles of green grass that were hidden under the trees from the late summer. This was no time to sleep, but exhaustion had won.

Even pushing myself to a stand and walking was a challenge. My muscles ached, and my head throbbed. But I beamed proudly at the stake I had driven into the dirt after several blows with a rock.

MJR. My fingers traced the carved letters. "This is my home now."

Like a pirate's sword thrust into sand, the wood held fast in the ground, reminding me of the adventures Wesley and I shared of Long John Silver and Jim Hawkins in their quest for treasure.

"Son, this is *our* home."

CHAPTER 21

Daniel ~ Sprung Up, September 16, 1893

The dust from the Rush had barely settled, and the sun still hung in the sky as a reminder the day had more to bring. Hammers pounded and saws gnawed an offbeat rhythm as the skeletons of buildings formed along a grid of beaten-down earth.

"You might want to tuck that lady's hat away." Finn led the way through the maze of tents that now defined the birth of a town. "There's nothing but serious business going on here. No time to look like a *quine*."

"And what would that be?" I caught up alongside and frowned at him.

"A woman. And not necessarily a bonnie one."

"You can't say she isn't gorgeous." I tucked the hat under my arm. "Besides, I don't want to ruin it."

"Daniel, the hat's been trampled by stampeding horses. Do you think she's going to want it wear it again?"

"Returning it would be a nice gesture, don't you think?"

"You're going to walk around with a woman's *tammy* for days, maybe weeks until you see her? You may never—"

I snagged Finn's arm and pulled him to a stop. "I'll find her." My determination surprised me. Or perhaps it was madness. "It's not easy—"

"You don't need to explain." Finn elbowed me in the ribs. "Good to know there's something stirring inside."

*****

Of all the accounts we heard that first day from those lucky enough to have secured a town site, none were as lively as our own Mr.

Bartholomew Reid. After interviewing at least two dozen others—including a banker writing loans atop a whiskey barrel, a bent-over farrier repairing broken hooves and shoes for a line of horses, and a grocer selling jugs of water that may as well have been gold—we stumbled upon our friend.

"Ah, familiar faces." Mr. Reid held up his forefinger, signaling us to give him a moment to finish his conversation with a man wearing worn leather chaps and a cowboy hat that had seen better days.

They stood in front of an ill-figured tent. Canvas draped unevenly over four wooden poles, partially driven into the dirt. At a hint of wind, the structure swayed, making the handwritten sign, *Simon, Levy, and Reid—Attorneys at Law*, flutter and spin.

After Mr. Reid shook the cowboy's hand, he joined us. "Ninth client of the day." He smiled broadly and patted his wide chest. "Already, disputes are boiling over who has rights to a parcel. Especially the cattlemen. They seem to think much of this land still belongs to them since they've been renting thousands of acres from the native people to graze their herds. It will be interesting how that will hold up in court."

"By the looks of some around here, it would be no surprise if they took the law into their own hands," I said.

"Regardless, it's nice to hear business is good for our friend." Finn gave one pole a slight tug that made it tilt even more. "You've either been too busy to build a proper shelter, or you don't know the first thing about raising a tent."

"After my day, I'm lucky to be alive." He tugged on his shirtsleeve that was garnished with small rips where buttons once adorned it. "How about some tea? Haven't been able to step away for food and supplies for worry someone will tear down my sign and steal the lot. See this?" He held up a scratched glass jug, its contents dusky as though used as a spittoon. "Bought it from a boy going up and down the rows. Poor kid. He could hardly walk with all that weight tied onto each arm and roped around his waist. Said his father sent him out to make extra money selling tea and water while he set up a hardware store."

"How'd you get the tent supplies?" I asked.

"Gave the boy a tip." He jingled the coins in his pocket. "Told him to have his father deliver some wood and canvas for a fair price."

"And?" Finn cocked his head, still eyeing the tent pole.

Mr. Reid pointed at the crooked sign. "You're looking at the most expensive law office in the new territory. If there's another place to buy hammers and nails, I'll patronize that fellow next time. Regardless, I'm happy to have my claim and be able to report the good news back East."

"How were you so lucky? There isn't an inch of land remaining," I said.

He blew out a deep breath. "Like I said, nearly lost my life or at least a limb." He motioned us under the canvas where we huddled in close quarters. "As you know, my plan was to ride the Santa Fe in as far as possible until I could jump off and run to a claim. Did just that."

Finn and I looked at each other in confusion.

"But first, let me tell you about the train ride." He leaned forward as if sharing a secret. "Never been in such a situation. Being a larger man, it was still feasible to squeeze into a space near a window, or I would have suffocated. People were pushing and shoving so hard it felt like the train would tip over right there on the tracks. Even ladies were throwing elbows. One swatted me in the face with a gloved hand, accusing me of touching her backside."

I cleared my throat to suppress a chuckle at the vision playing out in my mind.

"For a moment, her wild-eyed husband looked as if he wanted to kill me. But then the whistle blew, and everyone took hold of whatever possible as the train moved forward."

"Did you grab the woman's rear end?" Finn asked with a hint of a smirk.

Mr. Reid laughed, and his belly shook. "No, sir. Stuck my arm out the window and held to a leg dangling from the top of the car." He stretched out his arm to reenact the scene. "The top of those cars had as many or more people on them as inside."

"We saw that from where we were standing," I added. "Amazing the train was able to move at all."

"It moved, for sure. In fact, as we got into the territory, we neared the town sites faster than I had planned." Mr. Reid scooted on the ground in a hunched position. "I bent low and ducked under arms and bags to make my way to the open doorway."

Now Finn and I leaned forward so we wouldn't miss a word.

"I stood on the bottom step, holding onto the railing with one hand and my stake and bag with the other. The ground blurred— passing under my feet like a muddy river." He rubbed his nose with the back of his hand. "All I could think about was how unforgiving the rocks and dirt were going to be when I landed."

He paused, drawing us in even closer.

"I'm not Catholic, you understand, but I made that ..." He touched his forehead, chest, and then left and right shoulders.

"Sign of the cross," I said.

"Yes, and prayed to God that the fall alone wouldn't kill me. Or worse, the train wouldn't pull me under and swallow me like a giant beast." He squinted his eyes as if refocusing the events in his mind. "I waited until the smallest patch of green was a few yards in front of me, then jumped." He rolled his head side to side and rubbed his neck with both hands.

"Incredible," Finn mumbled.

"No doubt it was to my advantage to be full of girth." He patted himself on the stomach. "Must have rolled a good distance before jumping to my feet and running into the field."

"That's when you drove in your stake?" Finn's voice cracked.

"Not yet." He pushed himself to a stand, though he had to hunch over to fit under the canvas. "I wasn't the only one who jumped. There were others rolling down the embankment and running in all directions. Some were screaming out in pain, probably from broken bones." Mr. Reid pumped his arms, alternating them forward and backward. "Before long, a younger fellow was racing alongside me."

Like a final crescendo, he paused on a lingering note. "Most likely, the tenderfoot would have beaten me to the claim, but you won't believe what happened next."

"Go ahead." A detailed sketch was quickly forming in my mind.

"A section of barbed wire, maybe set by the railroad or cattlemen, was blocking our way." Mr. Reid resumed running in place, making the story quite fascinating. "The fellow made a bad decision. He tried to go over the top, but the sharp barbs caught and held him there. He was dangling from the top wire, his head nearly touching the ground and his feet up in the air."

"Poor fellow," I said, shaking my head.

He bent lower. "Knowing there was no chance for me to clear the fence, I decided to slip through the middle. It took some squeezing and caused rips in my clothes."

"Can't imagine why you aren't cut to bits," Finn said.

"There are a few to remind me of the day." He raised his pant leg, revealing a jagged cut and dried blood. "The back of my coat was tangled up in the barbs, so I left it hanging on the fence and ran as fast as possible at the marked sites."

"What about the man?" Finn asked.

"He was hollering at me to stop, but I kept going until my stake was securely driven into lot number nineteen. Had my sights on twenty-four, but this will do."

"Do you think he's still hung up on the fence?" Finn asked.

"No, sir. I may be determined but still have my dignity. Once my stake was in the ground, I went back and helped him from the snare."

"Really? You surprise me." I could hardly wait to put my pen to paper.

Mr. Reid laid his hand on his chest. "Even attorneys have a heart."

★ ★ ★ ★ ★

Finn wandered the area taking the last of the day's photographs while I sketched what played out in my mind of Mr. Reid's escapade and his claimed town site. The sights, sounds, smells, textures, and even the taste of the bitter tea, would eventually translate into a myriad of colors and compositions—an event coming to life in my paintings, and one I would never experience again.

Mr. Reid insisted we call him Bart since we had now become part of what he considered his greatest accomplishment in life. Again, he was in deep conversation with two dirt-covered cowboys in need of legal assistance. The young men were brothers and, obviously, under the strict authority of their father.

"If you don't get this straightened out, you'll have to contend with our father, Mr. Stanley Cooley." The shorter one shoved his hands in his pant pockets and puffed out his chest.

"And you don't want to do that," the taller one added. "It's best if you go on over to the land office with us tomorrow, explain that the claim belongs to us, and get this taken care of before our father has to get involved."

"Besides, that woman has no business staking a claim on her own." The shorter one spat on the ground. "Especially by the looks of her. She'll be calling all sorts of attention to herself, and—"

"Even if she rides a horse like a man," the other brother said, laughing. "It ain't safe for a woman with her looks to be out here alone."

I looked up from my paper. "Does she happen to have red hair?"

Bart stepped to the side, allowing the others to see me under the drape of the canvas.

"She might at that." The taller and most likely older brother cocked his head. "What's it to you? Do you know her?"

I shook my head. "No."

But I will.

CHAPTER 22

Mary ~ Alone, September 16, 1893

I finished unpacking the few supplies I was able to carry on horseback, including a bag of grain for Sadie. A blanket and small canvas roll would serve as tonight's shelter. Until I made my way back to the remains of the tent city to reunite with the Contolinis, a bottle of water, biscuits, jerky, and a couple of apples would have to be enough food to sustain me. Besides those things, I untied the rifle from the saddle and set the leather bag holding a meager supply of ammunition and a hunting knife on the ground.

Joseph had been right. Without Sadie, the chances of me getting land by trying to run—or even with the three of us in the wagon—would have been sparse.

Sadie nuzzled in my grain-filled hand. "Tomorrow, ol' girl, we'll head to the land office to register and then get you back to Joseph and Lizzie."

I shooed away the flies making her ears twitch. "You have an important journey ahead to get Lizzie to another doctor." Whether it was from exhaustion or nagging fear and concern, my eyes welled with tears. "But it's going to be hard to say farewell to all of you."

As I leaned my head into her neck and listened to her breathe, loneliness loomed like a late day's shadow—my only companion for many days to come.

＊＊＊＊＊

The not-so-far-off pounding of hooves startled me. Two riders approached from the slight hill to the north. Now that my hat was gone, I could only smooth my hair into the knot tied at the base of my neck. Just in case, I lifted the rifle and leaned it against my skirt. *Sure hope this is a friendly meeting.*

The riders slowed to a trot and then reined to a stop. One tipped his hat, revealing a sun-darkened face. "Ma'am."

"Good afternoon, gentlemen." I held my chin high.

The other showed a youthful face beneath tousled, blond hair. He was perhaps in his late teens or early twenties. "My brother and I have come to inform you that you're on our land."

"Probably through no fault of your own," said the first one, "being that it can be confusing who staked first." He pushed his hat back, displaying ebony eyes. "Unfortunately for you, these acres are under the rights of Mr. Cooley." The cowboy stood in his stirrups and pointed to the left. "Just over that hill is our family's marker, and it was well in the ground before you ever got here."

"And how would you know that?"

One brother squirmed in his saddle as the other loudly cleared his throat.

"We were already sitting around the campfire singing songs when we saw you ride on past." The boyish one chortled. "Didn't you hear my harmonica?"

"Nate, keep your wit to yourself." The other frowned. "Ma'am, I'm Ben Cooley, and this here is my younger brother, Nate. Our family, under the authority of our father, Stanley Cooley, has been raising cattle along the Kansas border and in this area for a long time."

"You're standing on part of our lease from the Cherokees," Nate added. "No one, not even a pretty lady like you, is gonna put another name on this acreage."

"If the members of your family are ranchers, then you are well aware those leases don't exist any longer."

Ben spoke first. "Our father is a founder of the Cherokee Strip Live Stock Association and—"

"And there's plenty of other laws that govern out here." Nate pulled his pistol from his holster and spun it around his finger.

"Are you threatening me, young man?"

"Not at all, are we, Ben?"

It was difficult to keep my voice steady. "Now, you listen to me. Mr. Cooley will need to find different grazing land." My stance widened as I raised the gun. "I raced for this land just like any other fair person and was the first to drive my stake into the ground."

Ben replaced his hat. "You don't seem to understand, ma'am. This land—"

"Is *mine*. That's the only thing to understand, gentlemen."

Nate leaned over and whispered something to his brother.

"Don't be a fool," Ben snapped. Slowly and methodically, he dismounted and walked toward me.

Whether instinct or panic, I lifted my rifle to my waist.

"Our family don't want no trouble with you, ma'am." Ben stopped a few feet away. "But what's ours is ours, and you need to pack up your things and ride on home like a good little girl."

I pointed the gun at Ben. "No trouble is wanted here either, but I'm not going anywhere."

"Lady, you'd be smart to put that down," Nate called from his horse.

The realization that he had his pistol aimed at me quickly called me back to my senses, but I kept the gun in place. Though my heart raced, determination helped me stand my ground regardless of where my next words led. "Here's the problem with your story, and you can share this with your father as well." The scene played over with vivid clarity. "You came over the ridge that borders part of the neighboring lot. Your timing couldn't have been better. That old man and woman were both crazy as a loon and most likely going to kill me. Guess I owe you something for saving my life."

Ben shifted his weight but kept his dark eyes on mine.

"One of you yelled out that you'd found the prime piece of land." I glanced up at Nate. "It was you."

Nate's youthful face appeared to age under the curse of his boiling anger.

Ben clenched and unclenched his fists. "Once we ran them folks off, we headed straight here. Ain't that right, Nate?"

"Yup."

"That's not what happened, and we all know it." My mind rehearsed galloping along the creek that eventually led to where I now stood. "While you were racing toward the open field—fixed on getting the claim before that old couple—I continued to ride alongside the river bed. It was the only path that made sense for a horse to run full speed. It was not nearly as rocky and would never cause an animal to lose its footing." The toe of my boot dug into the gravely earth. "Being horsemen, you would have taken the same path."

Ben's face reddened, and he took a step back.

"I got here well before either of you." My hand gestured to the stake in the ground. "In fact, you didn't realize you even wanted this site until you looked a bit further and saw what mine has to offer."

"Lady, you're lying." Nate spat on the dirt, leaving a dark mark inches from my feet.

I held my ground. "How odd that you waited to pay me a visit so late in the day."

Ben sneered. "What does that mean?"

"It means you made a mistake. When you reported the results of the race to your father, you realized this was the site you were *supposed* to claim."

The boys were silent as I contemplated my next move. They were probably doing the same. Before speaking, I prayed for the right words. "After all the excitement has settled and both your family and I have registered our rightful claims, we'll become good neighbors."

Ben backed away, then turned and mounted his horse. "Your story won't hold up with the law." He tipped his hat and smirked. "You've probably heard what's been happening to the Sooners once they've been found out. It's a shame a nice lady like you decided to cheat and slip into the territory before the official start of the race."

Nate chuckled. "Got that right, brother. Plenty of witnesses saw her sneak in."

The Cooley brothers turned their horses and, with spurs laid into flanks, rode away. When the last swish of the horses' tails disappeared over the ridge, I dropped to the ground and held my stomach. My body trembled from an unwelcome mixture of fear, anger, and disbelief, but my mind was steadfast. Their threat only deepened my resolve to make this my new home.

I stood and brushed the dust from my skirt. They would find out soon enough who they were trying to run off. With rock in hand, I drove down hard on the stake once more, securing its place in the barren soil.

This is my land!

CHAPTER 23

Daniel ~ Found, September 16, 1893

Drinking with a Scot can be risky, especially if that Scot is Finn. While many of the new arrivals continued to build the framework of their businesses well into darkness, many stopped to celebrate the success of the day. Bart was intent on doing just that. Fortunately for me, Finn was a willing participant.

"Mr. Simon and Mr. Levy, can you hear me all the way from town lot number nineteen?" Bart stumbled sideways and took another swig of whiskey. "I've got news for you. Remember the young buck you wouldn't make partner unless I got us land? I did it." He tossed the empty jug into the campfire where it shattered against the ring of stones. "Simon, Levy, and Reid—that's what the sign reads now."

As if giving applause, Finn released an overt burp. "Congratulations, Bart. They'll surely be doing a jig when they hear the good news."

"Not so sure." Bart plopped his large frame on the ground, sitting with his legs crossed and arms folded. His posture reminded me of a giant toad that could only sit and wait for something exciting to occur.

"Why would you say that?" I asked. "They'll be thrilled it was you who jumped from that train, not them."

"Truth is ..." He uncrossed his arms and held both palms up. "Most likely, their plan was to get rid of me. You know, cut me out."

"If that's what they had in mind, they could have fired you a long time ago," Finn said.

"Not that easy." He picked up a handful of dirt and tossed it into the flames. "My father, The Honorable Jacob L. Reid ... you could say he has a lot of influence." He tossed another handful of dirt, causing thick smoke to rise.

"Hold on. You're smothering the fire." I picked up the few remaining pieces of kindling lying nearby.

"That's probably what they were trying to do to me—snuff out my career. I'd bet you all the money left in my pocket they were taking wagers at the courthouse that ol' Justice Reid's plump kid couldn't run the race, let alone win it."

Perhaps it was the grit in the air, but tears seemed to pool in Bart's eyes. None of us spoke for a while. We sat staring at the dwindling fire, pulled into our own thoughts. As the orange and yellow flames flickered, my thoughts were only of her—the woman with the flowing red hair.

Finn spoke first. "Why don't you have your own business? You've already started it today."

Still in his toad-like position, Bart raised his head as if waking from a deep slumber. "The thought's crossed my mind. Problem is, I owe them a good deal of money from making my way here and getting these supplies."

"At least you didn't lose the whole of it on the train ride," I added.

"Again, thanks to both of you for waylaying the thief." Bart whistled in relief. "Losing all that money would have been the end of me. There'll be plenty of income once all these cowboys pay up. They won't get a lick of work from me till they have the funds to hire me."

"What about those brothers? Think you'll hear from them again?" My curiosity was more for my own need than Bart's.

"Plan to see them tomorrow. They're anxious to get that lady Sooner off their land—hopefully get her arrested as well."

"Sooner?" I jumped up. "She's no Sooner."

"Said they have proof. Not sure of it yet, but the truth will come out when the three of us meet with the marshal tomorrow. Something about an older couple who swear they saw her hiding out in the bushes and then making a run for it." Bart rolled to his side and stood. "Ah, heck—all that is confidential. I can't be talking about a case."

"What land are they fighting over? I need to find her."

Bart eyed me suspiciously. "Why are you so interested?"

"Not sure. I just need to talk to her." *Why am I so interested? I don't even know her—if it's even the same woman.*

"Could be a lady we saw racing," Finn offered.

"Of the thousands upon thousands of people, you think you saw this same woman?" Bart coughed and almost lost his balance. For a moment, a sense of foolishness laughed at me as well. With tattered clothes and bloodshot eyes, the young attorney held his head high. "Regardless, gentlemen, client confidentiality takes precedence. You will get no more details from me without the consent of the men I'm representing. Be assured … I know the law."

"This is no way to end the celebration of Mr. Reid's accomplishment. Here." Finn pulled a flask from his shirt pocket. "Let's have another drink." As he passed the silver container to Bart, Finn winked at me. My friend was up to his usual shenanigans.

"Gentlemen." I stretched my arms and yawned. "Time to turn in. I have more years behind me than either of you." I nodded to Bart. "It's much appreciated you allowing us to sleep under your tent until we make other arrangements."

"My pleasure," Bart called out to me as I walked away smiling.

✶ ✶ ✶ ✶ ✶

Daybreak greeted me with Bart's loud snoring and Finn whispering in my ear. "Section thirty. Township twenty-three. She's 'bout an hour's ride from here." He poked me hard in the ribs. "I even got us horses."

The smell of stale whiskey lingered on his breath, but Finn had come through for me. I clutched my bag and—just in case it would be her—the tattered hat. We headed down the road, trodden yesterday for the first time.

"How in the world?"

"Don't ask. Only know the boy with the bottles is quite a businessman. He sells more than water, that's for sure." Finn sprinted ahead with his camera case in one hand. "Hurry up. We've got to get the horses back before noon."

CHAPTER 24

Mary ~ Meeting, September 17, 1893

If it's possible to sleep with one eye open, I did. The Cooley brothers' accusations made me listen for approaching U.S. Marshals the rest of the day and into the night. My ears had to be keen to any screech, hiss, or howl nearby or in the distance. Or worse ... the sound of footsteps sneaking into my camp.

My thoughts traveled to a sight I would have preferred to forget. Joseph and I had watched a wagonload of accused Sooners, shackled and tied to slats and each other as they rolled into Arkansas City on their way to be tried for the serious federal offense. Word was, it often came down to one man's word against another, and the judge's favor. In my case, it would be one woman's word against three men. If it were true about the ranching family's position and influence, the outcome was already determined. I rubbed my wrists, hoping I would never feel the pain of tightened ropes or heavy chains around them.

* * * * *

Sadie finished the remaining bits of grain and eagerly nibbled on a patch of clover. I packed a few supplies for my ride to Perry, one of the four land offices available to legally claim my parcel and receive a deed of ownership. Fortunately, after walking to what I thought was the northeast area of my claim, I was able to locate the small pile of rocks and jotted down the numbers that designated the location and identity of my site. As a reminder to any wayward or late rushers, my blanket, canvas, and the sparse cooking items would be left behind as a reminder that someone had already staked this claim.

"It doesn't feel right riding away, Sadie. Not being here to protect my claim worries me." It would be different if Tuck were here—if I had my family. How was I supposed to hang on to this land by myself?

Sadie snorted, content on eating.

"A stranger could easily pull my stake and set their own." Sadie groaned with the tightening of her cinch. "No other choice though. Not a person to call on for help out here."

Determined to make an imprint on my memory, I walked to the top of the small mound to survey the land. Each cluster of trees and bushes grew thicker as my eye traveled toward the creek. Extending my arm and squinting one eye, I turned in a circle, following the curves and plateaus of the land with my hand. Patches of brilliant goldenrod, mixed with swaths of bluish-green, hazy sage and pink prairie rose spotted the landscape as though an artist had taken a brush to canvas, adding dabs of vibrant color. Tipping my face toward the wide-open sky, the prettiest blue, marbled with subtle swipes of white, greeted me. Brushstrokes by the hand of God.

Ashamed for not thanking the Lord for my safety over the last couple days, I sank to my knees and bowed my head. After a few moments, my eyes lifted once again to the sky.

"Father, I'm only a speck in this world—a tiny piece of life in all of Your creation. Insignificant. But I must be important to You. I don't fully understand why, but You took care of me throughout the race and all the moments up to this point. Thank You, Lord."

With hands folded, I spoke the rest of the words with more confidence. It felt right, only the two of us.

"There's more, and I hope that's all right." The endless blue sky sprawled in front of me like an ocean holding bits of heaven on this side of life. "Please, Lord, watch over my land. Wrap a hedge of protection around it so others can't take it from me. I promise to take special care of it—to make it a good home for Wesley." The ascending sun warmed my skin and bathed me in a calm that had been missing for weeks.

Perhaps it was the western breeze caressing the plains, but the sound of horses approaching from the east was unnoticed until they were well on my side of the creek and a stone's throw away. In one swift motion, I was on my feet, my heart racing as they rode closer.

"Ma'am," a man with an accent called. "Guid morning."

"Didn't mean to startle you." The other looked at me—not with the uncomfortable stare of some men, but with an odd expression, as if trying to recollect a memory. "We're bringing no trouble."

"Then what does bring you here?" My rifle was already tied to the saddle but, strangely, my heartbeat slowed.

"Only to introduce ourselves." The man with the accent gave a slight bow. "I'm Finn Allaway, and this is—"

"Daniel McKenzie," the second man added.

"We're on assignment from the Boston Globe to cover the race," Finn said.

"But the race is over." My eyes stayed on the one who must have been the elder of the two. His skin was tanned from the sun, but not leathered like the people who spent most of their lives outside.

"We're speaking with folks who participated in or witnessed the Rush," Daniel added. "If you'd oblige us your time, we'd love to hear what you have to say."

"And to take your photograph if you don't mind." Finn patted the leather case secured to the back of his saddle. "I take the photographs, and my friend paints the pictures."

"Who writes the story?" I asked.

"I do," they answered simultaneously.

"Hmm." My eyes moved to Finn but quickly returned to Daniel.

Finn pointed to himself and then at Daniel. "We both gather information, anecdotes—"

"About people we find ..." Daniel paused, as though waiting for the right word. "Fascinating." His announcement hung in the air as an uncomfortable silence joined our company.

Finn was the one who broke the silence. "Ma'am, what's yer name?"

I hesitated but somehow felt these two could be trusted. "Mary Roberts."

"Well then, Mrs. Roberts, mind if we talk with you for a short while? Take some photographs?" Finn pointed to Sadie, still eating the clover and not interested in the visitors.

I hurried off the mound. "Perhaps another time, gentlemen. It's urgent that I get on my way to the land office in Perry."

"Perhaps we interrupted you … praying." Daniel spoke softly, shyly.

"Absolutely not." My face grew hot, and my fingers fiddled with the leather straps securing my bag. "Only resting. There's a good ride ahead of me." *Oh, Lord, why did I just deny You? Am I that stubborn?*

For a moment, the truth welled in my gut—the real need to drop to my knees and pray. I unwrapped the reins from the ground stake and looped them around the saddle horn. "Sorry I can't help you with a story." My voice was terse as Daniel's eyes locked with mine. I grasped the stirrup to steady myself. "There are surely more *fascinating* people than me."

There is nothing ladylike or graceful about hoisting one's self onto a horse in long skirts, but I settled myself astride the saddle in as dignified a manner as possible. "Gentlemen, good day and much luck with your work." I gave Sadie a gentle kick.

"Wait," Finn called out.

I didn't stop. "Long ride ahead."

"The lines in Perry are stacked miles deep," Finn said. "You'd be waiting for days, maybe weeks."

I halted and turned in my saddle. "How do you know that, Mr. …"

"Allaway. We've been talking with plenty of folks. Most who made their way into Perry straight away after the race turned back to wait it out. Once they got word it was a waste of time to stand in another line, or—"

"Received a future date to return to complete the paperwork," Daniel said. "Could be several months from now. Four land offices in the entire territory can't accommodate forty-thousand claims."

Pulling Sadie around, I approached the men from Boston. "Then what do you propose? I need to be able prove this is my land … and soon."

"You'll eventually need that piece of paper, but for now, it's important to establish something that resembles the beginnings of a homestead." Finn pointed to the remains of last night's small campfire.

"A proper shelter is a good start." Daniel dismounted. He was taller than he appeared in the saddle. Broad-shouldered and muscular too. Gathering the reins, he led his mare to the post poking awkwardly from the earth. His stride was confident and upright—not a bow-legged saunter like a man who spent most of his days on a horse. Although, the gentle way he patted the horse's wither made me take note that he had spent time other than in the confines of a big city.

But as Finn dismounted, my senses kicked back in. "What are you doing?" My voice rose with each word. "I am well aware of my needs. No help is needed or wanted." Swinging my leg over the saddle, the hem of my petticoat snagged on my boot, sending me backward and tumbling onto the ground. Before I could get up, Daniel was leaning over me, his hand extended. For the first time, his eyes were in clear view. They were hazel—a mixture of pale blue, green with flecks of gold … turquoise.

Turquoise. The small stone Lizzie gave me before the start of the race. "Keep this safe with you," she said, wrapping her frail fingers around mine. "An old Indian gave it to me when I was a child. Told me it brought protection, especially from falling. Wisdom too, he said, for those who have eyes to see, ears to hear, and a heart to love. I've had it all these years. The best part … he promised it had been carved from heaven and slipped to earth."

I accepted his hand and rose to my feet. His grip was firm and seemed to linger. I looked up to thank him and our eyes locked.

There's kindness in your eyes. The thought fluttered into my mind like a delicate butterfly. Just as quickly, it skittered away—tossed in a storm—its wings now useless. *What do you see in my eyes? Fear? Anger?* I looked away.

As though he could read my mind, he stepped back and motioned for Finn.

"Is this all you have?" Finn walked in a circle around the folded blanket and canvas.

"Right now, yes. If you're right about the wait in Perry, I'll ride back to Arkansas City to meet Joseph and Lizzie."

"Your husband and child?" Daniel blurted. "Pardon me, ma'am, but there's something wrong with a man sending his wife—" His tanned complexion appeared to fade.

"Joseph and Lizzie are my dear friends. We traveled together from Missouri with the hopes of each of us getting land."

"My apologies. I figured you must be married." He nodded at my left hand, still adorned with a thin, gold band—a remnant of my previous life.

"My husband recently passed away."

He bowed his head. "My condolences. Please forgive me. I misspoke."

The details about Tuck's death were not shared, but Finn and Daniel were filled in about the Contolinis' change of plans, especially the importance of me returning as soon as possible to Arkansas City for Lizzie's sake. Besides, the anticipation to bring the good news of my success in the Rush was growing. Since I hadn't returned to their tent immediately after the race, they would have concluded one of two things—land was claimed, or there was an injury. In the latter case, Joseph would have come looking for me. "I'll get more supplies as soon as I can. There will be plenty to purchase as the new town sites will be coming alive in no time."

"They already are. Businesses are springing up overnight. But the horse? Your friends won't be able to leave her with you?" Finn ran his hand along Sadie's withers and spoke gently to her. "You're a mighty fine horse to run like you did. You were something to see. Kept up with the thoroughbreds, did you?"

"You saw us race?" I cocked my head in need of a response.

Neither spoke as they snapped branches and began assembling the framework of a lean-to. As much as I wanted to protest their help, common sense reminded me the shelter would be welcomed when the evening winds picked up and the day's blazing sun relentlessly scorched my skin.

"Well, did you?" I called out over the noise.

"Like Finn said, you were something to see."

"When the cannon sounded and the guns shot, you were up front with the best horses and men." Finn raised his hat in the air, swatted at his rear end, and galloped in a circle. "Even riding like a man, if you'll beg my pardon."

"Mr. Allaway," I called out over his hooting and hollering. "*You* are the sight to see."

It felt good to laugh as Finn reenacted the race—leaping over rocks and logs, then running up and down the embankment, panting and smiling.

*****

A temporary shelter now stood where only the open sky was above. Rocks were dug into the earth and firmly placed in a circle to establish a proper cooking area. Finn and Daniel gathered three substantial logs from the creekside to set around the fire pit—an indication to others that this lot was spoken for by more than one person.

Finn took a few photographs of my meager house and its surroundings. "How 'bout a few more?" He pointed the camera at me.

"No, please." My hand slid nervously along my temple. "I'm not presentable for my picture to be taken." But the camera let out a burst, capturing me in time and place.

I hadn't seen myself for days, not since catching my reflection in the general store window the day before the race. The trickle in the creek had allowed me to splash water on my face and to rub the grime from my arms and hands. My attempts to tame my tangled hair with a ribbon and a few pins were futile. Its natural wavy and unruly state won out—just as it had when I was a carefree child.

Finn poked his eye around the edge of the box before retreating behind the lens like a game of hide-and-seek. More bursts followed until my hand lifted to cover my face.

"One more?" He was charming, but that was enough notoriety for me.

"Perhaps another time." I tucked a loose strand behind my ear. "When my homestead is complete, you'll have more interesting subjects to photograph."

I approached Daniel. "Thank you for your help. You didn't need to do all this." My throat went dry. "I'd planned to take care of everything upon my return from town." My hand extended toward his.

He shook mine in return. "It was my … our pleasure."

Whether it was reality or only my imagination, he seemed to keep hold of my hand a little longer than necessary. For that brief, yet lingering moment, my heart skipped a beat.

* * * * *

My remote and lonely piece of land was becoming crowded. Once again, riders came over the hill. I figured it wouldn't be long before they returned.

"Who's your company?" Finn widened his stance and watched the riders slow to a trot.

"Cooley brothers. Their family thinks they should have my land." I fisted my hands to maintain composure.

Ben spoke first. "Ma'am. Gentlemen. Mrs. Roberts, excuse us for intruding with you having guests and all."

"Good day, Ben. Nate."

Daniel stepped forward. "Gentlemen. What can we help you with?"

"Ain't you the fellow from last night?" Nate narrowed his eyes and stepped his horse closer. "Ain't this a sight, Ben?" He motioned to his brother to pull up alongside him. "Asked if she had red hair."

"But said he didn't know her." Ben and his brother grinned like they had just won a high-stakes game of poker. "Sir, you're either a liar or that attorney has a loose mouth."

"What are you talking about?" I shot a look at the brothers, then back at Daniel.

"Surely your friends hightailed it out here to let you know you've been found out," Nate said with a smirk. "Too late, though. The law's already working in our favor."

"That's right," Ben added. "No Sooner is keeping what ain't hers. We have that lawyer filing a case against you today. Paid him a deposit this morning for his services."

Anger started to bubble inside. "You have no proof whatsoever."

"We have testimony from the respectable—" Ben began.

"And reliable," Nate chimed in.

"Mr. and Mrs. Roper." Ben sat back in his saddle and grinned. "The old couple you nearly scared to death when you came out of hiding in the thicket."

"Then you lathered up your horse with soap," Nate said, "and ran full speed, nearly running them down dead, till you reached this site."

Ben clicked his tongue in disgust. "Shame you scared 'em away before they could realize their own dream."

My mouth opened in disbelief, words refusing to come out. Those awful old hoots. I could only imagine what the Cooleys were willing to pay for their false testimony.

Daniel walked toward his horse.

Nate raised his gun. "I'd be careful what you're getting from that horse, Mister."

Daniel turned his head. "No need to worry, gentlemen." He slowly untied the leather strap on his bag.

Finn slipped his hand under his vest while I hoped the brothers kept their eyes on Daniel. At first, it was difficult to make out what Daniel pulled from the bag. It looked like a tattered piece of clothing of some sort. Finn nodded as if privy to Daniel's plan.

Holding the object aloft, Daniel approached and spoke loudly, "Your *chapeau*, madame." He bowed, almost theatrically, and offered my crushed and filthy hat.

My eyes widened. "My hat? It's hardly recognizable."

"But it's yours, I assure you." Daniel winked, yet his jaw was set as though it was important for me to pay close attention to what he spoke. "Like we said, you were quite a sight running that horse in the race. You didn't miss a step, even with your hat coming loose and all."

"The sash loosened while I was in full run." My fingers slid along the one remaining ribbon. "It flew off behind me and into the oncoming horses and wagons."

Nate leaned forward in the saddle, obviously trying to get a better look. "That don't make no sense at all."

"Surely it does, Mr. …"

"Nate Cooley. This here's my brother, Ben. You won't be pulling a fast one on the Cooley family. This lady friend of yours is a thief."

"What's she doing for you to play in her favor?" Ben scoffed. "Surprising what a pretty lady can get a man to do."

"How dare you talk in such a way!" I stomped toward the foul-mouthed brother.

Daniel stopped me, then addressed the brothers. "You might want to consider making an apology to Mrs. Roberts."

Nate frowned. "What for?"

"Yer not that ignorant, now are you?" Finn pulled his gun from underneath his vest.

Suddenly, three guns were raised, and no one spoke.

It was my voice that broke the silence. "I have the race documentation."

"Don't prove a thing," Ben replied. "You sneaked in before the race started."

"Yep, you holed up in the brush for a day—already had your choice lot picked out."

"Good thing I do what I do." Finn enunciated each word with exaggerated emphasis.

"And what would that be, foreigner?" Ben asked.

"Take pictures." Keeping his face raised, Finn bent over and patted the camera box on the ground. "Lots of pictures. In fact, some of the best ones are the actual Rush."

"Especially those of the red-haired woman wearing the ivory hat." Daniel smiled broadly. "Gentlemen, she truly was a sight to see. Too bad you missed the chance."

The brothers glared at me.

"This ain't over." Ben adjusted his hat and turned his horse.

Nate directed his words to Daniel. "I'm afraid it's you who are missing the chance. What a shame to be involved with the likes of her." He looked at me with such disgust and hatred that my stomach lurched. Then he turned and followed after his brother.

"Dunderheeds to be sure." Finn slapped his hat on his knee. "Idiots don't seem to recall the photographs won't show color. No red hair in my pictures, only shades of black and white, everyone looking the same."

"Not true, Finn." Daniel looked directly at me and paused for a moment as if finding the right words. "She was different than the others."

Silence followed until Finn stepped between the two of us. "Well then, Daniel, you'll need to paint her hair red."

A wide smile spread across Daniel's face. "I will. Hues of raw sienna, ochre, and red."

CHAPTER 25

Mary ~ Good-bye, September 18, 1893

Like the remnants of a carnival that had packed up and rolled into the next town, the tent city was a mere smattering of ashen campfires, trodden grass, and bits of broken glass and forgotten items. For the few people who remained, most were the unlucky ones who didn't strike a claim and were faced with which direction to travel next.

Some decided to stay put, hoping Arkansas City would bring new opportunities as other towns sprouted across the newly tilled territory. Others packed their few possessions and pointed themselves toward what was home, willing to relinquish their pride with heads hanging low—sure to face the naysayers upon return.

"Joseph!" I called out. "I did it."

He waved both arms above his head. "I knew you would." He poked his head in the tent's opening. A moment later, Lizzie crawled out, and Joseph helped her to her feet. I dismounted and ran to my friends. We wrapped our arms around one another, none of us wanting to let go.

Sadie whinnied, and we all laughed.

"That's my girl." Joseph opened his arms to her as if welcoming home a long-lost friend. He stroked her neck. "Didn't want to be forgotten, eh?"

"Impossible." Sadie's speed and agility were surprising. "You should have seen her go. She did all the work as I held on for dear life."

"We saw the start, but all that dust kicking up ..." Lizzie said.

"It looked as if someone set the prairie on fire," Joseph said. "Couldn't see much of anything, but we could hear it. Never heard such a sound. Thought the earth was going to split open."

"So loud, my entire body shook like I was going to fall over." Lizzie nodded at Joseph. "He propped me up the whole time till we couldn't see anyone left on the prairie."

"Except the poor souls who wrecked their wagons or fell off horses at the start," Joseph said.

Lizzie placed her hand on her cheek. "I still wonder what happened to the fellow on the bike after he tumbled into the ditch."

Joseph pretended to balance atop a large-wheeled bicycle, wobbling his arms side to side. "Like I said, he didn't deserve much better thinking he could compete on such a contraption."

Lizzie pinched his arm.

"Ouch, woman. It's the truth."

My heart warmed, relieved to be with my friends again. "You two haven't changed in the past forty-eight hours." I took Lizzie's hands in mine and searched her face. "But really, how are you feeling?"

She pressed her lips firmly together and seemed to search for the right words. "Let's just say, it's best Joseph and I aren't trying to start a new life out there." She glanced around me toward the open prairie. "That's for you now, not us."

Unexpected tears filled my eyes—perhaps some from exhaustion, but mostly spilling from my heart. The next few hours would be both precious and fleeting. After we unpacked my portion of the wagon at my lot, the Contolinis would head away from the setting sun, and I would say good-bye to my best friend—one I had been given the honor to travel alongside during what was most likely her last journey on this side of life.

"Mary," Lizzie whispered in my ear. "I know what you're thinking." Now she took my hands in hers. "I'm scared too, but you must understand this. We came into one another's life for a reason. There are no mistakes in God's plan. He has blessed me because of you."

"And you have blessed me." I reached into my pocket and then placed the smoothed turquoise stone in Lizzie's palm. "Your stone kept me safe."

Lizzie looked confused and shook her head. "No, child. The stone didn't keep you safe. It has no magical powers."

"But you said—"

"It would guide you? Provide wisdom?" The creases in her brow relaxed, and only the wrinkles earned from old age remained. "Those things don't come from a stone. Only God is that good." She pointed to the sky. "But I'd like to believe the Indian was right."

Together, we said the words, "carved from heaven and slipped to earth."

"Mary, make me a promise."

"Anything."

"Seek His wisdom. Ask for eyes to see, ears to hear, and a heart to love." She placed the stone in my palm and closed my fingers. "Especially a heart to love again."

"Again?"

"Yes, again. It's worth the pain that inevitably comes with loving."

"Are you sure about that, Lizzie?"

"It hurts worse to not love at all."

I breathed in deeply and closed my eyes, squeezing the last few tears down my cheeks.

* * * * *

Losing the horse that carried me through the biggest adventure of my life was hard enough. But wrapping my arms around Joseph's neck and kissing his stubbly beard threatened to shatter my heart.

"We'll find a way to check on you," he spoke into my hair.

After he hugged me and stroked my back, a long-forgotten memory surfaced of what my father did on rare occasions. But when Joseph wiped his eyes with his kerchief, I couldn't recall ever seeing my father cry.

"When you get a proper address, we'll send each other letters." He tugged on his suspenders with both hands. "I have a good feeling about where we're heading. Pastor Allen promised us those are good people he left behind."

Lizzie was quiet. She and I had said all that really mattered. Before Joseph lifted her onto the front bench of the wagon, we simply held each other, breathing in rhythm.

God, you placed so many years between us. But somehow, that doesn't matter in heaven. Please don't let this be the last time I see her, even if it's after this life.

Sadie faithfully led Joseph and Lizzie's wagon across the creek and along the tree line until they rounded a final curve. Only then did I slump to my knees and weep, not caring that I cried aloud. Only the birds and insects, perhaps a lingering rabbit, were my witnesses.

I was now completely alone.

CHAPTER 26

Daniel ~ Trouble, September 21, 1893

The last few days had been filled with sketching the metamorphosis of the landscape. Buildings appeared where before only grasses danced in the wind. Roads gouged into the once untouched soil—permanent scars on the earth. And although to most the new surroundings were positive—signs of growth and opportunity—to me they came with a price. My entire adult life had been spent enclosed by the dimness of a city. I had forgotten how captivating the open sky could be and the peace it brought when gazing at its grandeur and knowing there was more to my life than what the moment afforded.

"I won't be traveling back with you." I waited for Finn's response.

"Figured as much." Finn carefully wrapped the last of the film he would develop in the Globe's darkroom.

"You did? Think you can read my mind?"

"Just yer heart." He playfully punched my arm. "Makes sense. Been missing Elizabeth something awful."

"What will you tell McKelvey when only one of us shows up?"

Finn tapped the side of his head with his forefinger. "Steps ahead of you, my friend. I'll tell him you stayed on to cover one of the greatest events in the history of our country. *And* you'll give him one of your best paintings to gift to his wife."

"I will?"

"If you want your job when you return to Boston. You are coming home, aren't you?"

"Eventually." I lifted a bundle of sketches. "As soon as I complete a few of these."

"But why not in your studio?" Finn averted his eyes as he fastened the straps on his bag. "I know, I know. You need to be surrounded by the inspiration."

"I'll be back before you know it. But you're right. That's how we artists do our best work. And right now, my greatest inspiration is here."

✶ ✶ ✶ ✶ ✶

Approaching the spot where the creek curved and widened, I pulled on the reins. The enterprising young lad had been quick to raise the rental price for the mare when he found out I needed flexibility as to when she would be returned.

Now, the entire idea to ride out to see Mary seemed foolish. A woman choosing to come out here alone must want to be left that way. She had a fire in her to match that hair. It would be best for me to turn around and catch the next train to Boston.

A skein of geese honked overhead, a reminder that with the incorrigible heat the country had endured, cold winter temperatures would soon follow.

She'll freeze to death without a sod house for shelter.

It wasn't clear at first, but woven between the noise above, a cacophony of sounds came from ahead. Men's voices rang out, whooping and hollering. Similar to the deafening sound at the beginning of the Rush, a pounding reverberated in my chest. But this was different than the sound of racing horses. It was deeper, more guttural.

With my spurs laid into the mare's sides, I raced around the bend. In the open space at the base of the small hill, well over fifty cattle ran in a tight circle, mooing and snorting as a plume of dust rose into the air. Three wranglers positioned themselves around the perimeter of the herd and snapped long bullwhips in the air. The crack of the leather sounded like gunshots, and the frightened cattle stampeded.

In full gallop, I raced through the creek and across the field toward Mary's camp. I scanned the area, frantically looking for her while avoiding a collision with a wayward bull. The cowboys yelled and waved their arms in the air as the cattle lunged in awkward diagonals. The massive animals bumped into each other with enough force to make them crumple to the ground.

Then, like a rehearsed dance, the men sidestepped their horses, quickly gathering the herd back into a cluster. As suddenly as it had all started, the animals calmed, and the dust settled. If I hadn't seen it myself, I never would have imagined that chaos had ever occurred.

One of the men rode out to retrieve a younger bull that had slipped away. After he shooed the animal toward the others, he trotted in my direction.

Nate Cooley.

"Where is she?" My back stiffened, and my hands fisted around the reins.

"Your lady friend?" Sweat dripped from his temples. "Don't know." He motioned to the herd. "We been busy rounding up a runaway herd. We got no time to be worrying about the whereabouts of a woman."

"You're lying. You ran your cattle right through her camp." I swallowed hard at the vacant space where the lean-to had stood.

"Now why would we do that? True enough, some of our cattle split off and wandered down here to graze." He shrugged as if this were an everyday occurrence. "Those bovines have a mind of their own. Must have followed the creek and then found some tasty clover on the flat."

My teeth clenched as an unexpected anger filled me. "Stay off her land."

In his customary manner, Nate spat on the ground. "I'll tell my men to keep a better watch on the cattle."

*****

There was little left of the campsite. Broken branches and torn pieces of canvas were scattered as if a tornado had brought its wrath. A skirt, blouse, and wool coat were in a heap. A blanket and a few undergarments lay nearby. The ring of stones and logs rested in random places, wherever they settled after being kicked by the powerful hooves. I picked up a flattened tin mug and a dented cooking pot, then righted a torn sack of flour, leaving what looked like a drift of snow in the dirt. A water barrel lay on its side, the last of its contents dripping out of a bullet hole.

She had so little, and now look what's left.

"Drop what's in your hands, and get off my land before I shoot a hole in you."

Though the voice was low and menacing, I knew it immediately. Not wanting to scare her—or have her stay true to her threat—I dropped the items in my hands. "Mary, it's me, Daniel." I turned slowly, hands in the air, and faced her.

A shotgun pointed straight at my heart. "Daniel?"

"I'm so glad you're—"

"How could you do this?" Her lips trembled, but the shotgun stayed firmly in place.

"That's absurd. I would never do such a thing. I only came here to check on you." I stepped forward, but the look on her face stopped me. "It was the Cooley boys, Mary. They ran their cattle through your camp. See? There are hoof prints and manure everywhere."

Our eyes locked, but a shudder passed through me at my inability to stop what had happened. "I'm so sorry. If only I could have gotten here sooner."

A look of defeat crossed her face, and she dropped the gun. "I should have known. It's not your fault. Who knows what they would have done had you tried to stop them." She set the gun against the empty barrel and wandered around the remains of her home.

Everything inside me wanted to help her, but she seemed lost in her own thoughts. A world where—regardless of the danger—she needed to be left alone. First, she wiped dirt from a spoon and bent fork. After gathering shards from a broken plate, she tossed them into the remains of the fire ring. Like they had been freshly laundered, she lifted a skirt and shirtwaist and neatly folded them, then brushed off a torn blanket, shook it several times, and spread it on the ground as though preparing for a picnic.

I didn't want to stare but found myself mesmerized by her movements, drawn to her as though she were a siren, beckoning me during my journey. She raised a silver hand mirror in front of her face but dropped it where it had laid—shattered.

When she fell to her knees, my spell was broken, and I went to her. She lifted a nightdress and reached underneath it for a book. Its limp cover flapped open in her hands, and loose pages spilled on the ground. The strewn pages were familiar—Luke, Deuteronomy, Ephesians, James, Genesis …

With delicate movements, she turned the bound pages, inserting those that had been dislodged into their inspired positions. When the pages were replaced, she sat back on her heels and sighed. "My mother's Bible. I promised her I would read it." She lifted it to her chest and held it tightly. "Seems like it's time to get started."

* * * * *

Paying the boy extra for the horse worked out to my advantage. It took some time for me to help Mary rebuild the lean-to now that most of the support branches were broken.

Even though the cooking pot was dented, it sufficed to hold beans and grits and would serve its purpose for the rest of the food that was unharmed. Fresh water was going to be an issue when the creek dried up altogether, but we brought enough from the creek for the two of us, then rested around the campfire after resetting one of the logs.

"Leaving this morning, I wasn't sure what kind of neighbors I would find to the south, considering the others haven't been too hospitable." She picked up a small shard of glass and tossed it into the fire. "The Andersons seem to be good people, though." Mary shivered and wrapped a blanket around herself. "They were happy to get a claim in this area. Thomas' brother is starting a hardware store in the new town. Says he already has the framework together."

"You don't say?" I slapped my thigh and had to smile. "If he has a young son with yellow hair and light-blue eyes, he has a businessman on his hands. That boy has practically emptied Finn's pockets, as well as my own."

"Everything costs something, especially out here. It sure didn't help matters to have some of my supplies ruined."

"I'm just glad you weren't here. If something had happened to—"

"Where is Finn, anyway?" She stood and walked to the other side of the fire.

"He's headed back to Boston. Took the earliest train to get a good start."

"Why didn't you go with him? You work together, right?"

The light from the fire cast a warm glow on her face and made me pause to take in the sight. *She's so beautiful.* "I'll be heading back myself at week's end."

"Certainly. Figured as much. The newspaper is surely needing you back as soon as possible." She poked a stick into the fire to stir the coals.

You're a fool, Daniel. She has no interest in you. For all I know, she has another man.

"I'll be heading back to Missouri tomorrow. It would have been nice to have my deed before leaving, but since I can't officially register until December, there's no sense in waiting."

"Tomorrow?" I tried to sound uninterested. "Business to attend to?"

Her smile was rueful, making her even more attractive. "My son, Wesley. He turned seven last week. My mother's been taking care of him until I could bring him here." She tossed the stick into the fire. "I sure miss him. Feel awful we were apart for his birthday."

"How will you take care of a child out here?" As soon as the words left my mouth, her smile faded.

"The Andersons are delivering my portion of lumber when they get their load from town. With everyone needing to build, it may take a while to get enough for a sufficient house. But we'll be fine."

"But he's only a boy. You can't expect him—"

"I *said* we'll be fine." She pursed her lips before turning her back toward me.

Clearly, I had overstepped my place, but I couldn't help myself with thoughts of the two of them left alone out here. "He's not strong enough to help you build a house. Let me build a proper—"

She spun around, and the look on her face was intense. "Mr. McKenzie, I appreciate what you're trying to do, but I am perfectly capable of taking care of my son."

"But Mary ..." I stepped toward her, but she backed away.

"And myself."

Neither of us spoke for a few minutes. She busied herself cleaning the plates and pot while I gathered and stacked the sparse kindling.

When she spoke, her voice was sad. "Thank you for your help today, but it's best if you leave now."

A pit formed in my stomach that hadn't been there since I was a young man. I hadn't allowed myself to care for another woman in all the years since.

"No offense intended. Only respect for what you've done here. Not many women would have taken on this challenge on their own. Just offering help for a friend."

A deep sadness etched its way into her features. "A stubborn friend for sure, but not foolish. Life won't be easy. Whoever said it's supposed to be is a liar." She seemed to be trying to hold back tears. Maybe there were difficult memories locked behind her wall of determination and independence.

"Mary, you're strong, capable ..." I hesitated, but the next words surged from my heart, intent on being released, "and beautiful."

She stared at me with a quizzical look, as though my words sounded foreign. When she didn't reply, I silently cursed myself for being so bold.

After a moment, she turned away. "It's best if you go."

All of my being wanted to wrap my arms around her and hold tightly ... admit my heart had begun to feel again even at the thought of her ... tell her I cared about her and wanted to be with her. But

I walked toward the mare, unlatched the halter, and slipped on her bridle. My body was numb, only going through the motions. After tightening the cinch a final time, I pulled myself onto the horse and tipped my hat. "Best of luck to you, Mary. No doubt, you'll make a fine home for you and your son."

She pulled the blanket closer around her before I turned and rode away.

Whether it was the coolness of the autumn night air—a reminder that the harsh winter months were approaching—or a premonition that both our hearts could grow cold from fear, or perhaps pride, I shuddered.

CHAPTER 27

Mary ~ Reunion, September 23, 1893

With my forehead against the window from a mixture of exhaustion and excitement, the train pulled into the Kirksville station. As the distance from home shortened along the rail tracks, the more my absence from Wesley and my mother was realized. In turn, the greater the physical distance grew between me and my new land, I yearned for it as well. Oddly, my life was suspended between two worlds. It was difficult to know which to call home. Regardless, without time to send a letter, my family would be surprised to see me back so soon.

On the train, I had been able to scrub the grime off my face and neck and then tame my hair into a twist. Walking through town without a hat wouldn't matter. My head could be held high after my success in the Rush.

* * * * *

Wesley begged me to retell the details of the race several times over the dinner table. He giggled each time at the description of the Englishman dashing alongside me, especially when I attempted a poor British accent. Both his eyes and mouth widened at the thought of me straddling Sadie, racing full speed over the open plain like a man.

The run-in with the old couple near the creek and the cattle being stampeded through my campsite were not mentioned. Those were realities I hoped we would never face again. My only mention of Daniel was that he and his colleague from an East Coast newspaper had taken my photograph, perhaps to be included in an article about successful claimants.

Other than wanting to know more about the Contolinis and sharing her concern for Lizzie, Mother was quieter than usual. Just as when I was young, she seemed to know when I wasn't telling the whole truth.

After rinsing the dinner plates, I was busy cutting slices of apple pie when a knock sounded at the door.

"Expecting someone, Mother?" She didn't answer. Probably not hearing as well these days. Upon opening the front door, Sheriff Murphy's familiar crystal-blue eyes met mine.

"Mary." He tipped his hat. "Heard you were back and wanted to come say hello."

Caught quite off guard, I didn't respond.

"May I come in?"

"I suppose so." A chill passed over me as I stepped aside.

He placed his hat on the side table and followed me into the kitchen.

"Would you like some dessert?" I asked. "Mother's famous apple pie."

"She makes the best pie in town. I've enjoyed a few slices over the last few weeks."

"Really? She invited you over for pie?" *What could Mother be thinking?*

"You could say I took it upon myself to stop by to see if she had any word about you."

"As you can see, I'm fine. A landowner as well," I said proudly.

"You are fine, without a doubt." He stepped closer. "You are even more stunning than when you left, if that's possible."

I avoided his stare and drove the knife into the pie, placing a slice on each plate. "Let's take dessert to the others at the table."

He rested his hand on mine. "You need to know how much I thought of you. Each day I wondered if you were all right. Every evening my dreams were about you."

My mouth opened, but words didn't come.

"You don't have to say anything. You've been through a lot, I'm sure."

As he ran his fingers along the top of my hand, a cold shiver ran down my back.

"I want to hear all about it, especially when we have a chance to be *alone*." He carried the plates into the dining room.

An exasperated sigh escaped as my body leaned against the counter. *I need to get away from here as soon as possible.* This man was nothing but a bushel of trouble.

"Sheriff Murphy!" Wesley's voice rang out from the other room. "Did you come to take me shooting again?"

And get my son away too.

＊＊＊＊＊

Even after catching up on some much-needed sleep on the train, I pretended to be exhausted. "My apologies for yawning." I pushed away from the table. "Sheriff—"

"Mary, please call me David. We know each other too well for formalities."

Mother looked at me with an odd expression.

"All right then … David. You'll need to excuse me. My eyes will not stay open another minute. And you, young man …" I tousled Wesley's hair, "it's bedtime for you as well."

David folded his napkin. "Louisa, your pie was especially delicious tonight. Perhaps it was the company and good conversation." He stood and patted his stomach. "Mary, I'm sure there's more about your adventure you'll want to tell me after you've had a chance to rest."

Again, I had reservations about how much to share with this man. The logistics of my travels with the Contolinis, the long wait to register for the Rush, even the excitement of the race and pounding my stake into the ground, seemed like safe topics. Past those, he would not step further into the other life I had been living for such a short time.

"Mama's gonna have her picture in the newspaper." Wesley bounced up on his knees.

"Is that right?" David turned his full attention to me. "Now, that's a picture worth seeing."

My cheeks warmed, but not from flattery. "Wesley, don't go starting rumors. Plenty of people had their photographs taken at such an important event."

"Not someone that looks like you." David's lecherous smile sickened me. "Which paper was it?"

All three of them stared at me. "I … I don't recall."

Mother slightly cocked her head, an indication she knew I was fibbing.

*****

After Wesley was sent to bed for the third time, he finally fell asleep. Mother and I were able to settle onto the sofa under the warmth of the quilt and talk.

"All right. Are you ready to hear more?" I asked, tucking the quilt a little tighter.

She turned toward me and propped a crocheted pillow beneath her arms. "I'm listening."

At the description of the Ropers and their devious involvement with the Cooleys, Mother shook her head in disgust. When I described what happened to my belongings after the cattle ran through the campsite, she covered her mouth with her hand. "I'd say I can't believe you did it, but I can. From the time you were able to walk, you thrived on being challenged. Don't get me wrong. It doesn't make me feel good knowing everything that's happened out there, and I've been around long enough to know there will be more trouble."

"You're right. The Cooleys won't give up easily."

"It's the nature of many people, dear—greed and hatred."

"Thankfully, there are ones who are good. My other neighbors, Thomas and Lucy. And there's Lizzie and Joseph, Pastor Allen and his wife. And … Daniel McKenzie and Finn."

Mother leaned toward me with a twinkle in her eyes. "Tell me more about this Mr. McKenzie."

"He's an illustrator for a newspaper back East. Most likely, he's joined his friend, Finn, back in Boston by now. Finn made me laugh like no one ever has." I smiled at the memory of him galloping around the campsite.

"What else … about Mr. McKenzie?"

"He helped me rebuild my lean-to," I said, wondering where the conversation was headed. "He didn't need to do that." I started to get up from the sofa, but mother stopped me.

"You're twisting a strand of hair around your finger like you always have when there's more to a story. More you're not too sure you want to tell me."

I slumped back on the sofa and puffed out a breath. "You're right. There is definitely more to Daniel McKenzie. Honestly, I'm not sure what it is or what to think. He's such a gentleman. So caring. So giving. So …" *And those eyes.*

She was quiet, maybe giving me time with my thoughts, or maybe reminiscing about my father, trying to recall the feelings she had so long ago.

"Mother, there's nothing more important in the world than taking care of Wesley and giving him a happy life. No matter what Sheriff Murphy … David … or whatever he should be called thinks, I am completely capable of doing just that." Pacing in front of the sofa only helped me state my conviction. "I've found out the hard way it doesn't work out too well to depend on anyone else."

Mother's nod surprised me at first. She had suffered even more loss and pain in the course of her life than I had, but she seemed to have found a source of peace over the years that kept her from constantly raising her fists like me.

"You're right, my darling, you shouldn't depend on anyone else for your happiness. But never allowing yourself to love again …" She rose from the sofa with difficulty. Old age had made her shorter than me by several inches. But in my eyes, she was a giant—full of wisdom and grace.

"I don't have feelings for the sheriff … and never will!" My voice was loud and forceful, and I hoped Wesley was sound asleep.

"That's quite obvious, but he sure doesn't see it. Besides, who said anything about him?" she scoffed. "I'm talking about Daniel."

"I hardly know him. And besides, he's gone. Probably back to someone he loves."

"Maybe he's thinking of you." She spoke matter-of-factly, draping the quilt over the sofa arm and straightening a stack of books resting on the table next to her reading chair. "I suppose you'll never know."

Her words stung. Once again, my fears had tried to hide behind pride—a traitor to my heart. Could he still be there? Was there a chance?

Maybe it's not too late.

*****

"You've hardly been back a week, and now you're off again." Mother wrapped her arms around me as we stood on the platform waiting for the westbound train. "It's going to be awfully quiet without Wesley's constant chatter. That child asks more questions, especially while we read. I can hardly get to the end of a chapter."

"You love every minute." I lifted the heavy suitcase. "I can't imagine many of the other homesteaders are worried about having enough books. It's a good thing the Andersons have a wagon. They've offered to let me ride along with them into town any time I need supplies."

Mother opened her small handbag. "I've been saving extra money for a long time. An old woman doesn't need much."

She pushed a roll of neatly tied bills into my palm. I didn't want to accept her offer, but the little money I had left of my own was running out. Getting other supplies and, eventually, a horse or mule, were necessities if we were to make it through the long winter months.

"You take good care of yourself and that grandson of mine."

"I love you, Mother." I kissed her soft cheek. "I'll try my best to come for a visit in the springtime. Or you could come stay with us when the house is fixed up."

She took my face in her hands as if trying to memorize every detail. Then she and Wesley hugged until he squirmed out of her grasp, more interested in the approaching train.

"It really is breathtaking there. The sky goes on for miles. And the wildflowers … they're scattered forever, every color you can—"

"Hope to see all that and more someday soon." Sheriff Murphy stepped onto the platform next to me.

"Good morning, Sheriff … uh, David," I said.

"It wouldn't be right not to have a proper good-bye. You didn't tell me you were leaving town so soon. Caught wind of it late last night." His eyes were bloodshot and his voice gruff.

"I wasn't aware you needed to know my schedule."

He leaned in closer. The smell of stale whiskey lingered on his breath. "We haven't had time to talk privately. Excuse us, Louisa."

For the sake of Wesley and my mother, there was no cause for a scene. I allowed him to take my hand as he led me to the rear of the platform.

His tone was low, but he may as well have yelled by the anger in his voice. "Who do you think you are leading me on and then running out of town?"

"I have done no such thing." In an attempt to pull my hand away, he clasped it harder. "You're hurting me."

"This is nothing compared to the heartache you've caused me. All I've ever done is look out for your well-being—from the lousy man you called a husband to you following a crazy idea to be on your own in the middle of nowhere. A helpless woman without a chance in the world."

"How dare you speak of Tuck that way." I jerked my hand from his. "And what I choose to do with my life is none of your business." I stepped away, but he gripped my arm.

"That may be true, but what you're doing to Wesley out of your selfishness is—"

"Don't you ever tell me what is best for my child." My heart drummed, and the words spewed from my mouth. "And if you think I have feelings for you, they are only of repulsion."

He released my arm and looked as though he had been struck across the face.

I stepped back, afraid for a moment he would raise his hand to me.

Surprisingly, his eyes welled with tears, and he spoke softly. "Mary, I wanted to be alone with you while you were home. I planned to …" he cleared his throat "… tell you I love you and ask you to—"

The train's whistle screeched, and the rumbling engine drowned out the rest of his words. I turned and ran to Mother who gave me a quick peck on the cheek. With Wesley's hand in mine, we picked up our bags and stepped onto the train.

As the train rolled forward, David stood at the side of the platform. He raised his hand in the air and feigned a wave.

My intuition assured me it wouldn't be the last time our paths would cross.

CHAPTER 28

Daniel ~ A While Longer, September 26, 1893

After arguing with myself for a while, my heart won over logic. Or at least my thinking side was fooled into believing this was the right thing to do.

Once again, more bills were handed to the yellow-haired boy. This time the horse was hitched to a rented wagon filled with enough supplies to construct a sod house for Mary and her son before they returned.

I'd be on my way to Boston, back to my familiar life, before she returned. No thank you was needed, and I surely didn't want her wrath. Maybe my motives were selfish. While in the comfort of my apartment, my heart needed to know she and the boy were at least warm and able to make it through the winter. The guilt from ignoring the well-being of a child would be unbearable.

* * * * *

I named the roan-colored horse Crimson. She'd made the ride to Mary's property now for the third time, and there was no one else to talk to. Plus, it was a color on my paint palette that had been neglected for too long.

"You can eat the grass after you've helped me cut mine for bricks." I patted her neck and hitched her to the plow. "There's plenty of buffalo grass for both of us."

Getting the cutting plow was a stroke of luck. They were in high demand with most of the settlers needing to build a soddy as soon as possible. Few people on the homestead sites could get their hands on enough lumber to build a house, even if they could afford it. With so few trees, the earth itself was the best source for providing shelter.

The task of making foot-wide strips of sod at least four inches deep, and then divided into three-foot lengths, would be hard on my own. But the timing was good. The owner of the hardware store, who was the brother of Mary's neighbor, said late fall was the ideal time to build this way. The buffalo grass roots were dense by this time of the year and would hold the soil together.

Daylight faded as I crisscrossed the last of the strips that made the walls up to where the windows would be placed. Sweat dripped from the tip of my nose. Three walls, about waist high and a solid two-feet thick, adjoined the hill that served as the fourth and most solid support for the home. The embankment would add protection from the harsh winds that would surely come.

Ravenous, but too tired to cook anything of substance, I tore pieces of bread and jerky and gulped water. As the sky darkened, my bedroll and blanket welcomed me within the walls I had constructed.

After a couple more days of hard work, there would be a roof to sleep under. I gazed at the stars, captivated by the immensity before me. Millions upon millions of pinpricks allowed small hints of heaven's brilliance to shine down on earth. Deep breaths filled my lungs, melting away the pain in my back and my aching muscles.

I was alive under God's roof.

* * * * *

When I awoke, Crimson was nibbling on the stubbly grasses protruding from the sides of the soddy. "Oh no, you don't. You'll have to find your own pasture." I shooed her away and constructed the next portion of Mary's home.

Two window frames were set, and I was measuring for the door when a wagon, led by an ox, pulled onto the property.

"Hello, there." A man and woman sat side by side on the front bench. He waved, and my hand lifted in return.

When the wagon rolled to a stop, I noticed both were youthful.

"Thomas Anderson." He jerked his head toward the woman. "This is my wife, Lucy."

"Pleased to meet you." I tipped my hat to the young bride and extended my hand to Thomas. "You're Mary's neighbors. She speaks highly of you."

"We sure are. She's a delightful woman. So glad she'll be close by." Lucy's curly brown hair bounced when she spoke.

"Is she here?" Thomas pointed to the partially built house. "That's a mighty fine soddy the two of you are building."

"She's back in Missouri. Left a few days ago to get her little boy." The couple looked puzzled.

"She didn't mention she'd be leaving so soon, did she, Tom?"

"Not that I remember." He scratched his head. "Something must have made her want to get on her way."

Or someone. There was no way of knowing what her reaction might be when she returned to find a home already built on her property. *Best I not be here to find out.*

"Pardon me, folks. There's a full day's work ahead of me, plus some, to finish this house." I picked up a saw and set it to a piece of lumber.

"But we don't even know your name," Lucy called out over the noise.

"Daniel McKenzie."

"Well, Mr. McKenzie, we came over here to tell you—actually, Mary—about some trouble in the area. Tell him, Tom."

Thomas rested his elbows on his knees. "My brother, Roy, runs the hardware store in town."

"Met him yesterday getting all these supplies lined up." I gestured toward the sod house. "His little boy is one heck of a deal-maker. He's the one who got me the horse."

Lucy shook her head. "If we have even one child with the spirit of Jeb, I'll have my hands full."

"Lucy's expecting in the spring." Thomas put his arm around his wife.

"Congratulations to the both of you. Perhaps having another just like him would be the best thing to come along. He's a smart boy, for sure." I adjusted my hat as the sun was already high in the sky. "Now, what about this trouble?"

"You've heard of the Dalton Gang, haven't you?"

I nodded, recalling news that had made it back East about a group of bandits holding up banks and trains in the Midwest.

"Bill Dalton and Bill Doolin formed the Doolin-Dalton Gang. There's some others that have joined them," Thomas said.

"The Ingalls bandits," added Lucy. "There was news coming from Guthrie that they were wanting to loot the town on the opening day of the strip, with all the people and money coming into the area."

"Not sure what came of that," Thomas said, "but there are ruffians in this area. Roy said there's already been trouble in town. One of them tried to rob a businessman last night."

Lucy nodded in agreement. "An attorney."

The saw slipped from my hand. "Is he all right?"

"Not sure, but I think so. Rumor has it the rather large man handed over all the money he had, but it wasn't much." Thomas paused. "Do you know him?"

"If he's the one I'm thinking of, then yes."

"And the bandit wanted to shoot the man for wasting his time and mentioned a past grudge. The story goes that he changed his mind when some cowboys came out of the saloon and saw what was happening. The good man wanted to fight the bad man, but the cowboys held him back." Lucy crossed her heart. "Promise. That's what Roy's wife told me."

"Regardless, we wanted to let Mary know. She doesn't seem to be the kind to want to hear this, but we're worried about her being alone." Thomas furrowed his brows.

"And with only her boy." Lucy lowered her voice, as though not wanting anyone else to know of Mary's vulnerability.

I can't leave her out here alone. This house will only protect her from the rain and cold—not that kind of danger.

"Will you be staying on … with Mary?" Thomas stammered. "I mean … she's not … you're not her husband."

"No, my job is waiting for me back East." I picked up the saw. "My plan is to finish this soddy before she returns and be on my way." *I'm not even sure we're friends, let alone married.* "I'll leave her a note explaining the situation and ask her to check in with the two of you often."

"Oh, one more thing." Lucy climbed over the bench to the back of the wagon. "Tom, how could we forget?"

"I didn't forget, girl. We had more important things to talk about."

"More important than a cooking stove?" Lucy pulled back a tarp and patted the black object. "Nothing's more special to a woman than a place to prepare the meals—even if you're not married."

"It's an extra one Roy held for us. It fell off the back of someone's wagon in the race, and a customer brought it in to trade for some tools." Thomas swung his leg over the bench and eyed the piece. "It has some good-sized dents and a crooked leg, but it should work fine."

"We thought Mary could use it. We don't need two."

The thought of Mary keeping a fire outside in the cold months was difficult. Wood was sparse, and once the snows came and the ground was either wet or frozen, it would be nearly impossible to cook.

"That's kind of you." A sense of relief that there were some kind-hearted people nearby for Mary made me smile. "I'm sure she wouldn't argue with your offer."

After Thomas and I unloaded the stove and placed it in a corner of the unfinished house, I shook his hand and thanked both of them for being good neighbors. Hopefully, the danger they spoke of would stay far away from this area.

As soon as I finish here, I need to check on Bart. All the more reason to get to work.

* * * * *

Driving pegs into the last of the sod bricks would hold them securely in place. The house, measuring fourteen by sixteen feet with two glass windows and a heavy door, only needed a roof. Tomorrow, I would be up with the sun to lay the two-by-sixes for ridge posts and two by fours for rafters. Tar paper would be tacked down before a final layer of sod, grass side up, was positioned on top. Then the house would be complete, and Mary would return to find she had a home—whether she liked it or not.

I was exhausted, but sleep would not come. The night sky darkened, and stars emerged as though layers of paint were being added to a giant canvas. If only in my mind, I was being pulled into another world as the layers of space deepened—far from the open plains, and even further from the lights and sounds of Boston. It was a peaceful sensation, and for the first time in many years, I wanted to talk with God. Not just a recited prayer learned as a child or a plea for something, but simply to talk with Him.

Although it wasn't audible, He responded as we talked about many things—the responsibilities of my job, the lack of time spent with my own art, going back to Boston, the boy in the stables, and the relentless guilt associated with that memory. We talked about the new Oklahoma—its trials and dangers—and Mary. I prayed for her, then for Wesley, the boy I hadn't met.

Just before drifting off to sleep, I wiped a tear and smiled. It felt good to be alive.

* * * * *

It was time to step back and admire my work. The roof drooped on one end, but it was solid. Extra grass and dirt filled gaps in the walls and roof, enough to keep the wind and rain at bay. From a distance, the stove's pipe looked like a prairie dog poking its head out of a hole.

"Almost done, Crimson."

I ducked into the house. All that remained was tacking the oilcloth to the ceiling to catch any falling dirt, then trying it out for the night to get a feel for sleeping in a soddy.

* * * * *

My cup of coffee was a welcome friend the next morning after a restless night. The scurrying of a field mouse had awakened me a few times, especially when it ran along my leg. If a mouse was that eager to make the soddy its home, all sorts of insects—and even snakes— would find it welcoming too.

It would delay me even more, but there was enough extra lumber to make Mary and Wesley a simple bed frame. That was the least I could do. And maybe a small table.

Though it would be snug, the bed was big enough for both of them. She would need bedding and pillows, but those were things she would be able to buy in town. The table was placed in the corner of the room. It looked lonely without any chairs, but there was no more lumber. With no vase filled with flowers to welcome her home, I placed three cans of food in the middle of the table that were purchased from the grocer—tomatoes, green beans, and peaches.

I loaded the plow and a few other rented tools into the wagon. Generously, the Contolinis had given Mary their ax and shovel. She would need those for cutting wood for the stove and getting a small crop of turnips started before winter. The few trees wouldn't supply enough fuel for long. But sometimes good things come from bad. I picked up the shovel and got to work scooping the manure chips into a mound behind the house—the unintended gift left by the Cooley's cattle.

Again, the day waned, reminding me it was time to head back— first to return the supplies and horse, then check on Bart and say good-bye. And then board the train toward reality.

While harnessing Crimson to the wagon, I remembered the promise to leave a note for Mary. "Just a minute longer, ol' girl."

Crimson whinnied in response, or maybe she was simply eager to return to her barn. I took a piece of paper and pen from my bag and jogged into the house.

Dear Mary,

Your kind neighbors, Thomas and Lucy, paid a visit. They brought news there has been a group of bandits in the area—been some trouble in town already. The Andersons are anxious for you to visit often and let them know you and Wesley are safe. I promised to share their concern.

I reread the letter several times, trying to decide what else to say.

I hope you find the house and its contents suitable (the Andersons provided the stove). I know you intended to provide this on your own and surely you will make revisions and additions that fit your needs. My apologies if I interfered with your plans. However, extra time before catching the train out of town left me with nothing else to do. A change in the weather could happen any time. Hopefully, what's been done gives you a head start on your home. I wish you happiness and prosperity.

Sincerely,

Daniel

My throat felt parched as my eyes scanned the letter once more. The realization that I would never see her again hit like a blow to the gut. The room spun as I laid the paper on the table and staggered to the doorway. The fresh air attempted to clear my mind, but even the brisk winds sweeping over the prairie couldn't push her from my thoughts … or my heart.

Idiot. I chastised myself for allowing my emotions to betray me. But there was one more thing to leave her.

After grabbing my bag from the wagon, I dashed back into the house. On the small table, the canvas unrolled from its loosened constraint from the rawhide tie, obediently lying flat by the placement of three cans and my elbow at its opposite corners. Then I shuffled through the small tubes of paint and selected my favorite brush. I planned to paint her the sunset she would watch in the evening from her doorway—the same spectacular view that had greeted me each day since my arrival.

It wasn't my best work, but the finished painting was tacked on the small ledge built into the wall. Lifting my brush one more time, I stroked my name across the bottom corner, then ran my eyes over the painting, noticing the mixture of warm tones matched the color of her hair.

Before leaving the house for the final time, I scrawled a postscript on the letter.

P.S. When you look at the sunset, remember me.

CHAPTER 29

Mary ~ Return, September 30, 1893

For the last part of our train ride, Wesley pressed his forehead against the glass and watched the countryside whiz by. My hunch was that he secretly wished to see a band of Indians chasing buffalo alongside the train. Before we left Missouri, I tried to describe to him the actual setting, but for a child, imagination and dreams take precedence, as they should.

"One, two, three, four … forty-four, fifty-six …" He counted the telegraph poles until his numbers jumbled out of sequence. "Mama, how much longer?"

"We're almost there." I closed my eyes and pictured the land, wondering what he would think. *Good thing he's a little boy. Camping out should feel like an adventure.* I replayed the list of items we needed to get in town once we arrived. Hopefully, the livery stable would have an available hired hand who could take us home before dark. We'd need a horse or mule soon. I made a mental note to move the necessity higher on the list.

* * * * *

Luck was with us when we approached the barn in town. The stalls and corrals overflowed with horses, mules, and even some smaller donkeys that kept a safe distance from the others and stood in the corner of the enclosure.

"Too many mouths to feed." The livery manager propped his elbows on top of the fence surrounding the enclosure. "Give you a good price on that one over there." He pointed to a horse with a sway back and protruding ribs.

"Wish I could take that one in, give him some food." I wrinkled my nose as I looked around, hoping to convey my disgust with the condition of some of the animals. "But I'll need one stronger and younger."

"You'll pay more." He cleared his throat, followed by a raspy cough.

"That's to be expected, as long as it's fair."

"Sixty bucks."

I pointed to a black saddle mule. "What about that one?"

"Looks sturdy enough." The man coughed again.

"Has he been ridden? My son and I have to travel to and from our claim."

"Not sure." The man sounded as sickly as some of his animals looked. "What's your husband riding?"

I almost corrected him, but something inside told me it was none of his business. The encounters with the Cooleys reminded me that men still had the upper hand, especially in this frontier.

"A fine gelding." I pressed my lips together when Wesley gave me a questioning look. "Like I said, we need a strong animal to carry supplies and plow."

The man scratched his head, and I was sure some bugs took flight like flies on a pile of manure. "Here." I pulled fifty dollars from my bag. "The black mule will be fine."

He flipped through the bills. I waited for him to argue, but he called out to one of the stable hands to halter the mule. "A bridle and saddle? That will cost you more."

"Not today. I'll speak with my husband about what we need." I forced a pleasant smile. "A halter and lead come with the price of the mule, right?"

He grumbled under his breath.

"Much obliged." I extended my hand.

* * * * *

It was a long walk home leading the mule with Wesley straddling bareback. My next large purchase would be a cart and harness to use my time and resources efficiently.

"His name's Jim," Wesley said.

"Who?"

"Our mule."

I giggled. "That's an interesting name for a mule. Sounds more like a person."

"He sorta is. Jim's my new best friend."

I kept walking, my sights focused ahead, hoping it was the right decision to bring him here. He had to leave everything behind—his friends and school. Even his grandmother.

"Jim likes his new name. Don't you, boy?"

We both laughed when the mule let out an odd combination of a whinny and bray.

"You must be right," I said, "Jim it is."

It took me a few more steps to place the name. Ah, *Treasure Island*—Jim Hawkins. Yes, a good name for Wesley's new friend.

*****

My feet and legs welcomed the relief when we summited the small hill. Our journey to our new home was nearly complete. But when the house came into view—standing where only sticks and a flapping canvas were before—my legs nearly collapsed. Had someone stolen my land?

"Mama! You built a house!" Wesley slipped off Jim and ran down the hill.

My feet felt like cement. My arms hung at my sides, the lead rope loose in my hand.

Jim nudged me from behind, but all I could do was stare. Like a mirage in *The Arabian Nights*, perhaps the desert was playing tricks on my mind. My eyes studied the image in front of me. Sure enough, three walls of stacked sod joined with the embankment in the rear. There were two windows on either side of a door and a roof.

Wesley bounded out the door. "It's got a big bed too. Is it mine or yours?"

The mule and I hurried toward the house. "What in the world?" My finger pointed to a black cylinder poking through the roof.

"You're sneaky, Mama. You said we'd be cooking over a campfire, not on a stove."

Before entering the house, I stopped and ran my hand over the piece of wood that formed the doorframe. *Who did this?* Lucy and Thomas had their own home to build. And it was surely not the Cooleys.

Wesley was right. A bed, large enough for both of us, filled the corner to the right. It was only a frame, but I already imagined a feather bed with fluffy pillows and the quilt I would make before winter set in. My clothes were stacked in a neat pile near the bed. The water barrel, now useless with a bullet hole in its side, sat upright as a nightstand. On its top, a kerosene lamp shared the space with my Bible and another familiar object, though not mine.

I picked up the small hand mirror and ran my fingers over the detailed silver design, then held it in front of my face. The woman looking back at me seemed a stranger in so many ways. Everything inside me wanted to smile at her and see her smile back with excitement and joy over having returned to the surprise of a solid and welcoming home. But she hid any hint of gratitude with a frown—not willing to betray her hard-fought independence. And expose her fears.

"Come see." Wesley tugged my arm and led me through the door.

Behind the house, overturned dirt formed three parallel rows cut neatly into the earth. A piece of paper, poked through with a stick read, TURNIPS. The other rows were marked in the same manner—WHEAT.

"And there's a big pile of cow pies. Phew!" Wesley pinched his nose and looked around. "Do we have cows too?"

"I'm afraid not." I propped my hands on my hips and surveyed the area, still in disbelief at what had sprung up on my recently vacant property. "But someone's cattle left that mess."

How would I explain the house and garden to my son? I didn't really know what to say to myself. *Daniel McKenzie.* It had to be him. He was the only one who would have done this, even though I told him I could take care of my son … and myself. I looked back at the soddy. Part of me was appreciative, thankful to return to a sturdy home. The other part wanted to scream and release the frustration and anger that surged each time someone doubted my abilities.

You didn't think I could do it, so you had to do it for me.

But as the cobalt sky mingled with the remaining greens scattered among the wispy grasses, my memory painted a picture of Daniel's turquoise eyes. They smiled when he laughed, assuring me I was safe with him. In those brief moments when we caught one another's gaze, his eyes looked straight into my heart as though we knew each another from a different time, if only in dreams. My heart unexpectedly jumped at the thought of him. Did I truly miss him—secretly yearning for him to be part of my life?

"Where's Jim gonna sleep?"

Wesley's question knocked me from my thoughts. "Certainly not with us. He'll be fine tied up outside."

Wesley dropped the stick he was using to draw an X in the dirt. "But he'll get lonely. What if it rains or gets real cold?"

"I'll build him a barn before winter."

Wesley's big, brown eyes looked up at me, reminding me how much he looked like Tuck. "You're a good builder, Mama. I can help too."

It was tempting to let him believe I was the one responsible for our new home, but my conscience bore down on me like a hammer—the one I *didn't* use to set the door and window frames and construct the bed and table.

"Son, we have this wonderful home because of the kindness of a friend." *Go ahead. Tell him the truth.* "He must have had extra time to do this before he had to go back to where he lives."

Wesley picked up a small rock and threw it. "That's too bad."

"What do you mean? You should be thankful he offered his time and supplies," I answered curtly, though my comment was directed at myself.

"I am thankful. It's just too bad he isn't here anymore."

Wesley was right. It was a shame Daniel was gone. Why did I let my pride keep me from letting Daniel know my true feelings? It was obvious he wanted to stay.

How could I have become so hardened?

I ran my hand along my neck and over my ear as if a cruel intruder whispered the thoughts in my mind.

Wesley rubbed his eyes, a sure sign he was exhausted from our long journey. "Then we can't build a barn for Jim."

"And why would that be?"

His face reddened as his hands balled into fists—a side of my son I hadn't seen since the morning he found out about Tuck's death. "'Cause you don't really know how to build one like you said." He kicked at the dirt and shouted, "If it wasn't for that man, we'd freeze to death!"

"Wesley Roberts. Do not raise your voice at me." I stepped toward him, but he backed away and scowled.

"Sheriff Murphy was right."

I swallowed the lump in my throat and stared at my son. "About what?"

"About us needing a man to take care of us or we'll die out here." Wesley's eyes filled with tears. "Please don't let me die, Mama."

He attempted to push me away as I knelt and wrapped my arms around him. His little body heaved as tears reserved for only scrapes and bruises poured out and dampened my blouse—seeping into my heart.

* * * * *

Wesley wiggled out of my grasp and sat in the grass next to where Jim grazed. Far enough from me in the grasses, my son talked to the animal—most likely sharing his thoughts, and maybe his fears. Strangely, even though Wesley was with me now, a profound feeling of loneliness crept into my soul. Not alone like before, but lonely.

I stepped into the soddy and looked around once again. The sun no longer cast its direct light inside. Carefully, the glass chimney of the kerosene lamp was removed and the cotton wick raised. A box of matches rested on the stove. He had thought of such small, but important items. With the flick of a match, the wick lit and a warm glow filled the room. The bread, canned meat, and applesauce bought at the grocer before leaving town would suffice until tomorrow when the stove would get its first use with flapjacks and bacon.

The table looked lonely without chairs. At least he remembered most things. A smile spread across my face at the thought of Daniel carefully placing the items in the house. Chairs would be added when we could afford them. No hurt in standing for a while.

Before calling to Wesley, I lifted a note tucked under one of the cans and held it near the lamp. At the mention of the recent trouble, my heart raced. Joseph's rifle leaned against the wall. I gave it a quick nod, resolved that it would be used if needed. After breakfast, we would visit the Andersons, get more details, and thank them for the generous gift. The stove would help get us through the first winter. Someday, I would need to sufficiently return the favor. My body shivered—not from the brutal cold that was sure to come, but from a nagging doubt. Were Sheriff Murphy's words true?

As I read the signature and postscript on the note, my hands trembled.

I wish you happiness and prosperity.
Sincerely,
Daniel
P.S. When you look at the sunset, remember me.

The painting had caught my attention when I first entered the house, but I wouldn't allow myself to stop and take in its full beauty until now. Even in the dim light, the colors were vibrant, yet at the same time, soothing and calm. The brushstrokes, stretching across the vastness of the sky, were methodic and peaceful. *Daniel McKenzie.* As my eyes rested on his signature, I pictured the man who came into my life so suddenly, and left just as quickly—tall and broad-shouldered, golden, sand-colored hair ... and those turquoise eyes.

Moving to the doorway, my body leaned hard against the solid, wooden door. For several minutes, God's hand painted the sunset across the sky, the same palette as the painting propped on the shelf.

I will remember you, Daniel McKenzie. More than you can imagine. I wrapped my arms tightly around my waist and allowed myself to hope.

Will you remember me?

CHAPTER 30

Mary ~ Catch, September 30, 1893

The first night in our bed, Wesley and I both tossed and turned. At least we had a roof over our heads and weren't sleeping on the dirt floor. Once proper bedding was laid on the bottom board, rest would come easier.

But the main reason I couldn't sleep wasn't a lack of comfort. Much of the night, my unsettled mind jumped back and forth between the sheriff's comments, listening for any unwelcome footsteps outside the windows, and wondering what Daniel's real life was like, so far away from mine.

* * * * *

In the morning, our success with the stove to cook breakfast lifted our spirits, and the short walk to the Andersons' property made the morning even better. It was good to know honest people lived nearby.

Thomas and Lucy were nearly finished building their house. It was larger than ours and constructed out of a combination of sod for the walls and lumber to make a solid and well-pitched roof—a good thing as they would have their new addition in the springtime.

"Wonderful to have you back, Mary." Lucy hugged me. "And, Wesley, pleased to meet you. You're in for quite an adventure living out here."

"Pleased to meet you, ma'am. I like adventures."

Tom shook Wesley's hand. "Welcome home, young man. Your mother is lucky to have a son with such a strong handshake. That's the sign of a good man."

Wesley beamed, and I knew he and Tom were already friends. I giggled when Wesley followed with an introduction to his other friend, Jim.

"We're heading into town for more supplies to finish the house and start the barn. Come with us," Thomas said.

"What did you think when you saw your soddy?" Lucy asked. "Daniel's such a kind man. Too bad he had to leave so soon. After all, Tom and I think he's smitten with you."

Wesley looked up at me, and I quickly looked away, though I wondered if Lucy's assumption was true. "It's remarkable, but he didn't need to do all he did. I planned to take care of a home upon my return."

Thomas put his arm around his wife. "He wanted to do something kind for you and your son. Wanted to get you off to a good start. Seems to really care."

"Especially before the cold," Lucy added. "I'm planning on a long winter, especially having to wait for the baby."

I couldn't help but smile as she rubbed her hand over her stomach. "The baby will be the perfect gift of spring." The dried and parched prairie grass was so brittle it crunched and lay lifeless underfoot. "He or she will arrive when the grass is green and flowers return—so different than the brown that spreads more each day in every direction."

"Ladies, you can talk more on our ride into town. We need to be on our way, right, Wesley?"

"Yes, sir." Wesley took up Jim's lead. "The men have work to do."

Lucy and I grinned like two lifelong friends.

* * * * *

"Didn't expect to see the two of you so soon," Thomas' brother called down to us from the top of a ladder in his hardware store. "Figured you had enough lumber to keep you busy for weeks." He shuffled boxes around on a high shelf. "Be down in a minute. So many customers, I'm having to dip into my back stock."

"Take your time, Roy." Thomas tipped his hat to his sibling. "My brother, the businessman. Me, the farmer. Different from each other since we were boys. Good thing we have him though."

"And he, us," Lucy said. "Hard to believe two years have gone by since his Marjorie passed. As soon as our first harvest comes in, he'll be the first at our table for my home cooking."

Roy backed down the ladder, holding a handful of nails. "Ma'am. Roy Anderson."

"Mary Roberts."

"So, you're the lucky lady. Mr. McKenzie set you up real fine. He was in about an hour ago before the train arrived. Purchased some last items for his attorney friend's shop and ordered a couple chairs for you. I'll have one of my men deliver them to you when they arrive from—"

"He's still here?" I blurted.

"Well …" Roy rubbed his head. "Not sure if the train's come or gone, but it's got to be any time now." He glanced at his pocket watch. "Granted, the stopping point is more than a stone's throw from here, and I don't always hear it."

"It's been a pleasure, but I have to try and catch him."

Lucy and I exchanged nods, perhaps a woman's way of reassuring another to follow her instincts.

"We'll be here waiting," she said.

Wesley and I headed toward the door.

"Where we going, Mama?"

"To thank Mr. McKenzie for making us a home." I tugged his hand, and we hurried down the road toward the tracks east of town.

A makeshift platform stood alone in the field. Prior to the recent birth of the town, trains passed this area without a hesitation. Now, the Santa Fe made brief stops twice a day.

My breath was short as I scanned those gathered on the platform. Two women wearing plumed hats waited next to several cases. My guess was they decided to get far away from here and closer to the comforts of city life. Mostly men, some in suits, and others in dirty and worn clothing, turned their heads in the direction of the approaching train.

I stepped onto the wooden planks and saw him. Perhaps it was my imagination, but as though he sensed a presence, he turned his head side to side as if looking for someone. Our eyes met. For a moment, I couldn't breathe. My heart raced, and my head felt fuzzy—a distinct feeling I hadn't experienced in so many years. As he walked in our direction, I released Wesley's hand.

"Mary." His expression was unreadable. "I didn't think I'd ever see you again."

"I … *we* came to say thank you. The house is—"

"It's something special, Mr. McKenzie." Wesley beamed up at Daniel.

"And you must be Wesley." Daniel shook his hand. "I've heard wonderful things about you. Sounds like *you* are something special."

Wesley's smile broadened nearly ear to ear.

"I plan to repay you as soon as possible, send money for the materials and food you—"

"I don't want your money." He squinted as if my words hurt. "Please, accept it as a gift. You probably had plans to build it differently, and the roof is crooked—"

"It's perfect. The garden too."

His smile warmed me to my toes. "It's small, but I hope it produces well for you, at least until spring when there's more to plant."

The planks vibrated under our feet as the train pulled to a stop. I raised my voice over the rumbling of the engine. "I wish you safe travels." An unexpected pang shot through my chest, and I wanted to beg him to stay. "And a happy and prosperous future."

His eyes locked with mine. "Mary, more than anything, know that you're amazing."

The whistle blasted, startling all of us. Wesley wrapped his arms around Daniel's waist, almost bringing tears to my eyes.

"It's all right, dear." I tried to pull him away, but he held tightly.

"Please don't leave us. I'm scared." He looked up at Daniel with pleading eyes. "You'd keep us safe, wouldn't ya?"

Fine. My son had the courage to say the words that were in my own heart. "Now, Wesley, Mr. McKenzie has a job, a home, and probably a family." Was that true? I knew so little about this man, but I longed to know more. My thoughts were confirmed by the look on Daniel's face. The color had drained, and tears welled in his eyes as he wrapped his arms around my son. Did he feel the same about me?

"You'll be all right, Wesley. There are good people here. Besides, I'm counting on you to take care of your mother." Daniel knelt and held Wesley at arm's length in front of him. "Deal?" He extended his hand.

"Yes, sir." Wesley shook his hand and then sidled next to me.

The train inched its way down the tracks. With his bag in hand, Daniel stepped on board. For a last brief moment, we stared at each other. My mind told me better, but my heart sealed him into my memory as he held to the rail, looking back at me until the tracks separated our worlds a final time.

CHAPTER 31

Mary ~ Visitor, November 14, 1893

Over the next month and a half, Wesley and I worked hard to make our house feel like a home. Now, a part of me regretted my impatience to learn sewing and quilting when I was younger. While the other girls spent hours making new clothes and quilting with family and neighbors, my time was occupied with riding horses or fishing. But the balmy childhood days I spent on horseback paid off in the race for land.

"It's not pretty, and the pattern doesn't match, but it will keep us warm." I tied the last stitch and spread the quilt across the bed.

"Looks good to me." Wesley marched a toy soldier up one side of the bed and down the other. Bits of branches and twigs wrapped with strips of cloth and penciled faces came to life in his imagination as his soldiers set off to conquer their enemies.

"I'm gonna have a big battle outside."

"You're *going* to have a battle." I sighed, realizing how much work was ahead. "Young man, it's time we begin your schoolwork again. If you were in Adair, the winter session would be starting up about now."

My son rolled his eyes and trotted out the front door with his soldiers.

My fingers caressed the spines of the books that comprised our tiny library. There was *A Study in Scarlet* by Arthur Conan Doyle, two of Twain's *The Adventures of Huckleberry Finn,* and *The Prince and the Pauper. The New England Primer* was a gift from Wesley's schoolmarm to hold me accountable for his learning. Anna Sewell's *Black Beauty* was a favorite and sure to make me cry again. Alcott's *Little Men*'s cover was torn and pages frayed, more loved in our home than her earlier, *Little Women*. Still, they sat next to one another on the ledge, waiting to be revisited.

My fingers flipped through the pages of *Heidi,* another personal favorite. The orphan and I understood one another. We shared a need for freedom, especially in the beauty and tranquility of our surroundings. Even though I wasn't in the lush hillsides and snow-capped mountains of Switzerland, my landscape was just as inspiring in its own way. And just like Heidi, surrounded by vast and monumental beauty, there was a definite void in my world—a loneliness, or perhaps an emptiness that yearned to be filled.

The *Bible* remained on the nightstand. Lately, Old Testament stories had become my favorite to read to Wesley—many I hadn't heard since childhood. When Wesley slept and silence blanketed the room, portions of the New Testament were my companions. In those moments, I wasn't alone.

*****

Wesley was talking just outside the door, most likely to his imaginary soldiers. Or maybe Jim, who was still without a shelter and tethered close to the house.

"Who's winning the battle?" To my surprise, when I opened the door, a young girl close to my son's age jumped backward and hunched behind the scrub brush. A quick glance around told me there was no adult in sight.

"I've been telling her she can come play, but she won't talk." Wesley waved his hand, beckoning her to join him. "See, I want her to play with me, but she keeps hiding."

"Hello, dear," I called to the little girl, but she ducked again. Only the top of her head, crowned with curly chestnut hair, was visible. "I'm Mrs. Roberts, and this is my son, Wesley."

"I already told her my name. Even tried to give her one of my soldiers, but she ran away."

"Do you live nearby?" Leaning to the side to get a better view of her proved pointless. I didn't recall any neighbors nearby with a child her age.

"Sweetheart, it's not safe for you to be away from home by yourself. Are you lost?" I raised my eyebrows at Wesley, but he shrugged and went back to playing in the dirt.

As I approached the brush, the girl popped up, her eyes wide like a captured animal.

"No one's going to hurt you," I said softly.

She wore a pale, cotton blouse draped over a pleated skirt. Surprisingly, her clothes were clean and well-pressed—different than most of the poor children in town and the outlying properties.

"Here, why don't you come inside and have something to eat? Then Wesley and I will get you home." I reached out my hand, but the girl turned and ran. Going after her would surely frighten her even more. As she ran up the hill, she looked back only once. The fear painted across her face pierced my heart. I would have to find out more about her.

"You scared her away." Wesley stood next to me. "But she'll be back."

"How do you know that?"

"'Cause she's come here plenty of times. Watches me from over there." He pointed to the field. "I thought she might play with me this time … till you made her run away."

"Sorry, Son. Next time, I'll leave the introductions to you."

* * * * *

Sleep had barely found me when a pungent smell nudged me awake. Campfire? No, there hadn't been an outside fire since we returned. I jumped out of bed and opened the door.

To the north, an orange line of fire danced on the hillside. Making sure it wasn't a nightmare, I rubbed my eyes, but the thick veil of smoke drifted toward the house, carrying a stench that burned my nostrils.

"The hill's on fire! Wesley, get up!" Before running out the door, I grabbed the box of matches and shovel near the stove.

On Thomas' instruction, the grass around the house had been cleared to provide a barrier should a prairie fire occur. But even with the fire at least a hundred yards away, the intensity of the heat was brutal. The smoke forced me to cough, even though my nightgown was held close to my mouth and nose.

"Mama, I'm scared!" Wesley screamed from the doorway. "What about Jim?"

"Hold tight to his rope and stay close to the house," I yelled while scooping up dirt and throwing it in a ring around the perimeter of the house where the brittle grass rose out of the ground and met the cleared area. Jim brayed, adding to the eerie sounds of the crackling of burning earth and the wind sweeping the fire closer to our home.

It was a risky move, but I ran into the area of taller grasses in front of the approaching fire, striking a match, then another, and another, until the grasses caught fire and the flames danced.

Set a backfire if you can. Burn off a space and stand in it for safety. Thomas' words rang in my ears.

The other fire was gaining, burning high and fast—a horrific monster, intent on devouring everything in its path. I ran back to Wesley and pulled his face into my chest to shield him from the smoke. With each breath, my throat and lungs burned, and I realized how easily my next breath could be my last.

Like the clashing of opposing armies, the two fires met in the field in front of our home. The air exploded with a force not of this world, and then as quickly as it came, the fire subsided.

I stared in disbelief. The air, blackened and thick like a death veil, hung lifeless around our home. Crackles and hisses seethed from the ground—as if the Devil himself tried to emerge on my land.

"You're all right now, Jim." Wesley stroked the mule's neck.

"That's right. It's all over."

It took some doing to tuck Wesley into bed. The quilt, the pillows, our clothes … everything reeked of smoke. It would be a long time, if ever, that the reminder of this dreadful night would leave our home.

The rest of the night was spent looking into the darkness, watching for approaching flames and keeping a watch for the occasional red ember—the eye of a snake, coiled and ready to strike.

I'll find out who did this. It couldn't have been lightning on a clear night like this.

And it certainly wasn't an accident.

CHAPTER 32

Mary ~ Dark Days, December 22, 1893

The days shortened and snow deepened as Christmas approached. Several times, I spotted the young girl crouched behind the charred bushes—her red coat a speck of color against the black and white landscape.

Although she still kept her distance, her presence became normal. But approaching her or trying to talk with her caused her to skitter away—elusive as drifting snow.

"She must be cold," I said to Wesley while watching from the window. "It's not right her folks let her wander off. I have a mind to go after her and let her parents—"

"She likes coming here, Mama."

"I suppose so, but why do you think she's so scared of us?"

"She's not scared when you teach her. And she really likes listening to the stories."

"I beg your pardon?" I stared at my son, wondering what he knew that I didn't. He was sprawled on the bed, hands behind his head, and wearing a toothy smile.

"You know when I say it's too hot in here?"

"Yes, the stove gets warm. What does that have to do with reading?"

"If I open the door a little, she'll sit outside and listen."

"That's ridiculous. How do you know—"

Wesley held his finger to his lips and whispered, "I bet she's by the door right now." He motioned to me to open it and patted the space next to him.

It felt strange to have her outside while we were warm and protected. Nevertheless, I obliged my son, then opened to Matthew fourteen and began reading where we had left off.

And when it was evening, his disciples came to him, saying, This is a desert place, and the time is now past; send the multitude away, that they may go into the villages, and buy themselves victuals. But Jesus said unto them, They need not depart; give ye them to eat.

And they say unto him, We have here but five loaves, and two fishes. He said, Bring them hither to me. And he commanded the multitude to sit down on the grass, and took the five loaves, and the two fishes, and looking up to heaven, he blessed, and brake, and gave the loaves to his disciples, and the disciples to the multitude. And they did all eat, and were filled: and they took up of the fragments that remained twelve baskets full. And they that had eaten were about five thousand men, beside women and children.

Was the mysterious girl listening? If she was, did she believe in such wondrous miracles?

* * * * *

Wesley and I spent a chilly Christmas Day huddled inside. For a special treat, we stacked our flapjacks high and pretended the last drops of maple syrup trickled down like mountain streams. We grinned at each other and licked our sticky lips. The absence of gifts, carolers, and stockings hung by the fire was not important. At that moment I had all I'd ever wanted.

I savored the last, sweet bite. For the rest of the winter, our food would consist of salt pork, flour biscuits, a sparse collection of canned peas and beans, and turnips. Visits to town for supplies would need to wait until early spring.

Last week's ride into Perry to receive the official land deed had been enough of a challenge. The ruts and ice were so severe I feared the wagon wheels would snap or Jim would come up lame. Still, having the signed piece of paper in my hand was a tremendous relief—legal proof of being a landowner. The Cooleys no longer had reason to cause any trouble.

"Good thing we pulled the turnips before the first deep freeze." I lifted the heavy burlap sack. "They didn't have time to grow large like the ones back home, but they're tender and sweet."

Wesley frowned and his lower lip inched forward. "I miss Grandma. I miss her cookies and pie. And her Christmas tree." He looked around as though only now noticing the void.

"I miss her too."

"Are we ever gonna see her again?"

The question shot a pang through my chest because I didn't know the answer. "I hope so, but it's expensive to travel to Missouri." I ruffled his hair. "And we need to buy those chickens this spring so we can have eggs for breakfast."

"I'd rather see Grandma than have chickens." He plopped his elbows on the table and buried his face in his hands. "Besides …"

"Wesley?" I reached for him, but he pulled away. "What's wrong?"

When he raised his head, big tears pooled in his eyes and ran down his cheeks. "I want my friends. I got no one to play with or even talk to."

"I *have* no one—"

He wiggled from his chair and ran out the door.

I started to go after him but remained in my chair. He'd been let down so much. This wasn't the life he wanted. A snapped twig bound with cloth—one of Wesley's injured soldiers—lay on the table.

There was not even a present for him to open Christmas morning.

✳ ✳ ✳ ✳ ✳

For weeks after Christmas and well into the New Year, Wesley checked behind a cluster of bushes to see whether or not his gift for the girl had been received. Each time, he dragged his feet back to the house and shook his head.

"With the cold and all, maybe her parents decided they'd better keep a closer eye. Maybe she'll come back when it's springtime." I scraped the remaining beans from the bottom of the kettle. "I'm sure she's fine." *Please Lord, let her be okay. Don't let the influenza take any more children.*

For that reason, I didn't want Wesley around the crowds in town. Pneumonia and a deadly flu brought back horrible memories of families losing loved ones, especially their children. Besides, the paths the mule would travel to pull the cart remained horribly rutted from the relentless slush and ice.

James and William. My twins came to mind often, making me wonder what life would be like with three children. Everything would be different for Wesley if he had his brothers—playmates and confidants sharing the good and bad. *Perhaps I would still have Tuck.* That thought made me wonder even more what my life would be like in this new place. Having a man around to do what needed to be done would be a blessing, but maybe Wesley and I were still better off without him.

"She didn't like her present. That's why she left it and didn't come back."

"Absolutely not." I plopped a dollop of beans on his plate. "The rock is really nice, and you're right. It does look like a rose."

Wesley's latest interest was collecting rocks around our property. His most prized find was unusual—a cluster of orange-reddish rocks, each in the distinct shape of a rose. Thomas told him the rock was a rare find. A Cherokee legend claimed the rock represented the blood of braves and the tears of the women who made the devastating "Trail of Tears" journey across this territory.

I untied my apron and joined Wesley at the table.

"Mama, you're happy now. You got all this land." He scrunched up his nose, a sign he was deep in thought. "But it makes me sad the Indians starved to death and got sick when they got kicked out."

"Who told you that?"

"Tom." My son's eyes were bright with admiration. "He knows lots of things."

"Mr. Anderson's right." The beans on our plates, albeit a bland and staple meal, reminded me of our fortune to at least have something to eat. "I think about those people and wonder why we're here instead of them. It doesn't seem fair."

We ate our beans in silence. My mind swirled with thoughts of the vanished tribes—families with children, homes, and animals—relocated to desolate and undesirable areas while my home was built on what was once theirs.

Then, as they often did, my wistful thoughts turned to Daniel, wondering what my life would be like if he had stayed.

And Wesley? I imagined he was thinking of the girl—the mysterious child who had become his friend in an odd sort of way, without ever saying a word.

CHAPTER 33

Mary ~ Schooltime, May 9, 1894

After a long and lonely winter, spring kept its promise, bringing new growth and sunshine—and a gathering of children.

Lucy had spread the word among the women in the area that I had a gift for teaching and especially loved reading aloud from my favorite children's books. For most of the families, their homes had only necessities. Not many books, especially children's, earned precious shelf space.

Once chores were completed and children were allowed to slip away, my home became a gathering place for more than a handful from the nearby properties. A formal school wasn't established yet and most likely wouldn't be for quite some time until homes, barns, gardens, and fields were well underway.

For Wesley, new faces and an opportunity for friendships was nothing short of a miracle. He spread blankets for the younger children on the newly sprung grass and helped the older boys carry hollow logs from the riverbank to provide extra seating for the students.

It was a hodge-podge. Stewart and Seth were ten-year-old twins from Wisconsin. Their sister, Emily, was only six but kept the brothers busy keeping track of her whereabouts. To my relief, they took their job seriously. No doubt they didn't want to return home without the youngest and lose their privilege of going to school.

Twelve-year-old Luke and one-year-older brother, Aaron, were strong readers and quick with numbers. I made a mental note to remind myself they would be good help with the others who had little or no schooling.

My heart went out to William. He was clearly the oldest, although he wouldn't say his age. My guess was fifteen, maybe more. Tall and skinny, his arms and legs were not yet able to stay in rhythm with the rest of his body. He and his parents traveled from England last year to begin a carpentry business on the East Coast. Before his mother was able to disembark the ship, she became ill and passed away within a month. With hopes of mending his son's broken heart—as well as his own—the father decided to head West for a new start. I understood them well.

For the first few days, my time was spent getting to know the children—what they knew about arithmetic, reading, literature, and spelling—and, largely, what they didn't know. Even William read only a little and struggled with the basics of arithmetic.

My work is certainly cut out for me ... and I'm not sure how I was assigned this role.

Even though I had no formal training as an educator, I had always been a good student and often helped my friends and younger children with their studies. Several of my teachers had encouraged me to attend college to become an educator. But then Tuck came along, our children followed, and the desire to become a teacher was slipped into the attic of my life.

I smiled, and eager faces—several dirt stained—smiled in return, waiting for the lessons to begin.

* * * * *

"Mama, she's come back." Wesley tugged at my sleeve and pointed toward the field.

Curly, dark hair and a light-blue jumper were visible when she briefly stepped from behind the sagebrush. I waved to her and—like a turtle retreating into its shell—she jumped behind the plant.

I tugged Wesley's ear. "Let's hope she stays for school today."

Throughout the morning, the girl remained apart from the group but always within earshot of the lessons and story time. By lunchtime, while the others unwrapped sandwiches or chewed on jerky and handfuls of nuts, she inched herself outside the perimeter of the group.

Her small face was delicate and pretty—pink lips and porcelain skin framed by contrasting dark hair—like my favorite and only doll as a child. I tried not to stare, knowing the other children saw her as well. But the entire time, the others went along with their own business as if each of them understood and granted the quiet girl her own special and safe place.

As the children gathered to hear the next chapter of *Huckleberry Finn*, Wesley slipped from the group and sat a few feet from the girl. After a few pages, he extended an open hand to her. Resting on his palm was the rose-shaped rock.

Although the other children huddled closer, eager to learn what would happen to Huck and Jim on the foggy river, words stuck in my throat. Slowly, the girl scooted closer, peeked at the object in Wesley's hand, and then picked it up and cupped it to her chest. As if nothing out of the ordinary had just happened, they sat side by side on the blanket, holding hands and listening to the end of the chapter as though it were any other normal day.

* * * * *

The children returned most days, except for a particularly rainy stretch when the dirt stuck to our boots like molasses and lightning seared the sky. I remained inside with Wesley, but he watched from the window—waiting for the sun to break through and for his friends' return.

As new growth sprouts after rain, the number of students increased as well. Three more boys and another girl tagged along with the twins, bringing our class to a dozen. Clearly, we would need more books, small slate boards, chalk, paper, and pencils in addition to extra food and water to make our time spent together not only productive but enjoyable—and free from rumbling stomachs that were unwanted companions throughout the winter.

Although Lucy was due to be a mother any day, she had the gift of building community and worked hard to spread the word of my schooling needs. Families were abundantly generous. Four chickens, complete with a coop, arrived the first week. Gardening tools and packets of carrot, lettuce, tomato, pumpkin, melon, and bean seeds were sure to make my garden flourish.

Little Emily beamed when she handed me an envelope of sunflower seeds. "My papa says these will grow even bigger than me."

"Oh my. Then they will be very tall." I rose on tiptoes and reached toward the sky. "Please tell your father thank you from me *and* the birds."

William lived the farthest from my lot and walked well over five miles each way to attend school. The morning he and his father arrived by wagon remains etched in my mind.

"Good day, Ms. Roberts. I'm Lewis Hill, William's father. My apologies for not introducing myself sooner."

"It's a pleasure to meet you. You have a wonderful son."

"I appreciate that. He's a fine boy. Our carpentry business in town is keeping my boy and me busy. Our specialty is furniture." He nodded to William, who climbed into the back of the wagon and pulled back a tarp. "He's made something for you."

William lifted a rocking chair and carefully set it on the ground. "It's cedar." He rocked it a few times. "Please, try it."

The right words were slow to form, so I settled into the chair, rocking back and forth while William smiled the widest smile I had seen since we met. "It's absolutely perfect in every way."

"My son has a talent working with wood. That's why he won't be coming to school any longer."

I stopped rocking and stood, once again searching for words.

"Don't get me wrong, ma'am. I greatly appreciate what you've done. It's just that it's only the two of us and ... I need my son."

Compassion filled my heart. "I understand." *More than you know.*

Though not proper for a schoolmarm, I wrapped my arms around William and hugged him. When I stepped back, his eyes were damp—saddened perhaps by his father's decision, but most likely for the longing of his mother's touch.

"Please visit often and ... oh, wait." I ran into the house and pulled *The Adventures of Huckleberry Finn* from the ledge.

Before they turned their wagon toward town, I handed William the book. "Remember, Huck stayed true to what he believed and learned plenty about life through the process. You'll be busy helping your father, but you're always welcome here."

"Thank you, ma'am. I hope you enjoy the rocking chair."

"It means more to me than words can express."

The boy grinned and waved as they pulled away.

* * * * *

The rest of the morning felt incomplete. Not only did William's absence create a void, the mysterious girl—whose name or family we didn't know—hadn't arrived.

Wesley was distracted during our penmanship practice and watched in the distance for his friend to appear. Staying focused was difficult as the children recited rhymes from the primer book. Even the methodic repetition couldn't keep my mind on task.

Shortly before lunchtime, two riders that hadn't been around since autumn descended the hill—Nate and Ben Cooley. I gasped when I saw the little girl astride the saddle in front of Ben, his arm wrapped around her waist. They must have seen her walking alone and thought they'd help her get here quicker. But she wouldn't have told them where she needed to go.

When the horses stopped, Ben dismounted and lifted the girl to the ground. She skipped off and sat next to Wesley on the log. Wesley beamed at her.

Ben tipped his hat. "Mrs. Roberts."

"Mr. Cooley." I crossed my arms, wondering what kind of trouble was brewing. "It's been a while. Kind of you to help the girl find her way. Do you know her family?"

"She's our little sister," Nate called from his horse.

My jaw dropped, and before I could respond, Ben spoke. "Anna Cooley. Figured she didn't tell you that."

"No, she … uh … didn't. In fact, she hasn't talked at all." I glanced at the girl as she drew a picture on a slate board. "Your sister? Really? Did you know she's been coming here since back in the fall?"

"We figured as much," Nate said. "Ben and I weren't too happy about it, but our pa said to let her go see you. Thought a woman's influence might help her."

"What do you mean?"

The brothers looked at each other as if deciding how much to tell, and then Ben spoke. "Anna's mother, Pa's second wife, passed two years ago."

"The girl hasn't spoken a word since," Nate added.

Another child losing a mother. Life isn't supposed to be that way when you're so young. "I'm sorry. I didn't know."

None of us spoke for a long moment.

"Anyhow, our pa sent us here to make you a proposition," Ben finally said. "Though we still know this land you call yours should rightly be under our family name, we'll agree to leave you be and not press any charges as long as you continue to educate little Anna."

"Charges?" My blood started a slow boil, shocked at the nerve of the Cooley family. "You still think you have a claim to my land? I have the legal deed." Anger continued to rise as I chose my next words. "I should be the one pressing charges against you for setting my field on fire and nearly burning down my home with my son and me inside."

"We thought nobody was here," Nate blurted.

"Dang it, Nate." Ben threw his hat at his brother. "Pa's gonna kill you."

"I had a hunch it was you but couldn't imagine how anyone could be so evil." The words spewed from my mouth, and my stomach rolled. "You could have killed us."

"That was never our intention." Ben softened his voice. "The fire got away from us when the wind kicked up." He picked up his hat. "For all it's worth, none of us in my family would have been able to live with ourselves if someone got hurt."

My arms hung limply at my sides as I looked at Anna and the other children. They shared their lunches in what little shade was available on the north side of the house, peaceful in one another's presence—unlike the cruelty that coursed through the hearts of others.

"Tell your father I can't help his daughter." My next words were forced. "She isn't welcome here anymore."

Again, no one spoke. Ben approached Anna and whispered something in her ear. He took her by the hand and led her back to the horse. After he placed her on the saddle, he gave me a slight nod and hoisted himself behind her.

Anna turned and buried her face into her big brother's chest.

As the horses trotted away, Wesley jogged after them a short distance into the field. "Where ya taking my friend?" he called out, but there was no reply.

I sent the other children home after they finished lunch. For the remainder of the afternoon, I lay on the bed. My head pounded. But more than anything, my heart ached.

CHAPTER 34

Daniel ~ Memory, May 9, 1894

Several times over the last few months, I painted her in my memory. Today, she would be captured on canvas, allowing us to be together again—if only in my dreams.

The palette rested on the table—ochre, burnt sienna, raw umber, cadmium yellow, red, and sap green—ready to bring her hair, skin, and eyes to life. Before dipping my brush into the paint, my eyes followed the lines drawn earlier when I took her likeness from my favorite photograph by Finn.

Upon my return to the Globe, he had developed a handful of posed photos of Mary taken at her campsite. But my decision was easy. I picked the one in which she was unaware of being photographed—a natural and abandoned moment where her hair fell loosely, her eyes cast slightly down. Unbuttoned and rolled sleeves showed her forearms. Released from the heat, her collar draped open around her delicate neck. She wore a slight and somewhat mischievous smile—a hint of her adventurous spirit, ready for the challenges ahead.

Lifting my still-dry brush, I ran the soft bristles along the lines of her body. The curves of her skirt led to a narrow waist. Too many years had passed since holding a woman in my arms. I continued down her arms to the tips of long, slender fingers. My brush traced along her neck and chin and where long hair tucked behind an ear. Escaped strands swept across her cheek as if a gentle breeze blew into my room.

I followed the curves of her eyes and tried to recall their exact color when the sun warmed her face. I traced her lips, then set my brush in the tray and ran my fingers down the length of her hair—imagining we were together.

* * * * *

Without knocking, Finn bounded through the door. "She said aye! Elizabeth's going to be me wife."

I set my brush and palette on the side table. "Congratulations, my friend." I pulled him in and gave him a hug. "So, Arthur gave you his blessing. Good man."

"He did." Finn scratched his head. "But on the condition that I keep me job and work toward a promotion. He made it clear I'm to support his daughter and be a respectable and honest husband and father."

"Finn, I think you're blushing." I smiled at my friend, who in many ways still seemed like a boy, yet was ready to become a man. "His requests sound fair, don't you think?"

"Agreed. I plan to do all that and more for me bride." He cocked his head and questioned me with his eyes. "You understand then why I can't go with you this time."

"Go where?"

"Back to the territory." Finn cocked his head. "Didn't ye know?"

"You've lost me."

"I figured McKelvey popped the news the other day before he mentioned it to me." Finn was so full of life he seemed to lift off the ground. "Everyone knows you've had your head in the clouds since ye came back."

"What's that supposed to …"

Finn walked toward the canvas and stopped. He studied the composition, his head turning to the side like a puppy dog. I forced myself to stand tall, embarrassed for painting her likeness—especially unlike other traditional and modest portraits.

Maybe I've gone mad.

As if Finn read my mind, he shook his head. "No, yer in love with her."

I remained silent, but it was true. And the friend who knew me best saw right through my attempts to stay consumed with work and professional conversation at the Globe. Most likely, others had seen it too.

"And what exactly is McKelvey's plan?" I asked.

"The paper's ready for a follow-up story. It's been nine months since the Rush, and the paper wants to report on what's happening out West. The country is changing before our eyes, and that event had plenty to do with it. I believe his exact words were, he wants you to 'paint the changing landscape.'" Finn swirled my brush in the air. "Plus, he probably wants another one of your paintings to keep his wife happy."

"I don't know about his wife, but true enough, the city readers were fascinated with the lives of those people—two different worlds within one country." I tried to remain calm, but the idea of seeing Mary again sent a surge of excitement through me that couldn't be ignored. "But what about you? We're a team, remember?"

"Sure we be. But he's having me stay and cover the Pullman strikes. George Hardy's assigned to go with you this time."

"Hardy? He's not as good as you."

"Aye, good point." Finn pointed his finger at me. "But things are heating up, and the Feds in Washington aren't too happy about what the workers are threatening. Word is, well over a hundred thousand rail and factory workers are refusing to make or even maintain the passenger cars. Could bring the nation's rail system to a halt. Imagine that."

"Maybe old man Pullman should have cut the worker's rental rates as much as he cut their salaries." Without thinking, I had taken my travel bag from behind the easel and began stuffing it with brushes and paint. "Like you said, the country is changing."

"Indeed. Besides, Elizabeth doesn't want to wait much longer, and we're planning for a late-summer wedding. It's her favorite season."

"Are you sure you know what you're getting into?" I gave him a soft punch on the arm.

Finn winked. "I'll find out soon enough." He positioned his hat and started for the door. "You'd better talk with McKelvey soon before he changes his mind. And I'm planning on you to be the best man. Best if yer back before the wedding."

"I'm honored." I offered a theatrical bow before closing the door.

A ray of sunshine invited itself through the window and bathed the unfinished painting. *You are enchanting, Mary Roberts.* I breathed deeply and played her through my memory one more time. *I think of you often.*

I hope you think of me as well.

CHAPTER 35

Mary ~ Confrontation, May 10, 1894

My decision to march straight to the Cooley ranch first thing in the morning hadn't changed when I awoke. When Wesley refused to eat his breakfast and hardly talked to me, my resolve to meet senior Mr. Cooley and let him have a piece of my mind intensified.

How did I end up the bad guy in all of this?

"I'll be back shortly, and you need to do your schoolwork while I'm gone." My hair was secured into a low knot. No time to fuss with my appearance with urgent business to attend to. I considered riding Jim but decided the walk would let me gather my thoughts about what to say to the mysterious and powerful man. *How dare he think he could tell me what to do after all the trouble his family has caused. And to think he's never had the nerve to talk to me himself.*

Halfway across our field and heading for the rise, Wesley caught up.

"I told you to stay home. This is important business that is not yours, young man."

He lifted a folded piece of paper, unevenly creased several times. "Give this to Anna, please."

I bent down and looked him in the eye. "It's obvious why you're angry. You want her welcome at our house." Anna's sweet face flashed across my mind. "That's my wish too if circumstances were different. But her family can't ..."

Wesley looked like he was about to cry.

"I can't expect you to understand, but you have to trust that this is the best thing for us. Maybe for her as well. Something's not right that she won't even talk. How am I supposed to teach her if she won't make a sound?"

His lips trembled. "But she's my best friend. She doesn't have to talk. I know what she's thinking." He kicked the dirt. "Now she won't have a friend at all because of you."

"Wesley Roberts, that is not—"

"It's not fair, and you're mean!" He turned and ran back to the house.

Like brittle tumbleweed, I felt lifeless in the middle of the field, stunned and at a loss from Wesley's words. Was I really that awful? No, Stanley Cooley was to blame for all of this. My intentions were to settle here and be a good neighbor.

My hands trembled as I unfolded the paper and read his note. Now my heart ached even more. Wesley had written in his best penmanship and spelling for a young boy.

Dear Ana. I like your name. I hope you come back soon becuz your my best frend. I like how you draw picshurs to.
Your frend Wesley

Underneath the words, he included two faces, side by side. Both wore frowns and dots of pencil marks fell from the eyes.

My pace quickened. The sooner I told this man how I felt about his family, the better.

*****

Over the past few months, I intentionally hadn't traveled north onto the Cooley property. The town sites were situated in the opposite direction, and the Andersons' claim bordered mine to the east. Besides, it was best to keep my distance from their land. No sense in aggravating the situation even more.

As I followed the same stream that ran through my property—only a trickle a month ago but now a width that would be a stretch for me to jump across—I was taken aback by the house in the distance.

Thomas had mentioned the Cooley home was more than any other in the area, but my imagination could never have conceived the extent of it. A wood-sided two-story house perched like a queen in the middle of an open field, white with green trim detailed around several windows. On one end, a limestone chimney rose into the sky like a scepter. Behind the house, a line of cottonwoods painted a lovely backdrop.

To the west of the house, a barn loomed over a zigzag of pens and corrals, dotted with at least a hundred head of cattle. How the Cooleys built all of this since last fall proved they were undoubtedly an established, wealthy family. Behind the barn, a towering windmill spun in the breeze.

I had seen one of these contraptions through the train window upon my return from Missouri. An Aeromotor windmill was what another passenger informed me—powerful enough to pump water from a creek, or even a well if the Cooleys were lucky enough to drill down and strike precious water.

That's probably why they wanted my claim. The river widened even more on my property, providing a decent underground supply of water. Even though I'd welcome the shade and protection from their grove of trees, my property captured more wind power than theirs. Besides the rise behind my soddy, there wasn't much of anything to stop the constant gusts.

Still, their plot was more than sufficient, causing me to suspect our conflict had more to do with me being a woman than the actual site. Perhaps they wanted to bully me off my property so they'd have double the land. Many homesteaders had already expanded their acreage as neighboring claimants sold out for a decent profit—often deciding the reality of prairie life was none too glamorous and more difficult than they had imagined.

With chin raised, my feet followed the carved path leading to the house. Two rocking chairs paralleled one another on the front porch. The porch spanned the length of the house and wrapped around the eastern corner. A large wooden door, adorned with an iron horseshoe knocker, made me feel small.

Retreating down the steps and forgetting the entire conversation was a welcome option. I summoned my courage and lifted the knocker.

After a minute, I tried the knocker again. When no one opened the door, I stepped behind the chairs and looked in the window.

"What do ya think you're doing nosing around here?"

The gruff voice made me jump, sending me stumbling into one of the chairs. It lunged back and forth before my outstretched hand tried to stop its motion.

"Don't touch it!" A light-haired man with flecks of gray at his temples gripped the arm of the chair and brought it to a stop as if it were a spooked colt. He muttered something to himself and then turned to me with a scowl. The man was no taller than me.

"I'm ... I'm sorry. You surprised me. I didn't mean to—"

"You didn't surprise me. Been watching you all the way up the road." He took a kerchief from his back pocket and wiped his nose. "Figured you'd show up someday."

"Really?" I studied his light-blue eyes that contrasted with tan skin that wrinkled near his eyes and across his forehead. "Why is that?"

"My boys said you're a tough one. Not easy to break, like a wild horse." He squinted his left eye as if trying to confirm their description of me.

"I'll take that as a compliment." I extended my hand. "Mary Roberts. Stanley Cooley, I presume." My mind had pictured him much taller, older, and intimidating.

He ignored my hand, only to nod and then stuff his kerchief in his pocket before heading toward the front door. There was no formal invitation, but my gut said to follow him.

Surprisingly, the inside of the house was stark and silent. The walls were blank and the wooden floors bare. A wall hook held a limp coat, and a pair of boots sat underneath. It in no way resembled a home where four people resided.

In the room to the left, a small sofa faced an unused fireplace. An empty, rough-hewn mantel perched above it. There was no evidence of any family photos or decorations—unusual for the exterior grandeur of the house. Maybe it was the absence of his wife, Anna's mother. With her loss, a void had taken up residence.

On the other side of the entryway, a door remained closed. Up the staircase, I assumed there were bedrooms.

I followed him through the living room—a contradiction of terms—and into the kitchen. Not quite as lifeless as the other room, it had a round table with four chairs, a butcher block, and an overhead rack with a few pots and a large skillet. An icebox huddled in the corner, and wooden crates filled with food staples were stacked along the wall.

"Anna has been practicing her lessons." I pointed to the neat pile of papers and an elementary primer book on the table.

"She has." He pulled a glass from the cupboard. "Thirsty?"

I gave a curt nod, admittedly parched from the walk but wanting to remain completely capable and self-sufficient. "About your daughter. She's a dear little girl, and my son has become quite fond of her. However, I—"

"I expect you to keep teaching her." His response was abrupt, void of any desire for discussion regarding the matter.

"Excuse me?" My emotions refused to stay in check. "I don't owe you anything. In fact, it's the other way around. It's you and those boys of yours who owe me an apology. And quite frankly, restitution for all the hardship you've caused."

My hands automatically flew to my hips as my anger built. "First, you accuse me of being a Sooner, of all things, then threaten to send the law after me. Then your cattle destroyed almost everything I owned."

"Big clumsy animals. They got away from the men that day. Have a mind of their own sometimes." His tone softened, and as if it were another casual conversation, he settled into a chair and gestured for me to pull out another one and join him at the table.

Refusing to sit, I paced back and forth and continued to speak my mind. "Cows wouldn't know how to shoot a bullet through my water barrel."

He grinned beneath his silver-tinged mustache, inviting a solid punch if I were a man. I leaned within inches of his face. "And how dare you nearly kill my son and me in that fire."

He sat back and looked as though I *had* punched him. "I don't know what you're talking about. What fire?"

"The brushfire that would have burned us alive in the middle of the night had I not known what to do to squelch it." A lump filled my throat as I willed myself not to scream in anger or pummel him with my fists.

He pushed away from the table and stood. We locked eyes for a moment, each of us trying to make sense of the other's words.

"I'm not responsible for any fire. I'd never do that kind of harm, especially to a child and his mother." He shook his head as if disgusted with the thought.

"Your boys already admitted they did it."

His eyes widened and the color drained from his face. Without warning, he threw the drinking glass across the kitchen where it hit the wall and shattered into hundreds of tiny shards. "I'm gonna have a piece of those two when they get home." He laid a firm fist on the table. "We're a proud family, but not ignorant. And certainly not violent."

My heart raced as I backed away, intent on getting far away from this place. It wasn't worth restating that Anna wasn't welcome anymore. Who knew how he might react. Wesley's note was tucked in my pocket. It could easily be torn into tiny pieces and carried away on the wind during my walk back home. But lying to my son when he asked if the note was delivered simply wasn't an option. The innocence of children. How wonderful for them to see the world through different eyes—at least for a while.

I pulled the note from my pocket and set it on the table. "It's for Anna. A note from my son. Promised him it would be delivered."

He stared at the paper for a moment and then unfolded it, one crease at a time. It would have been an appropriate time to slip out the front door, but I found myself trapped in the moment—captivated by the sight of a rough and hardened man on the exterior who seemed to be a soft and caring person on the inside. At least that's what my intuition told me.

He was silent after he read the note, refolding it along the same lines as though retracing steps through the forest. His shoulders slumped in tandem with the ends of his mustache. I stared at him for a minute, unsure what to say or do. The rage that filled him moments before disappeared like a child's balloon deflated and lifeless.

I started for the door when he called out, "Mrs. Roberts. Allow me to show you something."

Common sense told me to keep walking, but curiosity made me stop. "I only have a few minutes."

"Then come with me." He started out the back door.

I hesitated, then followed when he waved for me to join him. We walked across the yard past a small garden and a chicken coop, then into the barn. It was dim inside as my eyes gradually adjusted and made out the line of horse stalls.

A horse's whinny rang out at the far end. "Quit complaining, Dusty. Your friends will be back shortly." He turned to me. "The boys took Anna and rode out to fix fences this morning. Left her little pony behind so they could cover more ground. Should be home before lunchtime."

The walls were lined with bridles, saddles, branding irons, and every imaginable ranching tool. A mountain of hay occupied the far end, and the sweet smell of barley filled the air.

"Good thing Jim hasn't seen this barn," I mumbled.

"Who's Jim? Thought your boy is Wesley." Stanley stopped in front of the last stall.

"Jim's our mule. Poor thing, he's been outside all winter."

"Jim, huh?" Stanley grinned. "That's a good name for a mule." He lifted the latch and swung open the half door.

Expecting a pony or some other animal to emerge from the stall, I was surprised when Stanley motioned me inside. He pulled back a tarp in the far corner. Underneath was a wooden trunk. A lock dangled from the side.

"A treasure chest? Wesley's favorite story is *Treasure Island*."

"It's a treasure, but not that kind." He knelt next to the chest and ran his hand along its top. "Haven't looked in here since I tucked her things away."

"I'm sorry about your wife. I lost my husband nearly a year ago."

"My condolences." He spoke softly, maybe from reverence for being near what must have been her personal items. "Wondered why you were here alone with your boy." He pulled a set of keys from his pocket. "Rushed on your own, did ya?" His eyes widened. "Ain't that something?"

I took his question as rhetorical and, perhaps, even as a side-handed compliment.

He fumbled with the lock and then raised the lid. Neatly folded and spread across the top was what appeared to be a wedding dress. Its white satin and laced sleeves contrasted with the darkness of the stall and the dark wood of the chest. As if it would break with his touch, he gently folded the gown to the side and slid his hand underneath.

I had no idea what he planned to show me or why he felt it necessary to share such a private part of his life. When he pulled a wooden box and a small, framed painting from the chest, my confusion mounted.

He sat back on his heels and held the box in his lap. "Flora was an artist." He flipped opened the lid. Brushes and paints lay side by side like they had been tucked into bed for an eternal slumber. "When the ranch house burned to the ground, I was able to run in and save this box, one painting, and a few of her other precious items. Everything else was consumed by the fire."

The thought of a fire destroying an entire home was devastating. "I'm sure she was happy you retrieved some things so special to her."

He breathed hard through his nose and took his time answering. "My wife passed away a year before the fire." His eyes were damp. "This is all I have left of her." He turned over the frame and showed a painting of a woman sitting in a rocking chair with a child on her lap.

His reaction when the chair on the porch was knocked ajar now made perfect sense. My fingers ran over the edges of the gilded frame as my eyes studied the faces, probably painted from a photograph.

Both Flora and Anna had dark hair. Anna's hair tumbled around her face with the unmistakable curls that caught my attention when she first hid in our field. Flora's hair must have been the same when she released it from the fashionable twist at bedtime—reserved only for her husband's eyes.

Mother and daughter were smiling—unusual for photographs of the day. I understood why she chose to paint them happy, content as they held one another.

"Anna hasn't spoken since her mother died." He took the painting from my hands and returned it to the chest. The wooden box followed and then the dress, spread evenly across the top. He closed the lid and secured the lock.

"Why did you show me those things?"

He pinched the bridge of his nose as if pushing back painful memories, and I wondered if he knew the reason. "Because I need to get my Anna back."

"But—"

"She trusts you and, especially, your boy."

"Mr. Cooley, I'm sorry for what's happened but I don't see—"

"You have to let her attend your school. She's smart as a whip. Comes home each time and practices everything you've taught her. There's a spark in her again." He stood and brushed the dirt from his pants. "For the longest time, she wouldn't leave my side. The two of us holed up in the house. Needed to be miserable together, I suppose. At least that way, we'd have each other."

We walked into the sunlight and both shielded our eyes. "But once she started sneaking off to your property, the boys and I knew something was changing for her. It's been hard to let her go on her own, but we agreed we had to let her do this."

"But why all the trouble? Your boys haven't exactly been gentlemen."

He ran calloused fingers through his ruffled hair, and it was easy to see where Nate got his likeness. "There's no excuse, and I take the blame for most of it. Been hard on the boys not to have me be the father they once knew. They're good young men, although they're in a heap of trouble for setting that fire." He extended his hand. "I promise my family will make it up to you somehow."

I wasn't ready to let the Cooley family off so easily and hesitated shaking his hand. But now the situation involved a child—one who desperately needed to be loved and accepted.

"How can I teach her if she won't speak?" As soon as the question left my lips, shame flowed through me. Anna was still learning—in her own way.

Stanley only smiled—that knowing smile of his that I would soon come to appreciate—and walked back toward the house.

CHAPTER 36

Late spring showers bathed the land. Once-barren fields were painted with far-reaching blankets of yellow coneflowers and black-eyed Susan, brilliant orange butterfly milkweed, and purple prairie clover. I pinched a pink blossom of horse mint and breathed the aroma.

Even though our school gatherings would end as soon as summer began, the children pleaded to continue story time.

"When your chores are finished," I said, trying to keep a serious face, "and your parents give you permission, you are more than welcome here."

"I want to hear *Heidi* again," Emily said. "She's my favorite."

"Me too, dear."

Luke's face told me he would rather read another boy's adventure.

"Next trip to town, I'll ask about other books. Ours are excellent, but it's always good to read something new."

Though her smiles and nods were more frequent, Anna clung to Wesley like his little shadow. The others developed unique ways of communicating with her. During playtime, Anna was brought into the fold and chosen on a team for Ox in the Ditch, Leap Frog, and Ante Over. It was food for my soul to watch the children play. Abandon and innocence was as much nourishment for their minds and bodies as schooling and supper.

The children didn't know they would eventually attend a state school—home during planting and harvesting seasons and in session from May to August, then November to April. Our small and informal school—inside the soddy on cold days and outside on warm—would someday be only a memory of their first years in the territory.

Selfishly, my heart sank when Thomas informed me the first bond had recently passed, and a school was under construction in Oklahoma

City. Like wildflowers bringing the fields to life, a love for teaching and helping the children learn blossomed in me.

Late one evening, after Wesley was asleep and my thoughts had time to meander, I asked God if this new passion had anything to do with Him. Could there be another purpose hidden in my travels so far from what I once knew? A reason beyond my determination to prove I needed only my independence to provide for myself and my son?

Have I been running after something ... or only running away?

The rocking chair, my precious gift from William, cradled me outside the door as my eyes gazed at the star-speckled sky. The vastness was captivating. And as though I felt His touch, God held my hand.

I breathed in deeply and then let the air flow from my lungs, along with the stubbornness, pride, and fears from my past. In the darkness and calm of the night, allowing myself to be still with Him, peace washed over me. It seemed like another lifetime when I was caught in the river searching for Wesley, at first terrified, but then covered in utter tranquility and peacefulness as I totally surrendered.

Another deep breath brought newfound clarity. The words *trust ... trust ... trust ...* bathed me like gently lapping water at the river's edge. If I would trust, He was ready to lead me into His endless world of possibilities.

"Father ..." I whispered into the darkness and realized I had never referred to or thought of God in that way. For some reason, it felt right after all these years. The only father I had ever known was never around enough to make an imprint upon my memory.

"Please reveal Your plan for me." Silence hovered until a gentle breeze brushed my hair. *But the Lord is in His holy temple; let all the earth keep silence before Him.* The verse played across my mind before more words were spoken into the darkness. "For the first time in my life, more than anything, I trust You."

Moonlight caressed my face as I leaned back and rocked. Then my eyes closed to the night sky. In its place, a familiar, yet distant face appeared—one that often visited my dreams both day and night.

Daniel McKenzie.

CHAPTER 37

Mary ~ Restitution, June 20, 1894

The pounding of hammers awakened me the next morning. Across the grass, some hundred feet away, Nate and Ben hammered in unison on the framework of what looked like a barn.

"Mama, Jim's gonna have a house too!" Wesley pulled on his trousers—clearly too short after a winter's growth spurt—and ran out the door.

My eyes ached, partly after a poor night's sleep from mosquitoes buzzing in my ears, but also from worrying about Lucy and Thomas' baby. Sweet Lila arrived in early May, healthy and pink. But over the last week, she'd been unusually fussy. I planned to head there shortly to see if I could lend a hand with meals and cleaning.

Gathering my hair into a tight knot and securing the buttons on my shirtwaist felt tedious this morning. At least I didn't have to wear the fussy and obtrusive leg o' mutton sleeves sported by some of the wealthier women back home. A brief glance into the small hand mirror confirmed my plain white blouse would suffice in this part of the country.

Before leaving, I lit the stove and filled a small pot of water. It looked like the Cooley boys had a long day ahead of them. A pot of coffee would do them good. An unexpected giggle escaped my mouth, knowing this job wasn't their idea.

"Good morning." My long strides toward the soon-to-be barn were in sync with the grinding of the saw.

"Mrs. Roberts." Ben tipped his hat. "Good morning to you as well."

"Ma'am." Nate wiped the sweat from his brow with the back of his hand. The day was already proving to be a scorcher. "Sorry we woke y'all so early. Pa said we needed to have this barn done for you in a day."

Ben took ten or so long steps, turned to the right, and proceeded the same distance. "Good thing it's not going to be a big one." He nodded at Jim, who seemed to be enjoying the activity in the yard. Big ears pricked forward, and pieces of grass poked from his mouth. "Pa said it needs to hold your mule, a cow or two, feed, and supplies."

"That's very generous," I said. "A lean-to for our mule would be sufficient. As you can see, we don't have any cows of our own, but we did have several visitors at one point." I winked at Nate. "Isn't that right, young man?"

"Yes, ma'am. If my memory serves me right." He rubbed his face roughly with the heel of his hand. "Speaking of that—"

"We also came to formally apologize," Ben added. "My brother and I accept responsibility for the trouble we've caused." He poked Nate in the arm. "Ain't that right?"

Nate mumbled something, and Ben gave him a harder jab.

"We're especially sorry for the brushfire." Nate looked at Wesley, who was practicing hammering nails into a piece of wood. "Honestly, like we told you before, it was an accident. It was my idea to set the fire so you'd smell the smoke and get scared."

"We didn't expect the wind to catch like it did." Ben shifted his weight from boot to boot as if recalling the dreadful event put him on edge. "We never would have forgiven ourselves if something happened to you and the boy."

"Then why didn't you warn us?" A shiver flew up my spine at the memory of that night.

Both boys were silent for a few moments until Nate spoke. "We got scared. Pa would've whopped us good if he knew what we'd done."

Wesley sidled up next to me. "I'm glad your pa didn't whop you, even though the fire almost scared me and Mama to death." He scrunched his nose. "But my mama beat that fire and smoke right up."

"Your ma's a tough lady," Nate said, then moved his gaze to mine. "That's meant in the best way, ma'am."

The full-grown bodies, awkward patches of facial hair, and gruff voices of Ben and Nate couldn't disguise that they were still young, ignorant, and, in some regard, innocent from serious ill intent. There was no sense continuing the battle with the Cooleys. Anna was welcomed in long ago, and she and Wesley were inseparable. Now that she was allowed to ride her pony to our property, her almost daily presence made her part of my own family.

"I ... *we* accept your apology." My stern look was a reminder for them to behave. "And I'll take your comment as a compliment." My hand extended toward Nate. "And never forget that I'm, as you say, tough. It wouldn't be wise to cross me."

He smiled and shook my hand. Ben did the same before cutting another piece of wood. "By the way, Pa's having us bring the milking cow tomorrow if that's all right with you."

"Cow? My goodness. He doesn't need—"

"That's the least we can do." Nate positioned himself behind the saw and set to work.

At the thought of fresh milk and cream to churn butter, my mouth watered. *That's what good neighbors do. They help each other.* With that thought, I remembered the boiling water and quickly ran inside to brew a pot of coffee for the boys.

Before setting out for the Andersons, I secured the flour sack containing at least a dozen biscuits baked fresh for them last night. A few extras were set aside for the Cooley boys. At the pace they were instructed to work, they'd be starving before lunchtime.

* * * * *

At the edge of the trodden pathway leading to Lucy and Thomas' door, a piercing cry cut through the air. I ran onto the porch, pushing the door open without knocking.

Lucy held Lila in her arms the best she could. The baby arched her back and screeched, her face contorting and reddening with each wail. With every burst of tears, her little fists tightened and shook.

Thomas looked at me wild-eyed and pale-faced. "She's been like this most of the morning. Couldn't get her to sleep last night either."

Lucy only nodded and continued pacing the room, rocking the baby and speaking softly. It were as though a stranger held the child. Lucy's bloodshot eyes and tousled hair made her look so different. Her face was sagging and gray, longing for sleep, or even a moment of rest. What happened to the confident, cheerful, and bubbly young woman who had become my dearest friend?

Wesley or one of the twins had cried out in pain from a stomachache or teething, but never like this. Lila's cry was one of pure agony, and her tiny body could only shake and heave. I prayed for God to show me how to help.

Thomas wrapped his arms around Lucy. Tears dripped down her face—a mother's heart breaking with the realization she was unable to comfort her baby.

"They'll be here any minute." Thomas kissed his daughter's forehead. "You just hang in there, my little darling."

"Who?" I glanced into the front yard.

"Rode into town before sunrise to get Roy. Figured he might know what to do or could bring the doctor with him."

Sure enough, two riders galloped across the field a moment later and dismounted. One was Roy. I figured the other must be the town doctor until he walked closer. He was dark-skinned, and long braids fell at each side of his face. His trousers and shirt had been patched more times than a quilt, and the brim of his hat flopped above high cheekbones.

"Roy." Thomas gave his brother a quick hug and glanced at the other man. He looked back at his brother. "No luck getting Doc Wilson?"

"This here's Adam. Friends call him by his Indian name, Adahy. He's come along to help the baby. That's what took me some time. I was lucky to find him this morning."

An awkward silence hung above the four of us like a cloud of unwelcome gnats.

"Pleased to—" I extended my hand just as Lila let out another cry. "Let's hope you can help her."

Thomas opened his mouth to speak, but my stern look shushed him. "Quickly now ..." The stranger was waved into the house, followed by

Roy. Before Thomas slipped in behind them, I touched his arm and whispered, "I've heard about him. William—the older boy who came for schooling—his father owns the carpentry business in town."

Thomas nodded but looked worried.

"William nearly cut off his fingers helping his father. This man … he saved his hand. Wrapped it with herbs and oils and completely healed him. Mr. Hill said he's a medicine man, a healer."

Thomas' face contorted as though wrestling with what to believe—the chance that an elderly Indian could heal Lila or the prejudices and hateful words that were as commonplace among most people as sipping tea on a summer's day.

"At least let him try. What else can we do?"

His mouth twitched with his best attempt at a smile before he stepped inside.

Lucy's eyes were wide as she clutched Lila to her chest.

"It's all right," Roy said to her. "Adam has a way with healing, but you have to let him see the baby."

Thomas went to his wife and whispered in her ear. Lucy's teary eyes darted between the baby and the stranger, but she placed Lila in Adam's arms.

As Adam whispered soothing words to the baby in an unknown language for several minutes, the intense crying subsided, replaced by sporadic whimpers. Attempts to hide our slight smiles didn't last long as the baby's cries were replaced with tiny hiccups.

The skin on Adam's hands was wrinkled and wore scars of hard use. Deep creases etched the back of his neck and alongside his dark eyes. *How old is he, and, more importantly, why is he alone in these parts?* Most of the Creeks and Cherokees were far to the east and southeast, scattered beyond the Arkansas River and into less desirable areas. Plenty of dark-skinned people, many whose families had traveled West for a new start after slavery ended, formed smaller communities. But for the native people, they were like tumbleweeds, blown across the open plains, uprooted and tossed by unrelenting winds.

"Boil water." Adam motioned to Roy.

"Here, let me help," I said.

Lucy and Thomas huddled next to Adam as he laid the baby in the cradle and massaged her stomach with the palm of his hand.

"Beautiful baby … curly hair like her mother's." The Indian untied the strip of rawhide on his leather bag and reached inside. He pulled out several handfuls of plant stems and leaves. "Gripe water. Make her stomach better."

"What's that?" Thomas inspected a purple sprig, a green stalk with feathery leaves, a variety of green leaves, violet berries, and a yellow and white flower. "Looks like a daisy."

"Chamomile." Adam plucked a petal and rolled it between his fingers. "Calm her belly. Fennel, peppermint, and aloe get rid of pain." He held a berry between his thumb and forefinger. "Tiny berry make her poop very much."

"I don't understand." Lucy teared up again. "You aren't having my daughter eat plants, are you?"

"Both of you. Mother and baby." He patted his chest. "Mother's milk, baby's food. What you eat, baby eats." He grinned, and the creases on his face deepened. "Hialeah will drink."

Lucy sniffled and swiped at her tears. "Who's Hialeah?"

Adam pointed to Lila. "Beautiful meadow. Her Indian name." He stood at the table, tearing off small parts of the plants and wrapping them in a piece of thin flour sack. When the water boiled, he took the pot from the stove and submerged the cloth. "Wait. Then you and baby drink."

"But how will she drink? She can't use a cup yet," Thomas said.

Adam pulled a small eyedropper from his bag. "Like mother bird feed babies."

* * * * *

I prepared lunch while Lucy rocked her peaceful baby. My friend was exhausted from worry and lack of sleep. When her eyes closed, the lines disappeared from her forehead.

As I stirred the ham and bean stew and cooled the hard-boiled eggs, my mind wandered to my own children and how much I loved them. Even death couldn't separate me from the profound feeling—so powerful that it often hurt. Strange how such a wonderful thing as love could be the root of so much pain.

The twins and I had too short a time together, and although I believed we would someday be together in heaven, it would be a long time until I held them again. But I had Wesley, and we were a family—even without a father.

Tuck. The once vivid memories of him faded more and more as the year passed. Like the sun-faded photograph of Mother on the ledge in the soddy, the image of my husband blurred and receded into the distant shores of my mind. Sometimes, he waded back into my thoughts in a certain way Wesley laughed. Or when I slipped on the same nightdress I wore while waiting for him too many nights. Then he floated away, back into the past.

Thomas tucked Lila in her crib while Lucy took a much-needed nap. He joined the other men around the table where they spoke in hushed tones as they ate. Two of them I knew as fathers, brothers, and husbands—honest and hardworking men.

I wondered if Adam had his own children and a wife. Did someone care for him as he did for us? He shared his gift of healing with white people—the race that brought destruction to his people's traditional way of life.

Within minutes, Adam emptied his bowl and consumed several eggs. I served him another full ladle, and he thanked me with a chip-toothed smile.

"No beans or turnips for Mother." He nodded towards Lucy. "Baby not like it—make her cry."

Thomas leaned in closer. "That's practically all me and my wife have been eating until the garden started to sprout." He scratched his head. "That's what was causing all this crying?"

Adam patted his stomach with a grunt.

Roy wiped his mouth with a kerchief. "Mary, thank you for filling our bellies. Your buttermilk biscuits were delicious." He pushed from the table. "It's time for Adam and me to head back to town. The clerks are probably wondering if I've abandoned them. Not complaining, but business doesn't slow down in these parts."

Adam quickly downed the second bowl and joined Roy and Thomas by the horses. Thomas shook Adam's hand before pulling money from his pocket. The Indian shook his head and turned to walk toward his horse.

There is so much we don't understand of each other. I scurried into the house, wrapped the remaining biscuits and eggs, and returned as the men hoisted themselves into the saddles.

"These are for you." I lifted my hands toward Adam.

He reached down and took the bundle of cloth. "Thank you. Share with wife."

"That's good. I'm sure she's as wonderful as you. Thank you for helping the baby." It was a relief to learn he had someone who loved him.

As the men rode away, Thomas waved and then turned toward me. "I'm ashamed of myself." He pushed his hands deep into his pockets. "Because he's an Indian, I didn't want him in my home or anywhere near my baby and wife. Assumed he was up to no good. Scared me a bit."

"Thomas, you're a good—"

"Not with thoughts like that." He rubbed his face. "I got nothing up on him. Never have and never will. Darn it, Mary. It disturbs me thinking he has so little, and I'm sitting like a fat hen. For all I know, my house is sitting on what was his land in the first place."

"Did he talk about that?"

"No, but Roy did. The Indians understand they're considered nobodies. Not even official citizens of the country." Thomas scratched his head as if trying to make sense of it all. "Not that they'd want to be. But because of it, they don't have land to call their own anymore."

"Why do you think he helped us?"

"It's a mystery to me." He kicked at a loose rock with the toe of his boot. "Maybe because the world still has some good people in it, and he happens to be one of them."

Thomas' words left me thinking as I silently walked back into the house. When the kitchen was tidy and the laundry folded, I kissed Lila on the forehead and started for home.

CHAPTER 38

Mary ~ Return, June 20, 1894

At the edge of the Andersons' property, my foot found the closest steppingstone before crossing the stream. A small pool waited patiently aside the slow current. From it, my reflection stared up at me.

In the gentle water was the person I had hoped to find again. For so long, she had been lost somewhere along the deep valleys and seemingly dead ends of life. As if wandering in a heavy forest, hoping to find light, she emerged from somewhere in my mind—a peaceful woman, no longer defined by the dark veil of fear and pride she'd worn for so long. She was free now, liberated by the promise that comes from trust and hope.

One by one, I tiptoed on the other stones and made my way safely across and onto my land. Anxious to see the barn's progress and hug Wesley, the field of knee-high grass welcomed me, and I ran into its embrace.

At the slight rise in the field, I stopped to catch my breath. The sun tilted toward the west, casting a glare that forced me to squint and lift my hand above my eyes to dull the blinding light.

Four silhouettes were in the distance. The small one was clearly Wesley, the others, Nate and Ben. The last figure seemed familiar. I took several more steps then stopped again.

Daniel.

For a minute, my feet wouldn't move. The old part of me wanted to turn and run, back across the creek and far away from where my heart urged me to go—someplace where pain and loss couldn't find me.

But my reflection in the water, if only in my mind, whispered a gentle reminder. *There is no place, at least on this side of heaven that promises those things. If you must run, run away from the past, and into the future.* Like wild horses on the gallop, my heart thundered, and for the first time in so long, it was not from fear and doubt, but from excitement and anticipation.

I must have looked like a schoolgirl released from the last day of school. I gathered my skirts and ran through the field. As our distance lessened, his silhouette faded, and his whole being came into focus. He wore a wide smile, and the sun danced off his hair when he lifted his hat. I slowed to a stop, unsure what to do next. Was he here for me or did he have other business to attend to? *Please be here for me.*

As if in answer to my questions, he opened his arms. Without hesitating or wondering if it would be proper, I fell into his embrace.

"Mary." He held me tightly. "I've missed you."

"It's you. You're really here." My fingers touched his cheek and then traveled alongside his eye. "Turquoise ... from heaven."

"Pardon me?" His look was quizzical, but he spoke softly. "I do know this. You are the one from heaven."

"Mama!" Wesley leaped through the grass and wrapped his arms around my waist. "Daniel's come back. Isn't it wonderful?"

"It is wonderful, Wesley. It couldn't be any better." The three of us stood wrapped together—me, my son, and the man who allowed me to trust ... and love again.

* * * * *

When the sun set, the men laid down their tools. To raise a barn in one day was a lofty goal. Surely Stanley would understand when his sons needed to return in the morning for another day's work. Jim had waited a long time for a barn. Another night without shelter would be fine. Besides, as much as the boys' hard work was appreciated, my heart was filled with joy when Nate and Ben rode away. Now I could spend time with Daniel—and find out the full details of why he'd returned.

He and I sat at the supper table while Wesley sprawled on the bed flipping through the pages of his gift from Daniel. *Beautiful Joe* was a new novel that was winning the hearts of young and old across the country. According to Daniel, the story about an abused dog had brought him to tears more than once as he read it on the train. At first, he had considered a different gift for Wesley, but as he followed Joe's story, he fell in love with the dog and knew we would as well.

More than once, we caught ourselves staring at each other. Perhaps we needed reassurance that our shared company wasn't a dream.

"It's good to see Nate and Ben have come around," Daniel said. "Not up to their usual mischief."

"Their father set them straight. He's an unusual man. Intent on wanting me out of here but then deciding he needs me as his neighbor and friend. But the past troubles are settled." The locked chest in the barn came to mind. "From what I understand, he loved his wife very much and is still heartbroken over losing her. She was an artist, like you."

Nearly every day of Daniel's absence, I had studied the painting on the ledge, absorbing its composition and color, following each brushstroke as if the painting held secrets of who Daniel McKenzie really was … and why I couldn't erase him from my mind.

Tonight, like so many other times, my fingers moved along the vibrant orange and pink horizon. "I remembered you, just like you asked." I felt his eyes follow me around the room. "Tell me, why did you come back?"

He was silent for so long it seemed he wasn't going to answer. When he spoke, his voice was full of emotion. "I couldn't forget you, not for a moment."

"What'd talking about?" Wesley rolled off the bed and settled into the chair next to Daniel.

"Young man, it's *what are you* talking about." I busied myself with clearing a few dishes. "Besides, it's nothing of importance. Only catching up."

"So why else are you here?" Wesley propped his elbows on the table and rested his chin on his hands. "Besides you couldn't forget her."

Daniel covered his mouth with his hand, but an embarrassed grin couldn't be hidden so easily.

"Young man, you have the ears of an elephant." I gently tugged his ear.

"To be honest, Wesley, I couldn't forget you either." Daniel settled back in his chair and stretched his arms high above his head. "And the paper has sent me back for a follow-up story."

"Is Finn in town too?" I hoped the answer was yes. Nothing like a good laugh with the young Scot.

"Ah, Finn. He's madly in love and getting married this summer. Our editor assigned him work on the East Coast. Good to keep him closer to his bride-to-be. A gentleman by the name of George Hardy is paired with me on the job."

A sick feeling overcame me, and my head felt as light as a dandelion puff. "Then you're leaving again … when your story is finished?"

Daniel was quiet and smoothed the faded tablecloth with his palm. Wesley looked back and forth between the two of us.

"So, that's the *real* reason you … came back." My voice wavered. "Things have changed plenty since you left. The town has tripled in size—hardly recognizable from the last time you saw it." Holding tightly to the back of the chair helped conceal my shaking legs as my words came faster. "There are farms and ranches in every direction, new roads, trains coming in …" Tears filled my eyes, and I pretended to look out the window. It was dark outside now. No breathtaking sunset—only my distorted reflection cast by the kerosene light on the glass, laughing at me. "You'll have quite a new scene to paint before you head—"

"Mary, stop." Daniel stood behind me, his hands on my waist.

An unexpected shiver ran up my back. Was the woman encased in the window a cruel reminder of my foolishness? To actually believe I could trust … and fall in love again?

His words were soft. "The truth is the Globe sent me here because everyone knew how miserable I was not being with you."

My breaths came in short gasps. Was he telling the truth? Or was he only wanting a woman … any woman?

"Mary." He took my hand and turned me toward him. "Please know this. I love you like I have loved no other. And I think you love me as well."

At that moment, it didn't matter that Wesley watched with wide eyes. The two of us stood holding hands, standing on the precipice of another world, unwilling to let the other go.

In my dreams, the words had replayed in my mind like an old, familiar song. I released them as though opening my palms and setting a captive bird free. "I do love you, Daniel McKenzie, possibly from the first moment I saw you."

He lifted my hand and gently kissed my fingers. My lips longed for his, and I knew Wesley would need to fall asleep soon.

＊＊＊＊＊

The next morning came quickly, and I hoped Daniel had slept comfortably in the half-finished barn. The door and windows weren't set, but the roof was complete, and fresh hay covered the ground.

Excitement surged within me when a knock sounded on the soddy. I smoothed my hair and opened the door.

"Good morning, Mary." He gazed at me with eyes full of love.

"And good morning to you, sir. Did you sleep well?" As I plucked a strand of hay from his shirt pocket, he held my hand over his chest. My legs weakened.

"I slept very well, especially dreaming about you."

Jim brayed from the yard, breaking the almost hypnotic spell that was forming between us.

"But Jim may be asking why he was second fiddle to me for a spot in the barn."

The scent of frying bacon and flapjacks wafted from the stove. A hearty breakfast waited in anticipation of the Cooleys' early arrival and another day of hard work.

Just as the sun lifted over the hill, not two, but four horses approached. A stocky cow swaggered behind one of the horses, tethered by a rope like an anchor to a ship. *Stanley Cooley.* It was about time he paid me a visit. And Anna. Wesley would be thrilled.

"Mornin', Mary." Stanley tipped his hat. "Thought I'd better see for myself if the boys' workmanship is up to my standards."

"They're fine builders. And truly, thank you for the barn and the milking cow."

The cow looked at me with her big, brown eyes. "She's amazing." I rubbed her long ears as her tail tried its best to swish away pesky flies.

"Stanley Cooley," I said, "I'd like you to meet a friend of mine, Daniel McKenzie."

Daniel shook his hand. "It's a pleasure, Mr. Cooley."

"Likewise," Stanley said. "Hear you're a reporter." His usual squint seemed to size Daniel up from boots to hat.

"Partially. Mostly a landscape journalist. Somewhat of a dying breed, so they say. I work with the writers and photographers then paint the subjects for the paper."

"Then you're an artist?" Stanley asked. "Hmm." He rubbed his hand over a stubbly beard. "Boys, better get to work before the sun cooks you alive."

"How about some breakfast first?" I offered. "Flapjacks and bacon are waiting."

Nate and Ben started for the house with Anna and Wesley trotting behind.

"I've been outvoted," Stanley grumbled. "But it sure smells good."

* * * * *

By late afternoon, the barn was complete with the added help of Daniel and Stanley. The cow occupied the first stall, and Wesley led Jim into the other.

"I don't think Jim likes it," Wesley whispered to me. "He looks awfully sad in there."

"He's fine. I'm sure—"

A loud braying echoed in the barn.

"See, he likes it better outside where he's free." Wesley stepped toward the barn door, but I caught him by his shirt collar.

"You leave him be. Those poor men have worked for two days."

Wesley wiggled out of my grasp. "Maybe when he gets to know Becky, he won't mind being locked up next to her."

"Becky?" I looked around, wondering what I had missed.

"Me and Anna named the cow. It's a good name. Just like Tom Sawyer's friend, Becky Thatcher."

"Anna didn't *say* that name, did she?"

"No, but she likes it too. Remember, I can tell what she's thinking." Wesley ran off to play with his friend.

Stanley tapped me on the shoulder. "Do you see over there?"

Just beyond the house, Daniel had propped a small easel earlier that morning with a swatch of canvas flapping lazily in the breeze. A wooden box filled with brushes and paint lay open in the grass. Next to the box was Anna. She was on her hands and knees, peering into the box as if she'd discovered a treasure. Delicately, she lifted a brush and ran her fingers through the bristles. She raised it to her cheek, and, like petting a kitten, ran it over her skin, back and forth, back and forth.

When Daniel stepped from the house, she dropped the brush in the grass and stood.

"Do you like to paint?" Daniel kneeled to her eye level. "I can teach you if you'd like." He lifted the brush to Anna.

She shrugged and held her arms to her chest.

"He's scaring her," Stanley grumbled and took a step toward his daughter.

I raised my hand to stop him. "No, wait."

Anna slowly offered her hand and accepted the brush. While Wesley climbed and jumped from the nearby plow time and time again, she watched Daniel prepare his palette—brilliant colors like the promise of a rainbow after a storm. As Daniel brought the blank canvas to life, Anna mimicked each stroke and swirl of his brush like a shadow cast beside the artist in the late afternoon sun.

I pretended not to notice, but Stanley wiped tears from his eyes.

He must be thinking of Flora ... and what his and Anna's life could have been.

Ben pulled a wadded kerchief from his vest pocket and handed it to his father. "Time to head home, Pa. Got plenty to do at the ranch."

Stanley nodded and called Anna to join them.

She frowned at him, then held her brush up to Daniel.

"It's yours, sweetheart." He wrapped her fingers around the handle. "Bring it with you next time. It will be your turn to paint."

Anna bobbed her head before she turned and ran to her father. He kissed the top of her head and plopped her onto the pony.

"Mary." Stanley straightened his hat. "Enjoy that barn and take good care of the cow."

"We will. Becky will be milked each morning and evening."

Wesley shook Stanley's hand. "And Jim'll learn to like the barn soon enough."

"You're a fine young man." Stanley slapped his thigh with his hat and chuckled. "Good animal namer too. Becky and Jim ... hmm."

Daniel shook hands with each of the men. "It's good to see a group of respectful and kind neighbors. That's how it ought to be. Mary and I both appreciate what you've done lately." He pointed to the barn. "Glad the past is gone."

"You planning to stay on?" Stanley questioned Daniel, then glanced in my direction. "Being a friend of Mary's and all."

"I hope to," Daniel said.

Stanley straightened his hat. "But sleeping in the barn with the animals isn't the best accommodation. The hotel or boarding house in town might have a room if you plan to stay on longer."

"The Globe is renting a room for my colleague and me. Hardy's been getting familiar with the area, and then we head south toward Perry. After that, we'll make our way back here. Might want to include your ranch in the story if that's okay with you."

Stanley tugged on the brim of his hat and didn't respond. These Cooleys were a private bunch for sure.

"In fact, best be on my way before dark. I have a close friend in town I'd like to see. Mr. Bartholomew Reid. You might know him. He's an attorney." Daniel mentioned Bart's name matter-of-factly, and I had to conceal my smile.

"May have heard the name, but can't recall anything past that," Nate said.

"Me neither," Ben added. "Those lawyers have sprung up like weeds."

Stanley huffed and adjusted his hat again. "Too many to count."

"He's a fine one if you ever need someone on the honest side of the law."

The men rode away without another word.

"That was witty, Mr. McKenzie."

"Don't want the Cooleys to get too comfortable. Let them know we're smarter than they are. I'd like to believe their intentions are only good moving forward. And that Anna, she's precious. But it's a rough world, Mary, and you know that's especially true out here."

"You're right. But I feel more comfortable with the Andersons on one side of my property and the Cooleys on the other."

Creases—or in Mother's words, worry lines—ran across Daniel's forehead.

"We'll be fine." I tried to reassure him.

His brows pinched together. "It pains me to leave the two of you even for a little while, but I need to get this story—"

"I know how to use the gun if needed. Besides, Tom's brother Roy said more lawmen are being assigned to the territory. Necessary since things are changing fast."

Daniel took my hands and pulled me closer. "Now that we're together, I don't want to let you go."

With my arms wrapped around his waist and my head resting on his chest, I listened to the rhythm of his heart. For the first time in my life, I was fully alive.

CHAPTER 39

Mary ~ Trouble, July 10, 1894

I bolted upright at the sound of footsteps outside the window. Could it be an animal? The wind? Maybe it was only my imagination playing cruel tricks.

Wesley lay at my side, eyes closed and small body curled in his usual position under the quilt. I heard the sound again and held my breath. Doolin gang? Outlaws? Black and white images ran through my mind of the evil faces posted on the yellowed sheets hanging outside Roy's store. Daniel? Surely, he wouldn't come in the middle of the night and startle me like this.

In the darkness, the faint silhouette of the rifle reminded me the gun leaned against the wall next to the door—out of reach from my bed. I cursed myself for my stupidity. I slipped out of bed and tiptoed toward the gun. Perhaps Jim had pushed the barn door open, or the wind helped to lift the latch, and he was wandering in the yard. Even though it was possible, my instincts told me otherwise.

Willing myself to remain still and listen, it felt like forever next to the closed door, the heavy gun resting on my hip. Most likely an animal, but I needed to make sure the mule wasn't out.

The blackness of the night met me as the door inched open. The moon was only a sliver, and the darkness was heavy, forcing me to blink a few times to focus. The outline of the barn—and what appeared to be its closed door—rose out of the ground. Holding the gun close to my chest, I stepped outside and turned in a slow circle.

"Anyone out here?" My voice wavered. "If so, my gun won't ask who you are." I was probably talking to a passing coyote.

When only the wind answered back, I went back inside and crawled into bed next to my son. Sleep escaped me even as daylight slipped in the window. My mind rehearsed the question, *What—or who—had paid me an unwelcomed visit?*

While Wesley slept, I wrapped myself in an extra blanket and went outside. It had not been my imagination. Footprints ran along the side of the house where the soil held to any sparse moisture. Not an animal's, but clearly those of a man.

At breakfast, over a shared bowl of oatmeal, my thoughts were troubled about who would trespass on my property and be bold enough to sneak around the house at night. Not wanting to scare Wesley, I said nothing of the happenings. Surely the Cooleys weren't up to no good again. To be sure, I decided to pay them a visit and ask for myself.

* * * * *

At first, Stanley was offended when questioned about his sons' whereabouts the previous night. But when he considered what I had been through and the reality of possible danger, he offered to have both of the boys watch over my home until Daniel returned.

"They can take turns sleeping in the barn. No one is going to want to cross my sons if anyone is being threatened."

"I appreciate your concern and the offer. But we'll be all right. Who knows, it could have been someone who lost his way in the dark."

"And you believe that?" Stanley shot me a stern look. "Could it have been that Daniel friend of yours?"

"Absolutely not." My arms crossed my chest in defiance. "He is *not* that kind of man. Besides, he won't be back for close to a week."

"I don't know." He scanned the horizon as we stood on his front porch, as though watching for a suspicious person to come along at any time. "My gut's telling me something isn't right." He sniffed the air like a hunting dog. "But I can't place it just yet." Even though Stanley couldn't have been much older than fifty, he had a fatherly sort of way, even toward me. "You never know. A man does things he's never thought possible when he loves a woman."

Now I gave him a look. "What kind of things?"

"Mary, don't play the fool. Anyone can see Daniel's in love with you." He wagged his finger in the air. "And don't act like you haven't got the same feelings for him."

I grinned at the scolding. He was right, and I could hardly wait for Daniel to return.

"At least take one of the dogs home with you. They bark up a storm whenever someone steps on the property." A large, black one with a white spot between its eyes and one crooked ear raised its head from where it lay dutifully near Stanley.

"So I noticed. That one nearly scared Wesley and me to death this morning."

Stanley nudged the mutt with his boot. "Just her way of saying hello."

* * * * *

My nerves calmed over the next few days when everything seemed back to normal. It helped having the dog tied up in the front yard. As though she understood her duty even at my home, she remained watchful and alert, just as Stanley promised.

Wesley wanted to name her, but I reminded him she wasn't ours to keep and would soon go back to the Cooleys. When he asked why we had the dog in the first place, I sidestepped a bit, mentioning she was only here to keep us aware of coyotes and wolves if they roamed too close to the house.

* * * * *

The next day, after returning from a visit to play with baby Lila, Wesley and I were shocked to find the dog hunched and growling in the yard.

"Stay away from her, Wesley. She's acting like she doesn't know us."

Stepping toward her with caution, I spoke softly. "It's all right, girl. We aren't going to hurt you." I knelt down and unwrapped the remaining part of a sandwich from lunch at the Andersons. At first, she growled, then whimpered when she smelled the smoked turkey.

"Here you go." The torn piece of meat invited her to sprawl out on her stomach and devour the food.

"Something scared her, Mama. She never acts that way."

"I think you're right. But she sure was hungry. Why don't you fetch some jerky from the kitchen?"

Wesley had barely stepped inside when he let out a yell.

The house was in shambles. The table and chairs were overturned. The bed was ransacked, and the linens lay in a heap. Food was spilled and scattered across the dirt floor, and the books—all but one—had been knocked off the ledge and lay haphazardly and smudged in the dirt. The photograph of my mother gazed at me through broken glass as though a spider had cast its web across her exquisite face.

Wesley's mouth hung open, and he began to cry. "My books are ruined." He lifted the newest, *Beautiful Joe*, as torn pages fluttered to the ground.

My heart ached for Wesley, but I couldn't pull my eyes from the corner of the room. My painting lay crumpled and torn, the center punched through by an angry foot or fist. My shaking hands picked up what remained of the drooping, lifeless canvas.

Split nearly in two, my rocking chair from William was splintered and broken, an ax dropped by its side. No wonder the dog was growling. The poor thing was tied up and couldn't defend our home.

My arms wrapped protectively around Wesley. His body shook as he tried to catch his breath, and I held him tighter. Tears poured down his face and soaked into my blouse.

"It's going to be fine," I said, stroking his back. "You're all right." Although my words were directed to my son, the reassurance was desperately needed for both of us at that very moment.

*****

"No more arguing!" Stanley slammed his fist on his kitchen table, making the cups clatter and spill coffee onto the tablecloth. "Someone has something against you, and they aren't messing around."

Whether the destruction of my house was against me personally or my home happened to be in the path of someone's rage—like the dangerous tornadoes that ravaged the plains and anything in their paths—we had avoided all of that to this point. I didn't plan to argue with Stanley.

"I'm going into town and demand the sheriff get out here and do something about what's happened." He paced across the living room. "If the law won't help, then I'll gather up my own posse."

Ben stepped forward. "Pa, let us go. You don't like going where there's other folks."

"We'll go right away," Nate added.

Stanley faced his boys with a somber expression. "I appreciate all you've done for me, especially since Flora died. It hasn't been easy for you either. In a way, you've lost both your mothers just like I've lost both my wives." He pulled his kerchief from his pocket and swiped it across his face. "But it's time for me to start acting like a grown man again." He looked at me with an odd expression. "We've got a good friend here in Mrs. Roberts. And she's more like family now, her and her little boy."

He headed for the back door. "And we're not going to let anything happen to the people we love." He lifted his hat from the hook. "Boys, saddle up. The Cooleys are heading to town."

* * * * *

After the sheriff circled the house a few times and kicked aside a broken dish on the floor, he pulled a small, leather notebook from his shirt pocket and made a few notes.

"Sorry you've got this mess to clean up, ma'am." He removed his hat and scratched his head. "The more people that come, the more trouble we have. But I can't say I've seen this sort of problem. Did you say anything has gone missing?"

"No, it doesn't appear someone was stealing from me. Whoever did this was evidently mad more than anything else."

"We did have a band of troublemakers a while ago. Nothing too dangerous but taking some things here and there and vandalizing property. It could be a few of them stayed around."

Stanley righted the table. "Either way, I expect you to keep a close eye out here. That's your job after all."

"That's partly true, Mr. Cooley. But there's an entire town under my jurisdiction. Believe me, there's plenty to keep me busy with the saloons alone. Some rough characters come through these parts."

"I appreciate you taking the time to ride all the way out here." I nodded at Stanley. "Isn't that right, Mr. Cooley?"

Stanley muttered something and stomped out the door.

"Tell you what I can do, Mrs. Roberts. The government has placed a few new lawmen in the area to help with the overflow of work. There's a new man who started last week. I'll tell him to check on you as often as possible. That should give you some peace of mind."

"It certainly would. Thank you."

Outside, the sheriff offered his hand to Stanley, who only waved him off and walked away.

After the sheriff rode away, Stanley helped me tidy the house.

"You're a mean old thing, Mr. Cooley," I teased, dotting a fingerfull of spilled flour on his nose. "But I like you that way."

* * * * *

When Daniel returned, it was impossible to assure him everything was all right.

"What do you mean he can send someone to keep an eye out here? You're in the middle of nowhere." He picked up the rifle and looked down the sight line. "You have to protect yourself."

"But I can't walk around with a gun hooked to my skirt." This was not the homecoming I'd imagined, but his concern and frustration were understood since he wasn't here to protect us.

"I'm sleeping in here," he said and then averted his eyes. "I mean ... on the floor. If that's okay with you."

"That should be all right. Just for a night or two until things simmer down."

Over supper, we tried to keep the conversation away from the damage to the house and our hearts. Most of the items could be replaced or repaired, except for my painting and the rocking chair. I didn't want William to know what happened to his handcrafted gift. I had brushed away the loose shards of glass from my mother's picture so she would continue to have a presence in my home.

Daniel told us about all he had seen on his travels to the south, then looping back to the west toward the northern part of the territory. Towns, farms, and ranches covered the territory like a patchwork quilt. Fences and roads crisscrossed the land—the thread tying it together. He flipped through his sketchbook and showed us the wealth of drawings—wide-stretching landscapes, some hilly and tree-filled, others flat and barren.

The detailed sketches of the people he encountered were fascinating. Young, old, black, white, men, and women. Almost all appeared tired and poor. Amazing how hard times showed on the faces of those who must face it daily.

Daniel and George Hardy proved a strong team. Though not the entertaining companion like Finn, George was a master photographer and captured the essence of the people and how they had changed the landscape forever.

"The hard part will be deciding which photographs to paint. My boss will have plenty..." His voice trailed off. "I'm sorry. Didn't mean to sound insensitive. The Globe will get the quality story they sent George and me to do."

"Makes perfect sense." An encouraging smile for a hardworking and dedicated man would have been the proper response, but it was no use. "Now that you're finished, when are you leaving?"

Wesley excused himself from the table. "I'm gonna talk to Jim and Becky." He lifted the lantern from the hook. "You two need to talk."

Daniel and I couldn't help but grin. "It's dark out there, so you stay close, young man," I called after him.

* * * * *

The time to talk was helpful. Daniel and I shared our concerns, worries, and even fears. We also talked about our hopes and dreams. It was apparent both of us longed to be together and couldn't imagine a future without the other. How we would make that happen would take more time.

"You and Wesley could come back to Boston with me." He reached across the table and laid his hand on mine. "I have a good job, and you could teach, but …" He lowered his head.

"What's wrong, Daniel?"

"You have a gift to teach, and the children love you. But if you want to be a teacher, then we couldn't marry, or you'd most likely be dismissed from the profession. That's just the way of things." One corner of his mouth turned upward. "I hadn't planned it this way, but I suppose that was somewhat of a proposal."

The jumble of emotions and thoughts kept me silent until they had time to settle in my mind. "I'm not sure how to respond … if that was a proposal." I slipped my hand away from his. "First of all, being a widow less than a year, it wouldn't be proper for me to consider marrying until more time has passed."

"My sincere apologies. I should have—"

"And you're right. I do love the children, and I am a good teacher. That's why it works here. No one cares—at least until the school system becomes formalized—if I'm married or not. I even make our own lessons and calendar. As long as the children are learning and happy going to school, that's all that matters." I tucked my hands in my lap to keep them from shaking. "Besides, leaving here and living in a big city on the other side of the country wouldn't fit."

"For me either. At least not anymore." Daniel's voice was soft, but his words were spoken with assurance. "Even though my home has been the city for a long time, it's different in the West." He stood and circled the table. "Here, I can see forever. It's easier to breathe, and the sun shines brighter." He knelt beside me and looked into my eyes. "It would be hard for most to understand, but coming here has set me free, especially when we're together."

My fingers touched his cheek and then ran across his lips. "I'm free as well. Especially when I'm with you."

He pulled me closer, and our lips met. We were together at last. And truly free.

* * * * *

The tender moment ended abruptly. Outside, Wesley screamed, and the pungent smell of smoke seeped into the house. The dog barked wildly and tugged at its rope as Daniel ran out the door. I followed, nearly falling over the remains of the rocking chair.

"Wesley!" My scream shot into the darkness. The only light was from the flames shooting from the roof of the barn, lashing like a dragon's tongue in a storybook. But the smoke and stench burned my eyes and nostrils. This was not a story or my imagination. This was real.

"Wesley!" I screamed again and ran toward the barn.

Daniel pushed the wide door aside on its hinges and ducked inside. As I tried to follow, a burst of heat nearly threw me to the ground, stumbling and gasping for air.

As I called their names, everything fell into slow motion. The crackling of the wood and sizzling of the tarpaper from the roof was the only response.

I righted myself in time to see Daniel rush from the barn with Wesley over his shoulder. He shoved my son into my arms. When he spoke, the angst in his voice erupted from a horrible and dark place. "He's all right, but both of you need to get away from here." Daniel turned and ran back into the barn.

"No!" I called after him. Terror from some unknown place ripped through my body.

"Mama!" Wesley tried to wriggle from my arms. "Jim and Becky!"

My arm went around Wesley's waist and held him in place. "You can't go after them." My voice cracked, and the tears came in a flood.

Protect Daniel, dear Lord, please ...

It must have been seconds, but it felt like time stopped altogether.

A moment later, Jim emerged from the barn, snorting and tossing his head as he trotted into the open air.

"Where are they, Mama?" Wesley buried his face in my lap.

I wanted to bury my face as well, fall away to another world where evil couldn't find me. But as I held tightly to Wesley, a figure staggered from the door, tugging a confused and scared cow.

"Stay put!" I yelled at Wesley above the roar of the fire. My command was firm, and then I ran to Daniel.

He could barely walk, staggering from side to side, but I knew he wouldn't leave the animal to be consumed by the smoke and fire. I took the rope from his hand. Becky resisted my pulls and dug her front hooves into the dirt. In that instance, the compromised barn moaned and leaned in our direction like a looming monster from a horrific dream. The reality that it would fall in our direction and crush whatever was in its way flashed in my mind. Dropping the rope, leaving Becky, and pulling Daniel to safety was the only option.

Maybe it was the air or seeing her friend Jim, but as if released from a giant slingshot, the cow lunged forward and sprinted toward the field. With my shoulder positioned under Daniel's arm, I half dragged him away from the fire.

"Wesley, get some water and dishcloths." I pushed out the words through the soot caught in my throat.

Daniel fell onto his hands and knees and coughed violently. The back of his neck was blackened, and his hair was matted, thick with ash.

"Here, Mama." Wesley set a bucket of water next to me. He handed me the cloths, and I dipped them in the water. I tried to place a dampened cloth on Daniel's neck, but he winced. When his coughing subsided, he rolled onto his side and drank from the bucket.

There was nothing we could do except watch the fire consume the remainder of the barn. The three of us held one another tightly, and with a raspy voice, Daniel prayed for us—thanking the Lord we were alive.

* * * * *

It hadn't taken long for the remnants of smoke to reach the Cooley ranch and, before we knew it, Nate, Ben, Stanley, and Anna were at our side.

"I'm sorry about the barn. You worked so hard building it." I hugged Ben as the dwindling flames illuminated his face in the darkness.

"We'll build you another." He returned the hug. "That can be replaced."

He was right. A barn could be raised again. Jim and Becky would have another shelter, and the burns on Daniel's neck would heal—though the next few weeks would be painful.

"Aloe. That's what we'll need to get from Adahy first thing in the morning." Stanley helped Daniel remove his charred shirt.

"You know of him?" I asked. "He was the one who healed the Andersons' baby."

"I've known Adahy for years. He's cured many of my ranch hands from various ailments. He used to be further south with the Cherokee until they got moved to the Eastern Wasteland. Poor soul. He isn't entirely part of his tribe since he's chosen to help the whites, and he doesn't have the legal right to be part of the white man's world."

When Nate joined the group, he held a broken lantern, his shirtsleeve wrapped around his hand. "It's still piping hot, but it looks like it could have started the fire."

"Oh, Wesley, didn't you fasten it to the hook? You know how careful you have to be around hay." Scolding him at the moment was wrong, but he needed to understand the seriousness of his actions.

His little body shuddered. "I don't remember. I was gonna go in the barn. But then I saw fireflies in the grass over by the plow." His eyes welled with tears. "Something in the barn made a strange noise, and when I opened the door … it was all smoky."

"The boy's telling the truth, Mary." Stanley pointed to the plow resting near the garden. "Son, is that your lantern over there?"

Wesley wiped his nose on his shirtsleeve. "Yes, sir."

"Then whose is this?" Nate held the lantern higher. "It was on the side of the barn, just outside the window, or at least, where the window used to be."

Daniel stood slowly as if every movement took great effort. I feared he might be injured worse than we thought. "Let me see that, Nate." He turned the lantern around a few times. "This doesn't belong to you, Mary."

"What are you saying, Daniel?" His silence scared me.

Stanley stepped forward. "He's saying someone set this fire on purpose." He pulled his pistol from his holster and cocked the gun. "Whoever it is … they ain't playing around."

✶ ✶ ✶ ✶ ✶

Stanley insisted we stay at his home for the rest of the night. None of us argued as the inside of my house reeked of smoke. We were all exhausted, and Daniel, though quiet, was noticeably in pain. Wesley was determined to bring along Jim, Becky, and the dog, so our short walk to the Cooley's turned into a journey.

When we climbed the staircase and headed to separate bedrooms, I kissed Daniel on the cheek. It wasn't a proper thank you for saving my son's life and rescuing the animals from a cruel death, but that night we didn't need any other words.

We knew our love was enough.

CHAPTER 40

Mary ~ Past, July 18, 1894

Perhaps it was the featherbed and soft pillows, but I didn't wake until the sun had been up for several hours. A survey of the room showed it to be clean and orderly, with fresh linens hanging next to the washbasin and a faded quilt draped over the arm of a chair. Like the rooms downstairs, it was void of any personal touches, but it was welcoming. It was as though the house was patiently waiting for happiness to return, to slip in its windows like a ray of sunshine.

I soaked a cloth in the basin and held it to my face. My hair smelled of smoke, and soot defined faint wrinkles I hadn't noticed before. A frown caused the lines to deepen. *Who was so intent on harming my property that they would go so far as to kill?*

In the confusion of the night, I had forgotten to pack a change of clothes. Since there wouldn't be women's clothes at the ranch, I reluctantly slipped on the smoke-filled skirt and blouse and made my way downstairs. The kitchen was quiet. An extra plate, filled with biscuits and gravy, waited on the table. Next to it was a note.

Mary,

Stanley, Ben, and I headed to town early to get the sheriff out here as soon as possible. Good to get a formal report and have him investigate what we suspect. Also, I'm paying a visit to my attorney friend, Bart. We might need his help once we get to the bottom of this. We brought the wagon to get more barn supplies. Stanley is set to replace the other one right away. It's not worth arguing with him. I already tried.

It's best you stay at the ranch with the children and Nate. That would give me the peace of mind all of us need under the circumstances.

All my love,

Daniel

P.S. By the way, you are beautiful when you're sleeping.

I folded the note and tucked it inside my sleeve. Outside the window, the children rode bareback on Dusty. Anna sat behind Wesley, her arms wrapped around his waist and her dark curls dancing in the breeze. As the pony trotted between the house and barn, they bounced up and down, both smiling as if they hadn't a care in the world.

I sighed. *As it should be.*

*****

Though the house was immaculate compared to the constant dirt and dust in the sod house, I tried to keep myself busy for a good part of the morning sweeping the floors and cleaning the kitchen. The smell of smoke lingered in the bed linens. After gathering them into a giant white ball, I strung them along the clothesline and hoped a strong breeze would chase the stench away.

As the morning wore on and turned to noon, my skin itched from my dirty clothes. I released the top button on my collar and dug my nails into my skin. Surely no one would mind if I got fresh clothes from home and hurried back. Besides, it might take several hours for them to return.

Nate was scrubbing the water troughs in the large corral. His shirtsleeves were soaked up to his elbows, and tousled hair fell into his eyes.

"That's hard work." I peeked through the railing. "But I'd consider taking a bath in one of those just to get rid of the grime from last night."

"Be my guest." Nate stepped aside and bowed. "Madame, your bath is ready."

For a brief moment, we allowed ourselves to laugh. It felt good.

"I won't be gone long. Going to my house to get fresh clothes."

Nate's smile faded. "You shouldn't be going there until the others get back." He looked toward the path leading to the house. "Can't be much longer."

"Honestly, it won't take but a few minutes. Just some clothes and a few other things we might need. Daniel would probably love to have his painting box. Might help take his mind off the pain from the burns until Adam can work his magic."

"But I was told to keep—"

"Nate." My chin raised. "Everyone's concern is well-intended and appreciated. The situation is serious, but I am a grown woman. Besides, there shouldn't be any danger in daylight."

Nate tossed the scrub brush into the dirt. "Then I'll come along right after the troughs are filled. In this heat, the cattle get meaner than Pa without enough water." He unlatched his holster and handed me his revolver. "Take this. You know how to use it, don't ya?"

I nodded and took the gun, hoping that wouldn't be necessary.

✳ ✳ ✳ ✳ ✳

The recent storm clouds had passed by without a hint of rain—stingy to share even though their bellies were full of much-needed moisture. Cracks cut across the dirt, and the green fields of spring were quickly turning brown and lifeless—reminding me that almost a year had passed since my adventure to go West began.

Wesley, Anna, and the black dog tagged along as I made my way down the path and up the rise toward home. The air was heavy and made the short walk feel twice as long.

At least water still ran through the creek bed. As we neared the path leading to the water's edge, the children and dog darted off. Soon, there was the sound of splashes in the lazy water that pooled around the bend. Although it was tempting to join them, the thought of clean clothes made me quicken my pace to get home.

Even though the smell of stale smoke lingered inside the house, it felt wonderful to cast aside my dirty blouse and skirt. Those could be washed later when the heat waned. I unfolded Daniel's note, read the last line again, and laid it on the nightstand along with the gun.

He thinks I'm beautiful.

Smiling, I loosened my hair and ran my brush through the tangles as I gazed out the window. To the left were the remains of the charred barn. Except for faint smoke rising from the cinders, it lay lifeless and defeated.

To its side was the garden. Untouched by the heat from the fire, it was miraculously alive. Stalks of corn and sunflowers towered over clusters of lettuce, frilly carrot leaves, and tangles of tomato, cucumber, and pepper plants. Runner beans crawled up sticks, poking from the ground like teepees. Pumpkin and squash vines coiled in the dirt, silent snakes waiting for autumn.

As I slipped on my cotton dress, a rider approached beyond the garden and at the far edge of the field. Daniel? No, but the horse was vaguely familiar ... although from where I couldn't remember. The rider drew closer until he halted near the hitching post. The brim of the man's hat was low and covered most of his face. My heart raced. Could this be the one making all the trouble? And to be so bold to return in the light of day? Before reaching for the rifle, something shiny on his shirt caught my eye.

The sheriff. Glad he decided to come today. Surely, Stanley had something do with that.

Quickly fastening the buttons on my dress, I hurried toward the door, but when it opened, I gasped and stepped back.

"Mary Roberts," the man fairly purred as he twirled his hat in his hands. "It's been too long. Much too long."

My mouth hung open until I caught my breath. "Sheriff Murphy. What are you doing here?"

"Come on now, Mary, you promised to call me David, remember?" A sick feeling overcame me at the touch of his hand under my chin. "It's mighty good to see you. You look wonderful. Good as ever." His head jerked toward the smoldering wood. "Although your barn isn't looking well. May I come in?"

I reluctantly stepped to the side and motioned him in, twisting my hands together, unsure what to say or do next. "Sorry. It's just that you surprised me. I never expected to see—"

"Me out here?" He glanced around the room. "Got reassigned. Promoted, you might say. With the population growing such as it is in these parts, there'd been advertisements for more sheriffs and deputies. They figured a solid and qualified man like me would be a good fit for such a lawless place." He was quiet for a moment as he surveyed every inch of the room. "Besides, it was time for a change of scenery. Not much happening these days around Adair."

"But we already have a sheriff."

He shot me a hard look, then his face relaxed. "I've been appointed to cover the areas around Enid and anywhere else that might need an extra lawman for the time being." He looked out the window in the direction of the barn. "Looks like you might need help."

"Happened yes … yesterday. Didn't take long to destroy the entire thing."

"Just the structure?" The expression on his face was unreadable.

"Our mule and cow barely got out. By the grace of God, Wesley wasn't harmed. Daniel got them out just before it collapsed."

His face darkened as he stepped closer. "Daniel?"

My skin crawled with the memory of the last time Sheriff Murphy had been this close—his strong hand digging into my arm. I moved to the other side of the table to put some distance between us and forced a grin. "A friend. Luckily, he was in the area and able to help."

"At night?" He smirked and then shook his head back and forth as if he found it amusing. When he stopped, his body stiffened, and he had a crazed look in his eyes that scared me. How did he know the fire happened at night?

With that thought, like an unexpected flood crashing through the walls of a canyon, the mere presence of the man was suffocating … terrifying. I forced myself to breathe and blinked hard to make sure he was actually in front of me. But his giant-like stature beneath my low ceiling and in my modest home confirmed he was no apparition.

Suddenly, everything made sense. Noises outside the window, footprints in the dirt the next morning, overturned furniture, the smashed rocking chair, torn painting. And the growling dog. The dog who was at the creek with the children and would be of no use.

My eyes shifted to the rifle poised next to the door and the pistol on the nightstand. As usual, David's gun rested on his hip.

He set the fire and almost killed my son. I was sure of it. As though bundling my nerves with a piece of twine, I willed myself to remain calm. "It might be best if you come back when my neighbors are here to help. I'm sure they'd like to meet you. Mr. Cooley has strong sons cleaning up the mess, but it will take more than them alone."

He was silent as his eyes traveled the length of my body, forcing me to relive a putrid memory.

"Good day, David." My words came with as much courage as I could muster.

"Wanting to get rid of me already?" His mustache twitched in an awkward way as if trying to control words waiting to spew from his mouth. "You're not being hospitable, now are you?"

As he stepped even closer, the stench of whiskey gave me more reason to fear him. "I've come all this way." He seized my hand. "The least you can do is—"

I pulled away, but his other hand grasped and dug into my arm. "You're hurting me. Let me go!"

He forced his mouth onto mine, and his bristly face scratched my skin. I tried to shove him away, but he held me tighter. For a moment, I was back underwater, unable to breathe, yet my body demanded me to kick and claw my way to the surface. I broke free and stumbled against the stove.

"Please don't do this." I pushed my hair from my eyes. "I haven't done anything to you."

He cocked his head as though my words were absurd. "You haven't? You've broken my heart. Isn't that worth something? Am I not good enough for you?"

He paced the room and then kicked the wall with his heavy, leather boots. Small dirt clods loosened from the wall and tumbled onto the floor. I knew in an instant he could destroy everything I had left in this world. My fingers wrapped around the fire poker shaft, but I froze when he stopped at the nightstand and lifted the note from Daniel.

He raised his head and glowered. "You whore! Your husband hasn't been in the ground a year, and you're already in bed with another man."

"That's not true!" I shouted. "How dare you—"

His large fist slammed on the table. "You could have become my wife—a respectable woman. But now you aren't worth more than spittle. I should have let you drown in that river." His face contorted, and then he lunged at me.

With every thread of my being, I swung the poker. It cracked him across the forehead, making him stagger and fall to one knee. He held his face as blood oozed between his fingers. I stared for a moment, shocked at my action. Then, as if someone whispered in my ear to flee, I scooted around him, took the pistol from the table, and ran out the door.

In an effort to run as fast as possible, my legs were defiant as if in a nightmare. Stumbling and unable to catch myself, my palms drove into the dirt. Then my eyes caught the sheriff holding himself against the doorframe. He seemed dazed, trying to focus through the blood dripping into his eyes. I stood, but before my feet could move, he charged after me.

I fumbled with the pistol and tried to raise it—at least to scare him. But he overpowered me and threw me back to the ground. A searing pain cut through my arm, and my fingers went numb. The gun slipped from my hand and skidded across the hard ground into the weeds.

He stepped back. "I'll show you what a man does to a woman

who's worth nothing." He sneered and then let out an eerie cackle. "This is how you can pay me back for saving your life."

I tried to hoist myself up, but the pain was so intense I collapsed. From the corner of my eye, something moved in the field. *Anna.* She was running toward the house from the direction of the creek, her mouth open and eyes wild.

"Run, Anna! Get help!" I cried out. She stopped, completely motionless. Only the browned grasses swayed around her legs.

"Who is that?" David growled and pulled out his gun.

"Leave her alone," I begged.

"What are ya doing here, girl? Go on." He raised his gun and shot into the air.

Anna remained still.

"What's wrong with you? Get out of here." This time, he pointed the gun in her direction.

I screamed and tried to kick him. "You're scaring her. Surely you wouldn't shoot a child. Besides, she can't speak."

"Good, she won't be able to tell what I'm going to do to you."

"No!" a small voice called out. *Anna's voice.*

David waved the gun wildly in the air. "Thought she couldn't talk. You're a liar as well as a whore."

With my last bit of resolve, I screamed again, "Get Nate! Run, Anna!" As she ran away, the only thing to do was pray. *Oh, God, please let me live to hear that child's voice again.*

David stood over me, his long shadow casting darkness across my body as though I were already in the grave. "Now, like I was saying." He rubbed his hands together and then tore the front of my dress.

Another voice I knew so well rang out, followed by the barking of a dog. "Leave her be!"

David turned. "Now, where did you come from? Sneaking around like that."

Wesley stood in front of the house with the black dog at his side, the rifle raised and aimed.

"Son, don't be stupid." David took a step forward and stopped.

"Put that gun down. You don't want to hurt anyone."

"Leave my mama alone, or I'll shoot you."

David shook his head as if my son had totally misjudged his intentions. "Wesley, no one's gonna harm your mama. Me and her are old friends. You and me too. Remember catching all those fish together?"

"I remember you teaching me how to shoot a gun, and I'm not afraid to do it." His small body shook, but he held tightly, one hand on the barrel, the other resting on the trigger. "Get off our property right now, or I'll have to kill you."

"You know if you shoot me, they'll put you in jail. It's a serious offense to kill a lawman." He nodded as though agreeing with himself. "They'd most likely hang you."

The clicking of his tongue reminded me of the old clock in Mother's kitchen, plodding on through the day. Could this be my son's last day on earth, as well as my own?

"Horrible way to die, Son, horrible." The dog snarled. "Now put that gun down. It would be a shame to have to shoot you or your dog in self-defense, now wouldn't it?"

"Don't listen to him, Wesley," I called out. "He's only trying to scare you. He won't hurt the dog, and he certainly won't shoot you."

"You're not in the best position to be saying much right now." A wad of spittle landed on the ground right next to my face. "Are you, Mary?"

Over the rise, a plume of dust filled the air as five horses and riders raced down the hill.

David glanced at me, then addressed Wesley in a loud voice. "The scoundrel who did this to your mother was lucky to get away before I arrived. Ain't that right, Wesley?" He turned back toward me. "Let me help you up." He leaned close. "And you'd be smart to keep your mouth shut. I bet you have quite a reputation around here anyway. These men will believe my story over that of a loose woman."

I pulled the fabric of my torn clothing together. "Don't touch me," I hissed. "And I'd never lie for the likes of you."

As he leaned over me, the dog leapt from the porch. A shot rang out, followed by Wesley screaming and running to the side of the dog lying in the dirt.

For a brief moment, David stared at Wesley and then at me. Like a cornered animal, he backed away toward his horse. But before he could untether the reins and pull himself onto the saddle, he was surrounded by the Cooleys, the sheriff, and Daniel.

"Who are you?" The sheriff pointed at David's badge. "And what in hades happened? Did the lady give you a beating?"

"She's crazy for sure. Not making much sense of what she's saying. Probably confused and scared. Looks like someone was out here right before I rode up." He wiped his face with his sleeve. "I'd only arrived to take a look at the damage to the barn, and she went off on me."

Daniel jumped from his horse and ran to my side. With one hand, I held the ripped pieces of my dress around me the best I could.

"Oh, my God. What happened?" He helped me stand as Ben ran over and steadied me. "I should never have left you alone." Daniel took my face in his hands. "Who did this?"

Everything around me blurred as though looking through a rain-pelted window. I wanted to release the torrent of tears that had been dammed behind walls of fear and pride for so long. But all I could do was barely whisper, "Him." I forced myself to look away from Daniel—a kind and good man—and toward Sheriff David Murphy—a cruel and evil being.

Daniel's body tensed, and when I glanced back at him, it was as though a different person stood in front of me. His eyes appeared to have fire coming from them. He ran at David.

"Daniel, no!" I shrieked.

Shots split the air as Ben threw me to the ground and covered me with his body. Time stopped. My world was captured in a nightmare, and there was no escaping the dark hole into which I tumbled. I imagined calling for help, but no one could hear.

Ben raised himself up and helped me stand. That's when I saw a body on the ground, a white shirt soaking up the puddle of blood.

264

Sheriff Murphy.

Daniel and the sheriff stood over the lifeless body.

"Fool of a man." The sheriff tapped the badge pinned to David's shirt with the butt of his gun. "Heard tell of a lawman down by Enid impersonating a newly appointed sheriff. You can be sure he wasn't sent here under my jurisdiction." He shook his head. "Must be the same fellow. That badge he's wearing says Missouri." He knelt and laid his fingers to the side of David's neck. "Wonder what brought him all the way out here?" He squinted at me, but I said nothing. "Too bad it had to end this way, but he pulled his gun first."

The sheriff glanced at the gun in Daniel's hand and then spoke firmly. "Good thing it was me who shot him. Ain't that right? We wouldn't want anyone being accused of murder, now would we?" He raised his eyebrows. "A man's got to protect himself and others, especially out here."

In the chaos, I hadn't noticed Stanley supporting Nate's arm. How long had he been here? And where was Anna?

Nate's blood trickled down his fingers as Stanley motioned to Ben. "Ben, find Adam and bring him right away." He looked at me as I held my limp arm as well. "Looks like there's plenty to keep him busy."

* * * * *

As the sun fell over the Cooley ranch, we talked in quiet voices—all but Anna. She remained silent.

Daniel encouraged me to tell him what David had said and done. A few of the details I buried deep where horrible memories were supposed to eventually disappear. But the way Daniel held me and whispered words of love, he understood David's cruelty and what would have occurred if Anna and Wesley hadn't been near.

Before long, Ben returned with Adam. Stanley greeted him with an embrace.

"Adahy. My home welcomes you again, but I wish this time it wasn't for healing."

The Indian clutched his bag of herbs and miracles. "Lots of bad in world. Plenty of good." He tucked his bag under his arm and lifted his palms, teetering his hands up and down. "Depends which side of scale you live." He dug into his bag and produced a vial of red powder. "Cayenne. Slows blood and closes hole fast."

Tears ran down Nate's face as Adam rubbed the cayenne into his wound. And when he twisted my arm in various directions, my head spun, and I was sure I would faint. With his thumb and forefinger, he determined a bone was broken in two places. Once the rawhide splint was in place, my body was able to relax as I sipped on the willow bark tea he insisted would lessen the swelling.

"Could have been a lot worse." Stanley carried a chair from the kitchen and plopped it next to Daniel. "The whole lot of you could have died, including me."

I held my finger to my mouth, reminding Stanley the children were present. Wesley hadn't left my side since we arrived in the wagon. Now, like a cat, he curled next to me on the sofa.

"You were a brave boy." I wrapped my good arm around him and pulled him closer, looking around for Anna. "Anna ..."

She sat alone by the window.

"Dear, will you come sit by us?" I patted the sofa seat.

She continued to look out the window, although there was nothing to see this time of night. I wondered what was going through her mind. How much did she see and hear today? *Poor child. I wish I could do something to help her.*

As though he read my mind, Daniel joined her by the window, sitting cross-legged like her. Stanley and Ben exchanged an odd look but kept quiet.

"You know, Anna, you were very brave too. Not many people would have been as courageous." Daniel paused and seemed to study the young girl. "You saved Mary's life ... with your word."

Anna gave him a sideways glance but said nothing.

"It's the truth." He looked out the window, and I wondered if that was the end of the one-sided conversation. But it wasn't.

"And even though today was scary and nothing like that will happen again, it was a good day, don't you think?"

Stanley shifted in his seat. "Don't know if I'd call it that. It was a—"

"Special day," Daniel interjected. "Yes. It was the day Anna found her voice again." He winked at her as she turned toward him. "Do you know the best part?"

Anna propped her elbows on her knees and shook her head.

"Now that your voice isn't missing any longer, you can bring it out as often as you like, even share it with others like you did today."

As though they were the only people in the world, they huddled face to face. The rest of us listened as she began to utter words and then sentences. Stanley sobbed into his hands, but the most audible sound was Anna's whispers.

When Stanley let out a tremendous snort, Anna giggled the loudest. He rose from his chair and gathered his daughter into his arms, kissing her all over her porcelain-skinned face.

"I love you," Anna said, pecking him on the tip of his nose with her finger. "It's all right now, Pa."

This was one miracle even Adahy wouldn't find in his bag.

CHAPTER 41

Mary ~ Present, August 18, 1894

Except for the incessant chirping of grasshoppers and the constant chattering of Wesley and Anna, the lazy days of August were quiet.

It had been only a few weeks since the dreadful event with Sheriff Murphy, and I found myself constantly looking at the spot where he laid in front of my home—still filled with disbelief at what he had done to die so violently. Part of me was saddened for him. What a shame to lose his life over displaced and distorted love. The other part was relieved, free from his roaming eyes and unpredictable rage.

The local sheriff had been unable to find any relatives. In the time I knew him back home, he had never talked about family or even distant relatives. A telegraph to Mother to inform her of his death and see whether she had any information came up empty, except to confirm the talk in town. People said he had suddenly left his position, supposedly off to pursue better opportunities in the West. He was a loner in the world and left it the same way.

Out of a strange sense of responsibility, shortly after his death I stood next to the deep hole in the ground while a deputy and a man who looked like he could benefit from a few extra dollars tossed shovelfuls of dirt onto a pine casket.

At first, Daniel and Stanley were adamant I not attend the burial of a man who had caused such trouble and grief. *Reserve that for those who lived a life deserving of honor and respect.* Daniel's words played across my mind.

Then, Stanley's response reverberated like the echoing of a drum— one so guttural that it reminded me again of my own humanness. *He that doesn't sin gets to throw the first stone.* At Stanley's version of the words of Jesus, the three of us bowed our heads.

Over the last year, the small cemetery had grown like a persistent bed of weeds, sprouting tombstones and crooked, wooden crosses—watered by the tears of mothers and fathers, children weeping for lost parents, and the sorrow of husbands and wives as a final good-bye was whispered.

It was odd, but I was compelled to be present when David was laid in the ground. Perhaps my conviction grew from an odd mixture of knowing him in the past, the kindness he showed to Wesley and my mother, and a sickening sense of guilt that if not for me, he wouldn't be dead. The memory washed over me again. David Murphy had saved my life a little more than a year ago when he pulled me from the river in Adair.

I stood between Daniel and Wesley and watched the last hints of the casket disappear under the soil. On that day, the three of us held hands, linked together by a love that was pure and unconditional. The best we could offer on this side of paradise.

* * * * *

Past the garden, Wesley and Anna placed wildflowers on the black dog's grave as they had done each day over the last weeks. The slight mound was sprinkled with petals from yellow bitterweed and blue-flowered chicory. A pile of stones rested at one end. Propped in the rocks was a small wooden cross, its pieces held together with twine.

Hero was scrawled in a child's handwriting across the horizontal portion of the cross. The children had been determined to name the dog before Nate dug a deep hole in the dirt, wrapped the dog in canvas, and placed its body into the earth. In their opinion—and I suppose they were right—the once nameless mutt was partially responsible for saving my life.

Death. There had been too much of it. My thoughts turned to my dear friends, Lizzie and Joseph. In my heart, I knew she had most likely passed in the year since we had embraced and parted company. I imagined Joseph soon followed after his beloved wife if for no other reason than a broken heart.

Tuck. My mind lingered on my first love, my husband for ten years and the father of my children. It had been a year since he died. In so many ways, it felt like forever. My eyes rested on Wesley, and I wondered how often he thought of his father and if he remembered him well.

No longer could I recall Tuck's voice, and his scent was long gone with his discarded clothes. Any hint of the touch of his cheek or the feel of his embrace had been erased from my memory. Even the clarity I once had of his dark eyes and curly hair faded from my mind—still present, but drifting further away as if into a fog. Strange how time plays tricks and steals away what I once thought would never disappear.

* * * * *

At the touch of Daniel's arms around my waist, I was brought back to the present.

"Are you all right?" Daniel spoke softly into my hair, and a tingle ran down my back. "You look so serious."

"I'm fine. Just sorting through all the blessings I have to be thankful for. And, Daniel McKenzie, you are right at the top of the list."

He grinned as though knowing there was probably much more on my mind.

"I promise. Everything is perfect." My smile was to remind myself how comforting it was to know he was near.

Although my broken bones would mend, it was my heart that needed to be protected. Daniel was long overdue to return to Boston and his job, and I dreaded the announcement that it was time for him to leave. When each day waned or we were forced to rest from the intense heat that lingered into the far end of summer, I savored each moment to watch him paint. Like a magic wand, his brush cast a spell as it moved across the canvas. Paints blended and spiraled as they birthed new colors. Shapes and images became defined, emerging from the painting as if he had called them forth. I was enchanted by him and hoped the spell would never be broken.

At night, after his brushes were cleaned and paintings left to dry, supper was finished and the day's work done, we walked hand in hand and shared our thoughts in whispers and laughs, hoping Wesley would stay fast asleep.

Later, when only the swooping owls, scurrying mice, and wandering coyotes were meant to be awake, Daniel walked me to the soddy door and kissed me gently—the perfect gentleman in the midst of a wild and untamed land.

I crawled into bed next to my sleeping child and thought of Daniel sleeping alone—except for the mule and cow—in the rebuilt barn. I imagined him holding me closely, dreaming about what our lives would be like if we were a family of three.

*****

When George Hardy insisted it was time to return to Boston, Daniel told me he couldn't argue with him anymore.

"George has been a good friend. He's stayed away from his wife and children much longer than he planned to give me more time with you. He even agreed to extend the story to cover Guthrie and Oklahoma City. He's photographed and written an entire section about what's transpired in those cities since the first run in 1889. Might earn himself an award or at least a promotion for bringing back a one-of-a-kind feature for McKelvey and the Globe."

"I understand." It was hard to keep my voice steady. "Besides, you have paintings to deliver to the paper, and your boss must be anxious to have the piece for himself and his wife. It's …" I turned and looked out the window to avoid his eyes. "It's of the sunset over the plains, just like outside our—"

Tears that I had forbidden to come now filled my eyes and blurred the orange, red, and pink skyline—a watercolor painting across the horizon. Behind me, hands gathered my hair to the side and lips kissed my neck and along my ear. *How can he do this when he's leaving?* I wanted to push him away, scream that I didn't love him and wanted him gone from my life. But I couldn't. My true feelings were exactly the opposite. I was deeply in love with Daniel and wanted to spend the rest of my life with him. But once again, he was leaving.

"Don't look," he whispered in my ear. "And don't turn around until I say."

I felt a bit foolish as the door shut behind me. I tried to peer out the window to see what he was up to. Just when my curiosity almost won out, the door opened.

"Don't peek, I'll tell you when." Daniel spoke with such excitement I couldn't imagine what he had brought into the house. After some shuffling, he spoke. "All right. You can look now."

I wiped the stray tears from my cheek and slowly turned around. At first, nothing appeared unusual in the dimness of the room until my eyes moved to the ledge. My hand went to my mouth as I stared at a painting—one where the other had sat before it was destroyed.

"Oh, Daniel. It's the best gift you could have given me. You've brought the sunset back into my home. Or is this the one you painted for Mr. McKelvey?"

"It's for you."

I stepped closer. "It looks so real. The colors are exactly like this evening, and the grasses that lead to the creek, they—" My eyes followed the meandering path until they reached two figures walking in the distance, holding hands while another smaller one ran ahead toward the peaceful water.

"It's us," Daniel spoke softly, wistfully. "You, me, and Wesley."

"It's the most wonderful painting in the world, but—" Whether imagined or real, a pain shot across my chest, and I realized a heart could truly break. "Don't do this to me. Not to Wesley either."

"Mary, look again."

Through my tears, I looked at the painting.

"At the bottom," he urged.

My eyes traveled downward to carefully painted words, tucked into lavender and lapis dotted flowers and swipes of emerald and forest greens bathing in the last light of day.

Be with me forever and a day ~ Daniel

Both of us were silent as I reread the words, although I wondered if he could hear my heart pounding.

"Are you asking me ..." I looked at Daniel with wide eyes.

"Yes." He knelt and took my hand. "Mary Roberts, will you be my wife so I can love you forever and a day?"

I wanted to find the right words—words as perfect as his painting—but all I could do was gaze into his eyes.

"We could marry within the month. After I arrive in Boston—"

"This is my home. I don't want to leave."

"I'm not asking you to do that." He shook his head and seemed to search for the right words. "I never would have imagined my life in another place than what I've always known. But then I found you. And for some reason that can only be God's plan, this is where I want to call home." He kissed my hand. "But only with you."

"But you're leaving. What about your work at the Globe?"

Daniel stood and walked around the small room. He squeezed his chin as though in deep thought. "I've been there a long time and have given the paper my best work. Nothing goes on forever, and the way things are growing across the country, there are plenty of newspapers springing up." He stopped in front of the painting. "Besides, I'm most passionate about painting. And you. There will be time to paint while we work the farm—maybe take on some cattle and sheep and expand the crops."

"I'd want to continue teaching the children," I added. "They've become my passion. And you too." It felt good to smile and to say exactly what was in my heart.

"Then ..." He held my hand again. "Will you marry me?"

"Daniel McKenzie, I would love to be your wife ... forever and a day."

We stepped outside and watched the brilliant colors intensify across the sky as though orchestrated only for us.

As the colors faded and darkened, Wesley bounded in from the field after keeping company with Jim as he grazed. Over supper, we shared our good news with him and talked about what life would soon be like for our family of three.

* * * * *

At our invitation, the Cooleys and Andersons arrived before Daniel left for the station. We wanted to announce our engagement so the marriage could take place soon after Daniel returned.

Once the news was shared, cheers rang out, pats on the back and handshakes followed for Daniel, and I received a big kiss on the cheek from Lucy.

"I knew in my gut you two were meant for each other. Knew it from the first time I saw him. He was obviously smitten with you." She gave me a tight hug. "When can we start planning your clothing and the food and—"

"Let's see Daniel off first. Then we can begin," I said as Lucy feigned a pout.

Daniel shook Stanley's hand before the older man pulled him in and gave him a hug.

"I'm proud of you, Daniel. A smart man wouldn't let a woman like Mary slip away."

"No, sir. I had no intention of letting that happen. I'll be sure to include a word about the Cooley Ranch in the article once I sit down with Hardy."

"Better be more than a word. It's a big ranch that deserves a big story in my opinion." Stanley puffed out his chest. "And it wouldn't hurt business either. Maybe some of those rich Bostonians will invest in my cattle."

Before Daniel and Ben headed toward town in the wagon, Daniel huddled the men together. I couldn't hear them, but I suppose he was asking them to keep a close eye on Wesley and me, keeping us safe until his return. When he finished with the men, he turned his attention to me.

"I'll hurry back as soon as the apartment is closed down. There's not much, but at least Finn and his bride-to-be can have all they want. Hopefully, that will help make amends with Elizabeth for Finn delaying their wedding until my return."

"It's too bad Finn and his new wife can't be here for our ceremony. I know that would mean a lot to you."

"It would indeed. Finn adds a unique touch to everything." Daniel held me close. "Have you thought about asking your mother to come?"

"Yes. It would mean the world to me to have her here. To get to know you and see her grandson would be—"

"And to be with you, my love." He kissed my forehead. "She's known you longer than anyone, through the tough and easy times. This is going to be a grand time that the two of you need to celebrate together."

"Daniel McKenzie, I love the way you think."

"And I love everything about you."

CHAPTER 42

Mary ~ Together, September 14, 1894

To help the days pass quickly, my time was spent mending the soddy like a pair of well-worn trousers and chasing away unwelcome mice and snakes. In the evenings, I wrote new lessons for the upcoming school session and read with Wesley until our eyes became heavy. Each day kept a steady rhythm—like methodic beats of a metronome—in anticipation of Mother's arrival and Daniel's return.

I visited Lucy often to plan what we would cook for the reception following the small ceremony at the town church. The menu would consist of roast veal, plenty of summer squash, green beans, juicy tomatoes, and freshly baked sour dough bread. Apple and peach pies, strawberry and raspberry preserves mixed into sweet cream, and baked custard would be a treat for dessert. Plenty of sweet cider would quench our thirsts after dancing to the lively music of the fiddle player.

"I've already spoken with the other women, and you're not doing any of the cooking on your special day." Lucy bounced Lila on her knee while we talked. The baby was plump and happy and squirmed to resume crawling on the dirt floor.

"You have your hands full with this one." I brushed the dirt off her knees. "You need to spend your time keeping Miss Lila out of trouble, not cooking for me."

"Nonsense. I wouldn't miss the chance to help make your day special." She gave in to Lila's wiggles and set her on the ground. "Speaking of that, I have a surprise for you." She opened a large trunk at the foot of the bed. "Close your eyes."

I squeezed my eyes shut and waited.

"Okay, open them."

Like an angelic apparition, Lucy held a delicate, lace and pearl-beaded wedding gown in front of me. The train pooled on the floor like a waterfall cascading into a hidden mountain spring.

"Oh, Lucy … it's stunning."

"I want you to wear it."

A lump filled my throat. With Tuck, a simple white linen dress was my only option. A gown fit for a princess never crossed my mind. "It's not proper for me to wear something like that, is it? Not since I was married before."

"It will be fine without the veil. We'll put lavender flowers in your hair and bouquet. No one will give it a second thought. It's not like you have many other choices. In my opinion, the shop in town has awful styles."

"Where did you get such a lovely wedding gown?"

"It was my mother's." She ran her fingers over the lacy neckline. "I wore it once and don't plan on needing it again. Thomas is stuck with me forever."

"Lila will need it someday." The baby scooted around the legs of the table.

Lucy giggled as she watched her daughter. "But that's a long time from now. Good thing." She wiped a smudge of dirt from Lila's forehead.

My fingers caressed the silky fabric—soft like new-fallen snow—and imagined how it would feel on my body. It would be so different than the worn cotton dresses of summer and the scratchy wool skirts in the winter.

"Put it on." Lucy laid the wedding gown on my lap. "See for yourself."

I took off my clothes and, with Lucy's help, slipped on the gown and fastened the long line of buttons. When she positioned me in front of a full-length mirror—another find from Roy's shop—I was speechless.

"Mary, it fits you like a glove." She lifted the hem. "The brown boots will have to go, but other than that, it's perfect. Don't you think?"

I loosened my hair and then gathered it again into a twist as wavy strands framed my face.

"And that hair ... you could wear a potato sack and be absolutely stunning."

"You are the dearest of friends, Lucy Anderson." I hugged her as I held back the tears that threatened to spoil this lovely dress. "Even though it will be a tiny wedding, will you be my matron of honor?"

Lucy screeched, and Lila let out a cry, making us both laugh.

"I was hoping you'd ask. I'd be honored."

* * * * *

Trains seem to take a long time to arrive when you're waiting for someone special. When the three o'clock train pulled alongside the platform a half hour late, my breathing resumed a regular pace. I had been worried about Mother traveling alone from Adair and prayed her travel would go smoothly.

When she stepped off the train, I was a child again—one who had found her mother after being separated in a crowd.

"Mother!" One hand waved frantically as the other held tightly to Wesley. When she saw us and waved back, we ran to her. The three of us huddled together and held each other as if the train would pluck one of us away as it rumbled and lunged on to its next destination.

"Wesley, my boy." Mother kissed him cheek to cheek. "You're so big—practically turned into a young man. And my dear Mary ..." She held my hands, and her eyes searched mine. "You seem so happy. It was evident from the telegraph." She touched my splinted arm. "Your arm. Is it almost healed?"

"Only another week. Adahy says the splint can come off before the wedding."

"Adahy?"

"We have a lot to talk about. But we'll have plenty of time for all that. For now, it's so wonderful you decided to come. It means everything to me that you're here." I lifted her bag. "How was the travel?"

"Besides being a little tired from the long ride, it was actually quite an adventure. Met several interesting people." If even possible, her hair appeared whiter than before, but her eyes remained sharp and clear. "Reminded me we live in a big world with plenty to see and do. Adair is nice, but it's only a speck of the country."

"Mother, as always, you amaze me."

Wesley could hardly keep his boyish excitement under control as he helped load her bags into the back of the wagon. With a little effort, we helped Mother pull herself onto the seat and headed home.

* * * * *

My soon-to-be family felt complete when, two days later, Ben brought Daniel home once again.

"Nearly three weeks was too long to be away from you." Daniel scooped me into his arms and spun in a circle.

"I hope you don't plan to go away again anytime soon." I kissed him quickly, anticipating when we could embrace for hours once we were husband and wife.

"Not a chance." He turned his attention toward the soddy. "And this must be your lovely mother."

Mother stepped from the doorway. "I see you are intelligent as well as handsome."

"Mother, this is Daniel McKenzie. Daniel, meet my mother, Louisa Johnston."

"Ma'am. It's more than a pleasure to meet the woman Mary speaks so highly of. You've raised a lovely, delightful daughter who will soon be my wife."

"And I'm sure you will make a fine husband. Love her like she deserves to be loved, and be a good father to my grandson." Mother took Daniel's hand and seemed to study him. "There's something about you I already feel good about. Hmm? Must be those eyes."

Daniel, Ben, and Wesley unloaded an odd assortment of items from the back of the wagon. When it was time to close his apartment,

Daniel couldn't bring himself to leave his easel. The unassembled pieces were bound together with rope until we could find a place in the small soddy or barn for him to paint. He brought a case filled with clothing, including a coat and tie to wear for the wedding. A few household items clanged around in one wooden crate. Another contained art supplies, and the last held books—favorites he planned to share with me and Wesley during the long winter months.

After harvesting the last of the summer food from the garden and enjoying an early supper, Daniel kissed the tip of my nose before bridling Jim. "I'll be staying at the ranch house until the wedding to give you time with your mother and … whatever it is women do before they get married." He lifted the saddle onto Jim's back and tightened the cinch. "Two days from now, we'll get to share a home." Daniel motioned to Wesley to join us. "Son, thank you for letting Jim come along with me. The Cooleys are bringing the three of you to the church in a larger coach—only proper and fitting for the bride."

* * * * *

Even though the church was a speck in the middle of the open plain west of town, in my eyes it was a castle, awaiting its queen. The skirts of the wedding gown filled most of the space in the coach, and the puffy sleeves made it difficult for anyone to share my seat. I giggled along with Mother and Wesley as the three of us did our best to squish together as we bounced along on our way to the church.

It didn't take many of our friends to fill the tiny building. From the back, I glanced along the pews and smiled at my schoolchildren and their families. William Hill, looking even more like a young man, was seated with his father. Roy and his wife sat beside Thomas, who was trying his best to hold Lila so Lucy could be at my side.

My mother sat in the front row, her hair pulled into a tight bun. In her favorite yellow outfit, she looked like a delicate songbird.

To my right, seated in the back of the church, were Adahy and a woman. Her hair was white like cotton and her skin tanned and leathery. *His wife*. He looked at me and patted his chest—a sign I took to symbolize love.

Ben, Nate, and Stanley whispered among themselves until the piano played. The minister, a slight and aged man, gestured to Daniel to take his position at the altar. Bartholomew Reid stood to his side, beaming at his appointment as the best man.

Like a fairy dancing in the forest, Anna went before me, scattering pink and purple wildflower petals on the wooden floor, their scent lingering like perfume. Wesley was her caboose, a piece of folded velvet across his palms in which the rings rested. Mine would be a long-held treasure that belonged to Daniel's mother. For Daniel, I had purchased a simple gold band at the only jeweler in town and had it inscribed with our wedding date.

The minister gave a slight nod, motioning to me to walk down the aisle. With a deep breath and a heart full of hope, I stepped forward.

I had heard the words before—long ago when I was young and innocent, ignorant about the challenges, hardships, and heartbreaks life brings. Though nearly the same words were shared—words meant to forge an everlasting bond—they held new meaning.

"I, Daniel James, take you, Mary Louisa, to be my wife, to have and to hold from this day forward, for better or for worse, for richer, for poorer, in sickness and in health, to love and to cherish until death do us part. I promise to love you forever and a day."

The minister raised his eyebrows as Daniel spoke the additional sentence. Then he grinned and nodded at me to speak.

"I, Mary Louisa, take you, Daniel James, to be my husband, to have and to hold from this day forward, for better or for worse, for richer, for poorer, in sickness and in health, to love and to cherish until death do us part."

I glanced at the minister who gave a quick wink.

"And I promise to love you forever and a day."

When the minister pronounced us husband and wife, Daniel and I kissed to the applause of our friends and family. We turned and started out the door to begin our new life together.

CHAPTER 43

Mary ~ Apparition, September 28, 1894

For someone who had kept a private and lifeless home for many years, Stanley was the perfect host. "Good thing I insisted the reception be at the ranch," he told me. Holding another tray of food, he pushed the screen door open with his foot. "It's about time we wake the place up. It will be good to hear a fiddle and kick up the dirt with some dancing."

Children chased each other around the yard as the guests chatted about the weather and the work that needed to be done on the farms. Congratulations were offered through mouthfuls of food and laughter. Even the chickens—a much-appreciated gift from Stewart, Seth, and little Elizabeth's family—clucked along with the excitement and merriment of the party.

When William and his father presented not one, but two mahogany rocking chairs, I was at a loss for words—overwhelmed with the love and generosity of the community.

Adahy's wife stood quietly at his side as her husband talked with Stanley, Daniel, and Bart. When I joined them, she pulled a shiny object from beneath the scarf that draped over her blouse and extended her arms toward me.

"For the new couple," Adahy said. "My wife make for you."

It was a silver bowl, inlaid with turquoise stones, surrounded by intricate etchings. I had never held something so intricate, and I cupped it in my palms like a robin's nest.

"Thank you." Her dark eyes smiled at my words. "It will always have a special place in our home."

"Another guest is here, Pa." Ben jerked his head toward the path leading into the yard. "But I don't recognize him. Is he a new hand?"

"No one I know. Haven't hired anyone lately," Stanley said. "A friend of yours, Mary?" I stepped to the side of our gathering to get a better look at the man walking into the yard. His shirt hung loosely, and his pants were worn at the knees. Drooping on one side, his hat covered part of his face.

Not wanting anyone to feel unwelcome at our celebration, I decided to greet him. "Welcome. Have we met?"

When the man removed his hat, curls fell around his face. He brushed them aside and stared at me with hollow brown eyes.

"Tuck!" I felt the blood drain from my face.

Daniel ran to my side. "What's wrong? Who is this?" He looked at me and then at the shadow of a man standing with his hat dangling at his side. "Sir, I don't believe we know you. Please state your business here."

When I lost my focus and began to sway, Daniel steadied me. My head shook in disbelief and shock.

"What's happening? Do you two know each other?" Daniel's voice became stern.

Could it be that my eyes betray me from the exhaustion of the day, or perhaps being overheated? I asked myself. No, it was Tuck in the flesh. And although the past year had obviously not been kind—and he looked several years older than when I last saw him—he was most certainly alive.

"Sir, you're upsetting my wife. I'm going to have to ask you to leave."

"No, Daniel." My voice quivered. "It's … it's Tuck. My … husband."

Daniel's face contorted as if he had been punched in the gut. "Your *husband*? Unless I'm mistaken, you and I just got married, and your first husband is *dead*."

Stanley strode up, demanding to know what was going on. "Mister, I don't believe you're invited to this affair." He looked at Daniel's pale face. "What in the … what's going on here? Do my boys need to remove this man from my property?"

Daniel looked at me with sad eyes that longed for an explanation. "Ask Mary. I have no idea what's going on."

He started to walk away, but I grabbed his arm with surprising strength. "Daniel, wait. I'm as surprised as you. He must be a ghost." But as Tuck stood yards away, surrounded by the three Cooleys, he was just as real as Daniel who stood by my side. My mind whirled with the possibilities. "He can't be here. He was killed over a year ago."

"Did you ever see his body? Was there a funeral, or at least a burial?" Daniel ran a shaky hand through his hair.

Suddenly, I was struck with a sickening realization that all I knew was what Sheriff Murphy had told me. How Tuck had gotten into a drunken brawl with another man at a bar somewhere in Colorado, drew a knife, and was shot in the chest.

"That filthy man lied to me." Nausea roiled as reality set in. With my hand to my mouth, I ran into the house and locked myself in the water closet. Inside the dim room, my horrified reflection stared at me from the small mirror on the wall. Only minutes before, I was the happiest woman on earth. Now, the woman looking back at me was terrified and confused. If he hadn't been killed, and Sheriff Murphy went so far as to lie to me for his own selfish reasons, why had Tuck come back now? Then another thought struck me with brute force.

Wesley! Oh, my God, has he seen his father?

I bolted out of the house, knocking into Lucy and another woman tending to the food. "Where's Wesley? I have to find him."

"Mary, what—" Lucy put out her hand, but I didn't stop. "The children are riding the pony in the field."

I lifted my dress the best I could and dashed down the path toward the open area, nearly collapsing when I spotted Tuck kneeling in front of Wesley in the middle of the field. Daniel and Stanley stood to the side of them, keeping a close look but allowing a conversation to take place.

"Wesley?" I halted a few yards away.

The corners of his mouth drooped, and his face was stained with tears. "Mama?" His voice shook along with his body. "It's my daddy."

More than anything, I wanted to be on the other side of the world from this man yet desperately needed to be with my son. As if I were ten feet taller than my true height, the instinct to do anything to protect Wesley swelled inside of me.

With a swift movement, I stepped forward and pulled my son close. From somewhere long ago, a proverb surfaced in my mind. *Let a bear robbed of her whelps meet a man, rather than a fool in his folly.* Recalling the strange image the verse had conjured when I first heard it, now it made sense. In Tuck's case, it would be worse for him to meet his own fool's folly. This mother bear would kill to protect her child.

Part of me wanted to tear Tuck to pieces, instill the same fear and pain in him that had taunted me even before his supposed death. Another part seethed at the notion of what the man who hid his evilness behind a shiny badge had been capable of doing—destroying our lives and ultimately losing his own.

Anger, confusion, fear, and hatred boiled inside me like a poisonous venom waiting to be unleashed—ready to spew its wrath upon this man who could ruin everything true, honest, just, pure, lovely, of good report …

Unexpectedly, like a welcome visitor, the rest of the words of one of my mother's favorite Scriptures slipped from my mouth, allowing me to pause. "If there be any virtue, and if there be any praise, think on these things."

Here in front of me, Tuck knelt in the grass like a wounded animal. The poisonous brew still bubbled in my gut, but it was sprinkled with an odd sense of compassion, mixed with remorse.

"Wesley, go play with the other children for a bit." I prodded him in the direction of the others who, by now, had made their way to the table filled with desserts. "Get some pie before it's all gone."

"But, Mama, you said he was dead." Wesley dug his hands into the skirt of my dress, his eyes locked on the man in front of him.

"Evidently, I was mistaken." My lips brushed the top of his head.

Tuck stood on wobbly legs. "We'll talk more, Son. Let me have a few minutes with your mother." He nodded in the direction of the other children. "Be sure to cut me a slice of apple pie." He gave the weary grin of a man who didn't have an ounce of happiness in his life.

Wesley backed away, never taking his eyes off his father, and then turned and ran up the hill to the house.

I glanced at Daniel, then moved closer to Tuck. Just as before, the smell of whiskey was evident. "What are you doing here? I've believed all this time you were murdered in a fight, far away in Colorado."

"By the filthy son of a—" He wiped the sweat from his face with a dirty shirtsleeve. "It wasn't enough for Murphy to falsely accuse me of stealing a horse. You remember that, don't you, Mary?"

He was innocent after all, just like I suspected.

"It's true. There was a fight. Got beat up pretty bad and wondered if that was the end." He pulled aside his collar. "Took a bullet just below my shoulder. Can't use my right arm much anymore, but it didn't kill me. Living proof, ain't I?"

"Then why didn't you come home? Why did you leave your son without a father?"

Daniel stepped closer. "Yes, why show up now … find her all the way out here?" Daniel towered over Tuck and could easily overpower him. Not to mention, Stanley stood nearby with his hand close to his revolver. I put my hand on Daniel's arm, hoping to assure him Tuck wasn't here to hurt anyone.

"Had to stay clear, far away from Adair. At least until I heard Murphy was dead. He swore if I came back, they'd find me floating in the river face down."

My hands knotted into fists. "He threatened to kill you?"

"Pretty much. Said plenty of others had it in for me, and if I wanted to keep on breathing, I'd better stay away." Tuck scratched at his dirty hair. "I wouldn't put it past him to have shot me himself. He was that crazy over you."

"You knew that?" Another surge of anger rose, and I wanted to slap this man who had made a vow to love and protect me. "And you ran away to save yourself?"

Daniel paced behind me.

"Mary, I loved you. Not expecting you to believe me, but I still do." He winced as if the thought was painful. "I was a coward—a drunken coward."

"Your pathetic excuse is too late." Daniel placed his arm around me. "In case you were too dense to notice, you arrived in time to celebrate our marriage. Your *widow* became my wife this morning."

Stanley placed a firm hand on Tuck's back. "It was a nice reunion, but it's time you be on your way."

Tuck twisted out of Stanley's reach. "Mary and I have unfinished business."

"And just what would that be?" Stanley's words were brusque.

"When I got to Adair, I went to pay a visit to my dear mother-in-law. The neighbors said she had left for her daughter's wedding. Told me Mary had met a man in the new territory where she and I had planned to homestead." As he spoke, Bart escorted Mother across the field to where we were gathered.

"Well, lookie who's here?" Tuck stretched out his arms. "It's a family reunion."

"Tuck Roberts, if you weren't standing right in front of me, I'd never believe it." She held tightly to Bart's arm. Her porcelain skin was even more pale than usual.

"It's me, Louisa. Come back to life, according to some."

"Mother, Tuck was about to tell us why he came all the way here."

"Ain't it obvious? To find my wife and son. A man has a right to his family. No one can argue against that. Ain't that right, Louisa?"

Mother glared at Tuck. "How about telling us the full reason?" Her frail body stiffened. "There was a time in my life I liked you, Tuck Roberts, proud to call you son-in-law. But when your life turned sour, you rotted away with it."

Tuck smirked, apparently devoid of any obvious guilt for his motives. "According to the law, since I'm obviously not dead, the land Mary claimed belongs to me, being head of the household."

"How dare you! You think you can—" I lunged forward, only inches from his face before Daniel pulled me back.

"Take what belongs to me? Looks like you have plenty of good things going your way, and I got nothing." Tuck staggered sideways.

"You're drunk … like you always were. I want no part of you, and nothing I have belongs to you." Like fire lashing out from a pit, the words came from a place deep and wounded, intent on destroying anything they could reach.

He laughed—a sick and cackling sound—as if he had gone mad. "There's not much you can do since the law is what it is. Got me some legal advice before making the trip this way. Your marriage this morning was nothing but an act since you're still bound by the law to me."

Bart stepped forward and spoke up. "I'm afraid your legal counsel was incorrect, and your logic is misguided. Once Mary was a widow, she became the head of the household. She registered for the race in her name and signed the deed of ownership under her name as well. She married Daniel under the honorable impression of being a widow for more than a year."

"But I'm not dead, and there lies her problem," Tuck shot back.

"Mary, did you ever receive a certificate of death or any statement that your husband was deceased?" Bart narrowed his eyes, confirming the seriousness of the situation.

"I can't remember. It was such a difficult—"

"Mr. Reid," Mother said. "I have the document. Sheriff Murphy gave it to me the day he came to my house and told us about Tuck. It's signed and dated." She turned to me. "Mary, you were upset, and I didn't want to make matters worse. It was put with my other papers and kept in my closet. One of my friends back home could mail it to us."

"Even if that's true and you have the paper, Murphy forged it." Tuck began to shake, and tears filled his eyes. "More than anything, I want my wife and son back."

All of us stood silent as the distraught Tuck held his face in his hands and wept. When he settled down, I asked if he would speak with me privately for a few minutes.

Daniel remained nearby, but the others walked toward the yard, following the melody of the fiddle as the notes carried over the plains.

It was surreal to talk with someone who was supposed to be permanently gone from my life. There would remain a small, reserved place for Tuck with the other fond memories that made up the past. To some extent, even the drinking and lonely nights when he didn't come home and had most likely found temporary love in another woman's arms had been forgiven. My head swirled with confusion and ambiguity in a vain attempt to make sense of his return.

Looking at him now, I tried to find a glimmer of the old Tuck—the one from when we were first married—in those once wide, brown eyes. But somewhere between the drink, his lustful wanderings, and a false sense of striking it rich with little or no hard work, he had fallen into an abyss that was too deep to ascend. Together, my eyes, mind, and heart tried to make sense of the tattered and weathered man I once believed would be in my life forever. "What happened to you, Tuck? You aren't the man I knew. Not on the inside or the outside."

He shot me a stern glance, and his cheek twitched. For a moment, it seemed possible he would be bold—or ignorant—enough to harm me. But then his face relaxed, and a crooked smile appeared. "You always were the better of the two of us. Strong and determined you were."

"I tried to do what was right." My throat tightened at the memories. "I was faithful, and you weren't. You left your family like a coward, and it looks like the drink and your false dreams got the better of you."

Tuck put one hand in his pocket while his other arm remained limp. "Whiskey makes a man do things he shouldn't. Those other women kept me warm, that's all. But my dreams were real. If it hadn't been for you and the boy, I would have left sooner. Yep, woulda caught the lodes before they were emptied … been a wealthy man by now."

It was surreal standing in the field with Tuck, adorned in my wedding finery like a shiny pearl, and longing to be loved by the man I had married just hours ago. "Tuck Roberts, I don't love you and never will again. You need to go."

He stared into the distance as though my words had far to travel to transcend his distanced heart. After several minutes, he spoke. "Earl's needing help farming in California. You remember my old friend, don't ya?"

The name was vaguely familiar, but maybe this was another of Tuck's misguided notions.

He glanced around. "More fertile than this godforsaken land."

"So why exactly *did* you come here?"

"Guess to see it with my own eyes. Pathetic. To think you left Adair for this."

"That's why you came? Not even to see your son?"

He rubbed his scraggly beard as he kicked at the dirt. "Yeah, to see him too." He glanced toward the house and the gathering of people. Fiddle music drifted over the open field as laughter and friendly talk weaved its way through the notes. "Seems like he has a good life here. You're a good mother. Knew how to keep loving even after the twins …" His voice trailed off as he again stared into the distance—perhaps the clouded and painful past.

My emotions were battling within me. More than anything, I wished this to be a disappearing nightmare. "I'll be sure to tell Wesley you love him, but you have to be on your way with the next train."

"I need to see him one more time. Gotta tell him myself that I love him. He needs to know his father isn't all bad." His voice was strained, and he sounded sincere. "Just for a few minutes, and then I'll be gone."

I looked to Daniel for his approval. He had become strangely silent but nodded his consent.

"Agreed. But only for a short time." My heart ached, wondering if this was the right decision. "He's confused and scared. What do you suppose he's thinking after going through losing his father, just to have it happen again?"

I started to walk away to get Wesley, but then turned and faced Tuck. "And our marriage. It needs to be ended legally."

"You mean a divorce? We'll see about that. Maybe I still love you and don't want one."

"You were dead to me, Tuck!" My hands cupped over my heart, the only thing possible to protect it. "I loved you once, but you threw that love in my face. And in your son's face. I married Daniel today. We love each other. He loves Wesley like a father should." Tears came again. "This is my … *our* home now, our future. It's not yours, Tuck. This isn't what you want. *I'm* not what you want."

He was quiet for a long moment. "That's it? This is how our story ends?" He smiled a brown-stained, crooked-tooth smile. "But you always liked happy endings in all those books you read."

"I still do. But you're not my happy ending."

When we walked into the yard, the music stopped. Except for the children who continued to play, the rest of the party stared at us. This would make for lively dinner talk for weeks to come.

With Wesley close by my side, the three of us went into the house. In his own awkward way, Tuck did his best to explain things. My son nodded several times as if trying to understand. When Tuck opened his arms, Wesley fell onto his chest. He held his son until Wesley wiggled free and took my hand.

I swallowed hard and searched for the right words before walking Tuck out the front door and onto the same path from which he had arrived like an apparition.

"You look like you could use some food. Here, let me get you—"

"I'm fine." He ran his fingers over a mangy beard. "Better get back to town and be on a train headed further west by tomorrow's end. Got some extra time before helping Earl. Just may find what the others have missed. Must be plenty of gold still hidden in the hills." He cupped his hand to his ear. "I hear it calling my name." He took my hand, lifted it, and kissed the tip of my fingers. "Take care of yourself and my boy."

As he turned and walked away, there was only one last thing to say. "Tuck Roberts. Take care of yourself as well."

Tuck raised his hand in the air and continued walking until Daniel ran past me and stopped alongside him. Their voices were out of range, but nods and a handshake were shared before Tuck ambled away and disappeared in the distance.

"What was that about?" My arm slipped under Daniel's, and my head leaned into his shoulder.

"Had to thank him."

"For what?" This day continued to be full of surprises.

"For trusting me to take care of you and Wesley. The man's clearly had a hard life, mostly by his own doing. But at least on some level, he realizes it." Daniel turned toward me. "He knew he would never be able to be the husband and father you and Wesley deserve."

"He said all that?"

"Some of it, but I did tell him Bart was taking care of the paperwork to dissolve the marriage and would have him sign before he leaves town. Also promised him a little incentive money if he makes sure to stop by the law office before hopping a train. Bart's having his father contact the justice of the peace in Adair to assure everything is taken care of and see what needs to be done on that end—just in case Tuck ever changes his mind and decides to stir up trouble."

"For some reason, I believe his leaving this time is forever."

"You're probably right. Even though I don't really know him, when a man turns his back and walks away like he did, he's already closed and locked the door to that part of his life. The way he shook my hand, he threw away the key as well."

As we returned to the reception and our guests in the yard, we held hands.

"Forever is a long time, my love." I stopped and gazed into Daniel's eyes, silhouetted by the colors beginning to brush across the sunset sky.

"Forever and a day is even more, and I plan to spend it all with you." He pulled me closer, and we kissed to the music of the fiddle and the distant laughter of those who had become our family and friends.

CHAPTER 44

Mary ~ Future, November 22, 1894

After the wedding, I convinced Mother to stay until the end of November when winter would deliver its first breath of cold air. The soddy was clearly too small for the four of us. Fortunately, the Cooleys offered an extra room with a comfortable bed for my mother. Wesley even spent a few nights at the ranch house, allowing Daniel and me time to enjoy easing into our marriage.

Daniel had already spent time sketching plans for additions to the sod house. A separate room for our bed and a studio space would expand to the east. Wesley would sleep in the main area near the stove so he would easily stay warm on bitter cold nights. Daniel and I would have to keep each other warm without a stove nearby—a welcomed inconvenience.

Before the expected snows would arrive sometime in early December, we enjoyed rocking side by side in the cool, late autumn air. The suffocating heat of summer had lifted like a blanket tossed aside. Now, the dried grasses danced in the field.

"While we're at it, should we build another room?"

Daniel looked pensive. "For your mother? Have you talked with her about staying?"

"Not really. I mentioned it a few times, but she said she'd miss her house and garden. Besides, she has plenty of friends, and the store owners tell her she can work for them as much as she's up to it."

"Then she'll have to visit more often. The trains are coming through all the time. This big country is getting smaller by the day."

My own thoughts kept me quiet until Daniel spoke, "Then why another room if your mother isn't ..." His eyes widened. "You're—"

My hands went to my stomach. "It's too early to know for sure. But I think so." I leaned back in my chair. "We've never really talked about having our own child, have we?"

"No, we haven't."

"I'm getting old, Daniel. What if I can't carry a—"

"Mary, if God's giving us a child, it will be a blessing beyond my wildest dreams." He knelt in front of me and laid his head in my lap. "But if He doesn't, just having you and Wesley is more wonderful than I ever imagined."

* * * * *

We celebrated Thanksgiving around Stanley's large dining room table, set with Flora's elegant china, crystal goblets, and silver flatware.

"She would be happy to see everything looking so perfect." Stanley kissed Anna on the top of her head. "She loved pretty things, just like her daughter." He sat proudly at the head of the table. Before we began eating, he shared a prayer of thanks.

"I'm beginning a tradition in my home." He surveyed the eight of us gathered around the table. "Before we enjoy this lovely meal, each of us has to share something we are thankful for." He nodded at Nate to begin.

"I'm thankful that the livestock are healthy, and it looks like we'll have a profitable year." Nate poked his brother to follow.

"I'm thankful for Susan Billings. She's the cutest thing that's arrived in the county in a long time."

"And she has her eyes on you too," Nate chimed in, making us all laugh.

Mother was next, and she seemed determined to hold back the tears. "I'm thankful for all of you—for making me feel like part of the family. Daniel, I thank the Lord you came into my daughter and grandson's lives. And, Mary …" Her eyes moistened. "You have grown from the daughter of my dreams to my closest companion and friend.

You've reminded me, in the words of the Lord, to *forget those things which are behind, and reaching forth unto those things which are before.*"

"I've never forgotten that verse, Mother, and I still have the note you gave me." I leaned over and kissed her cheek. "Life is to live, and I thank the Lord for you every day."

"Touching, Mary." Stanley tapped the table as if to keep order of the proceedings. "Is that all you want to say?"

I shook my head, and through my own tears and sniffles, added how much I loved everyone at our table and thanked God for blessing each of us.

"This wasn't intended to be so emotional," Stanley growled and pointed at Daniel. "You're next, so help me out with this."

"I'd like to say I'm most thankful for the twelve cattle you gave us for our wedding gift, and of course I am, but ..." Daniel hesitated. "What I'm most thankful for is my wife, and ..." He leaned over and placed his hand on my stomach. "Our new addition—set to arrive in early summer."

"Praise God." Mother held her napkin to her mouth and began to weep.

"That's the most wonderful news yet. Congratulations to the three of you." Stanley nodded at Wesley who was smiling ear to ear. "That deserves a toast."

We raised our glasses, and the soprano clink of the crystal brought music to our ears.

"Now the children. What do you have to share?" Stanley nodded at Wesley.

"I was going to say Anna 'cause she's my best friend. And I love the puppy you brought me, Mr. Cooley." He scrunched his lips together as if in deep thought. "And I'm still thankful for those two things, but I'm excited now that I get to be a big brother."

Before it was Anna's turn, she slid off the chair and disappeared into another room.

"What in the world is she doing?" Stanley leaned to the side, straining to see the whereabouts of his daughter.

Anna reappeared, half carrying and half dragging a large picture frame until she leaned it against the wall next to her father's chair.

I nudged Daniel. "Did you have something to do with this?"

He winked but didn't answer.

"I'm thankful you gave me Mama's paints and brushes." She stepped to the side of the frame. "It's for you, Pa."

No one spoke. We were all mesmerized by what we saw. Slowly, we left our seats and gathered around the painting. It was the ranch house and barn. On the porch was the row of rocking chairs, one occupied by a man in a brown hat. Next to him sat a little girl with dark, bouncy hair.

"That's me and you." She pointed to the chairs. "There's Wesley riding the pony, and Nate with the cows."

"Look," I said. "That's me reading a book on a picnic blanket, and there's Daniel painting at his easel in the field."

"Where am I, Anna?" Ben came closer to get a better look. "Oh, that's me on the wagon. Probably going to town to see Susan."

A blue sky with puffy white clouds filled the space around a tall windmill, and the rooster weathervane pointed to the west. Cows, horses, goats, chickens, dogs, and even a horse with long ears that I figured must be Jim, filled the painting. A creek ran along the bottom. Along its banks, dots of blue, yellow, pink, and orange paint covered the canvas with flowers. To the side, Anna had signed her name.

Stanley remained silent, too busy wiping tears from his eyes.

"Do you like it, Pa?" Anna climbed into his lap. "Daniel taught me how to paint. You know, he's a pretty good artist."

Stanley laughed and hugged his daughter. "Yes, I know that, and you have a gift like your mother. She would be so proud."

*****

Like my growing belly, the number of children swelled in our tiny schoolhouse over the ensuing months. On warmer days, we spilled onto the area in front of the soddy, but most days found us packed inside with little room to move.

"If the baby arrives on schedule, we'll be done for summer break, and then we could resume in the fall." I explained the situation to Daniel, knowing it would be necessary to stop teaching for more than one reason.

Parents were questioning whether it was permissible for me to teach now that I was married, and a few stopped sending their children when word spread I was pregnant. In most towns, male teachers outnumbered the women, and women who married gave up their profession to take care of their husband and family.

"I know it's hard to imagine not teaching," Daniel said as he and I talked quietly near the warmth of the stove. "But it sounds like the schoolhouse that's planned for the north side of town will be finished by the end of summer. The children will be required to attend there even if they'd rather be with you."

"It's so far for them to travel each day. It will be well over an hour each way for those living on the outlying farms and ranches." I scooted my chair closer. "When it's cold and snowy, many of them may not even go to school."

"They love learning. You've given them that gift. That's what will keep them going to school."

I leaned back and ran my hand over my stomach. "It's hard to understand. I thought God had sent me to do the Run so I could be independent and make my own way—prove that I never needed to rely on anyone else again."

"And?"

"He brought wonderful children, like Anna, into my life so I could teach them to read and write and learn to do all their other studies. I really thought teaching was my calling, and now it's slipping away." I leaned forward and took my husband's hands in mine. "But then He brought me you."

"And soon our baby." Daniel ran his finger over my weddi ring. "For a long time, you and I thought we'd find happines independence—protect ourselves from losing anyone and the pain that comes with the loss."

"But now we have others to love and care for … and worry about."

He placed his forefinger gently across my lips. "I believe more than anything, God's in all of this. I don't understand why He asks us to use our gifts and callings at different times in our lives, but the one thing I am sure of, He's asking us to simply trust."

He kissed me softly, reminding me that forever and a day, we would continue on this race together we called life—the greatest Rush of all.

First of all, a heartfelt thanks for journeying back in time with me. The present is oftentimes demanding and the future may seem ominous, but there's something special about the past that draws us in. It wraps us up like an heirloom quilt—a reminder that in many ways, we are part of it.

When I first began researching for this book—poring through old letters, records, and maps, reading books and articles, visiting sites in Oklahoma, and listening to family members' recollections and retellings—I wasn't sure how much fact about my ancestor's story would be woven into the novel. To my pleasant surprise, a great amount of *RUSH* is true.

Mary Louisa Johnston Roberts Chessher (1860-1944) was the real name of my great-great grandmother. She was described as, "(Having) cut quite a figure, narrow-waisted, red hair, fair of skin. Not afraid of anything, an independent woman with an unquenchable spirit."

Her husband, Aaron "Tuck" Roberts, left her and young son, Charles Wesley (their real names as well), to seek gold in Colorado after their two older sons died from pneumonia. Believing her husband was dead, Mary temporarily left her son in Missouri with her mother and successfully did the land run on her own, claiming 160 acres. She lived in a soddy, homesteaded, and taught school on the prairie. Mary did remarry, and yes … Tuck made a surprise "return from the dead." It was quite uncommon for those days, but a divorce proclamation was issued.

My grandmother, Mildred Roberts Owens, was born in a foursquare house with a tin roof that eventually replaced the soddy. Her father,

Charles Wesley Roberts, moved his family to Colorado in 1912, and that's where another story begins—perhaps another book to write—because history keeps making itself and there are tales to be told.

If you enjoyed the story, please consider sharing a review on Amazon, Barnes & Noble, and Goodreads. Word of mouth is still the best, so tell a friend about *RUSH*.

Also, book club discussion points, actual photos, and other informational links about this fascinating time in history are on my website.

I'm honored to be a part of the reading community—let's stay in touch via my newsletter and blog—available at www.jaymehmansfield. com.

Here's to the unquenchable spirit in all of us!

Jayme H. Mansfield

CPSIA information can be obtained
at www.ICGtesting.com
Printed in the USA
LVOW03s1601030418
572132LV00004B/971/P

9 781946 016294